MW00768827

ALSO BY STEVE BROWN

Black Fire
Fallen Stars
River of Diamonds
Woman Against Herself

The Susan Chase™ Series
Color Her Dead
Stripped To Kill
Dead Kids Tell No Tales
When Dead Is Not Enough

World War Two Series
Of Love and War
America Strikes Back

Read the first chapter of any of
Steve Brown's novels at
www.chicksprings.com

At this web site you can also
download a free novella

Hope this
will keep
you reading
late into the
night
[signature] 11-04

radio secrets

radio secrets

STEVE BROWN

Chick Springs Publishing
Taylors, SC

© 2000 Steve Brown
Cover design © Boulevard Productions

First published in the USA in 2000 by
Chick Springs Publishing
PO Box 1130, Taylors, SC 29687
e-mail: ChickSprgs@aol.com
website: www.chicksprings.com

All rights reserved. No part of this book may
be reproduced or utilized in any form or by any
means, electronic or mechanical, without prior
permission in writing from the Publisher except
in the case of brief quotations used in reviews.

Library of Congress Control Number:
00-133401
Library of Congress Data Available

ISBN: 0-9670273-6-5

for mary higgins clark

"Physician, heal thyself."
—*Luke 4:23, The Holy Bible*

acknowledgments

Thanks to the usual reading group for their assistance:
Missy Johnson, Ellen Smith, Mark Brown,
Bill Jenkins, and Susannah Farley of the
Richland County Library, and, of course, Mary Ella.

This is a work of fiction. Names, characters, places, and incidents are the product of the author's imagination or are used fictitiously. Any resemblance to actual events, locales, organizations, or persons, living or dead, is entirely coincidental and beyond the intent of either the author or the publisher.

one

"Time to go, Lister."

Raymond opened his eyes and looked through the bars. He lay on the bottom bunk. Above him lay William Andrews. Raymond knew his cellmate was pretending to be asleep so he wouldn't have to say goodbye.

Who gave a damn? Raymond didn't want to say goodbye either. Andrews was a punk, and Raymond had set him straight the first day they were locked up together. The trouble with kids these days was—out on the street they had a piece, in the joint they had nothing, and the fish couldn't fight worth a damn. They were so used to pulling a gun, they didn't know how to defend themselves. It hadn't taken long for Raymond Lister to straighten out William Andrews.

Raymond got up and took one last look around the cell, his home for the last twenty years, twenty-two days. In the corner sat a seatless toilet, and near it, the wash basin, its shelf, and a metal mirror—all so familiar. The wall opposite the bunk beds was covered with pinups from midway up. Below the pinups, nothing. There was a shelf, but one end of it was empty. Until the day before, half the shelf had been filled with books, all kinds of books. It had taken Raymond a year and a half to learn that the boredom of a lifetime stretch could be eased by more than workouts in the weight room.

Still, nothing was posted on the wall below the shelf. Nothing could come in the way of Raymond projecting her face on the wall opposite his bunk. Anytime he wanted, day or night, Raymond could roll over and see her face on his half of that wall. That open space had come to the attention of the warden during one of his walk-through inspections.

"Really, Lister, you should have something on that wall."

"There *is* something on that wall."

The warden was taken aback. "Explain what you mean. I see nothing there."

"It's what *I* see—what *I* remember there."

The warden eyed his prisoner. He didn't need another weirdo in this particular cell block. They already had the slasher down the hall, the flasher across from Lister, and the prison's jailhouse lawyer, who had brought Raymond to the attention of the parole board, saying, no matter how brutal the act, a lifetime stretch was too long for any rape. And, finally, Lister's victim had not appeared before the board to plead her case.

"Then," said the warden, "all I can say is you must have a very vivid imagination."

"That I do, Warden. That I do."

A blank wall gave him plenty of room to see her, and sometimes late at night, during the long hours before falling asleep—because The Woman was robbing him of the best years of his life!—Raymond tried to see what she might look like after ten, then fifteen, and eventually twenty years.

Certainly she would've aged; added a little gray, some wrinkles, a bit of weight around the middle. Hell, twenty years did a lot of things to people. They had to him; more so to a woman. At first, Raymond had wished The Woman bad luck. But as he grew older, he realized he wanted her to prosper, to be successful. That way she'd pay dearly for what she had robbed him of.

A call from the turnkey and the cell door opened. Alongside the turnkey stood a guard.

What the hell were they thinking! He wasn't about to try anything. Twenty years in this damned place. Raymond didn't want to be here another twenty seconds. And that's all that kept him from spitting on his cellmate lying on the upper bunk pretending to be asleep.

Vernon Pinckney opened the door to the studio where Jean Fox did her radio talk show. It appeared he'd arrived in the middle of something. Fox was upset with her engineer. Again.

"Got to pick up the pace, Kyle."

"I've got it, Doc."

"No, you don't. You're off the mark. Pick it up."

Jean's frown turned into a smile as she saw Pinckney standing halfway inside the studio, halfway out.

"We're still on for lunch?" he asked.

Fox continued to smile. "You're fattening me up for the kill, aren't you?"

The network manager returned the smile. "Nah, Jean, I figure you'll be making the killing."

At the metal gate the warden offered his hand. "I wish you luck, Mr. Lister"—the first time in the last twenty years Raymond had been addressed in such a manner—"and I'd like to give you my hand on it."

Raymond looked at the hand, then the guard standing close behind the warden. Beyond the gate was a second gate, its fence fifty feet from the first, then the gravel road, and miles and miles of open space. Guard towers every fifty yards. No place to run, no place to hide, and that's why few tried to fly. There was just no way to get small in that much space.

He looked at the warden. "I thought I'd been paroled. What else I got to do to get out of this fucking hole?"

The warden withdrew his hand and nodded to a guard. The guard signaled the tower, a latch was thrown electronically, and the gate swung open toward the other gate, fifty feet away.

Before Raymond walked through, the warden said, "In the nine years I've been here, no one who's shaken my hand has ever returned to this prison."

That stopped Raymond cold, hands becoming fists at his sides. *The bastard!* Always playing their fucking mind games! Raymond told himself to control his anger. He wasn't going anywhere, he wasn't going to screw up the rest of anyone's life but his own if he let this asshole get to him. And if *this* asshole could provoke him, he wouldn't last twenty minutes on the outside.

Raymond let out a breath, flexed his hands one last time, and followed the gate as it swung back, then waited for the first gate to close behind him before the second could be opened. Cautious bastards! Probably figured he'd try to sneak back in.

Fools! He'd never return to that damn hole whether he shook hands with the warden or not!

"This is Dr. Jean Fox, and welcome to the real world, Lynn."

"Oh, thanks for taking my call. I've been trying to get through for days."

"I'm glad you did."

"Dr. Fox, my fifteen-year-old-son ran away from home again."

"Do you have any idea where he is?"

"Living with friends across town. I tried the tough love approach, but it's not working, and now I'm wondering if I've alienated him completely. He has younger sisters and they don't give me any trouble."

"I take it you're divorced."

"Yes."

"How long?"

"A couple of years after the last girl was born."

"Is their father still in the picture?"

"I'm afraid not."

"Have you been to talk to your son, you know, to see if he will come home?"

"Oh, yes, I meet him at the principal's office. One of the counselors sits in with us."

"Did your son tell you why he ran away again?"

"He said I've got to get rid of my boyfriend, but I don't think—"

"Boyfriend? You have a live-in boyfriend?"

"Yes, and my son says he has to move out, but I don't think a child should tell an adult what to do."

"Lynn, as you know, I'm not keen on live-in lovers."

"But a child telling an adult—"

"Lynn, it's not a good idea to have a man in the house. The kids become attached, you get ticked, and out the door the boyfriend goes. What does that teach your children about relationships? You're their primary role model."

"I don't want to lose my boyfriend."

"Would you rather lose your son?"

Silence on the other end of the line, then, "I'm doing that, aren't I?"

"I'm afraid so."

"Dr. Fox, I don't have good luck with men."

"But that's another call, isn't it? Lynn, your son needs you, and kids—especially teenagers—don't need this complication in their lives. I thank you for your call. Regina, welcome to the real world."

"Dr. Fox, I listen to you every day and I just love your show."

"Thank you."

"I read your books, too. I've got both of them."

"Good. Why did you call?"

"I've got this problem with my husband."

"Yes?"

"He cheated on me with someone at work."

"And how do you know this?"

"I found the letters from his girlfriend."

"You asked him about the letters?"

"Oh, yes, he admitted that he 'slipped up' is how he put it."

"Are there children involved?"

"Yes."

"Then we need to do something to save this marriage, don't we? Is he still carrying on the affair?"

"He broke it off when I found out."

"That's always a good sign. Will he go for counseling?"

"I haven't asked."

"If you don't ask, you'll never know, and if you won't ask, you might be the problem, not your husband."

"Me? I'm not the one who cheated."

"No, but you might want to use this affair to beat up on your husband. I say let it go and work on your marriage. Your children need their parents together. Barry, you're on the air with Dr. Jean Fox."

"Dr. Fox, my brother's married a divorced woman and now she's letting him boss her child around."

"Your brother bosses the child around how?"

"You know, no elbows on the table, sit up straight, and there's rooms you can't bring food into."

"Barry, there *are* rooms in the house you can't bring food into."

"But is it my brother's place to tell the little girl what to do? This is the woman's child."

"Sounds to me like your sister-in-law got just what she wanted, someone to help discipline her child."

"But it's not right—"

"It's not any of your business. Stay out of it."

"I don't think—"

"It doesn't matter what you think. This is between your brother and his wife."

"But that's not right."

"Barry, why can't you stop meddling in your brother's affairs?"

"I'm not meddling—"

"Barry, I can't talk to you if you're not going to be honest with me. Valerie, welcome to the real world. What can I do for you?"

"Dr. Fox, my son is twelve and he wants to call me by my first name."

"It's a rite of passage, showing you that he's not a kid any longer."

"But I don't want him to call me by my first name."

"Then tell him what the penalty is. Tell him what you're going to take away if he continues to do this. Do you have a husband living at home?"

"Yes."

"Perhaps your husband should take your son aside

and tell him he's being disrespectful to his mother. Will he do that?"

"I think so."

"If you're not sure, perhaps the problem is with your husband and not with your son."

"Dr. Fox, you don't think it's right for children to call adults by their first names, do you?"

"My daughter started calling me by my first name when she was twelve."

"What did you do?"

"Sent her to her room and told her not to come out until she was going to be more respectful."

A taxi waited in a stand of trees; an empty picnic bench sat alongside the taxi, as did a trash can. Mothers, daughters, and wives often sat in the shade of those trees waiting for visiting hours to begin. Sometimes a woman would come and sit and just stare at the joint. That had to be a real thrill.

But The Woman never came. If she was smart she'd be long gone. If she was real smart, she would've disappeared from the face of the earth.

"Taxi, Mister?" The cabbie was some kind of foreign guy, dark skin, black hair, skinny frame. Raymond figured he could easily break the guy in half. After all, he was the prison's arm-wrestling champ. Just another way to pass the time.

"How much?"

"Twenty bucks."

"I'll walk."

As Lister went by, the cabbie asked, "How long you in for, Mister?"

"Twenty." Outside the wall, a twenty-year stretch became a badge of honor, not the grind it'd been inside.

The cabbie whistled. "Never picked up a twenty-year fare before. It is ten miles to the bus station. Ten bucks and I will drop you at the door."

"I'll still walk," said Raymond, moving away.

"I have a living to make, Mister."

"Not off me you don't."

"Ten bucks. My last offer. You walk, you net five."

Raymond stopped and stared at the funny-looking guy. Twenty years inside the joint had made Raymond wary. Inside, he'd plenty of time to wait and see what the other con wanted. Outside, maybe it was best to ask a few questions.

"What you mean, net five?"

The little man glanced at the sky. "Hot day and a dusty road. That new suit will have to be cleaned before you apply for a job. State of Florida gives you a new suit. You should protect your investment."

So Raymond got into the cab. Not only had he learned to listen, but he had learned a thing or two about investments. Everything Raymond owned had been sold and salted away in a savings account while he'd been inside. His sister said she did it to give him hope. Car sold for a couple of thousand, pickup for another thousand, several guns and rifles, electronic goods, all netting close to five grand, now worth almost twenty through something called certificates of deposit.

He couldn't wait to get his hands on that fucking money! Twenty thousand dollars would go a long way in finding The Woman and making her life miserable. If he ever got away from this damned place. The funny-looking little guy couldn't get the cab started. He twisted the key again and again, but no sound came from the engine, not even a whine.

"Sorry. Been having trouble all week."

Raymond was out of the car and signaling for the hood to be unlatched before the driver knew it.

"Raise the hood," ordered Raymond.

The driver sprung the release, then climbed out and followed him to the front of the cab. "Maybe I should call dispatch. The boss—he don't like people fooling around with the vehicles."

Raymond grabbed the cables and twisted the connections of the battery, first one way, then the other. Whitish-gray flakes fell off as he fiddled with one connection, then the other.

He stood back. "Now try it."

The little man stared at him.

"Well, you want me to do it for you?"

"No, no. I do it."

The cabbie hustled back into the cab and cranked the engine. It turned over, and Raymond slammed the hood, then joined the driver in the front seat.

"Thanks, Mister. I don't make any money with the car in the garage."

Raymond eyed the man. "Worth a ride into town?"

"Sorry, Mister, but they send me here to pick up a fare, they expect me to bring one back."

Raymond took a breath and let it out. In his lap his hands opened and closed, over and over again.

Watching those hands, the driver said, "I hope you understand. I could get in big trouble."

Raymond looked at the prison and the life he was leaving behind. His breathing became more controlled and his hands fell still. "I understand, sport. Believe me, I understand."

The driver opened his mouth to say something, glanced at those huge hands, and decided against it. He put the cab into gear and started down the road.

Tony Nipper stuck his head in Jean Fox's office. Nipper ran the station that originated the *Dr. Jean Fox Show*. It was Nipper's job to keep the talent happy, and Jean Fox was the goose that had laid the golden egg, a real find, a natural.

Fox sat behind a table in French Provincial style. Around the room, the straight-back chairs, credenza, and miscellaneous pieces were also in French Provincial. On the walls hung paintings by Fox's daughter, a good-looking girl, but much too headstrong for Tony Nipper's taste. Nipper thought Fox used the table/desk to her advantage with those long legs of hers. Some said Fox should color her salt and pepper hair, but Tony thought the hair, that narrow face of hers, and the long legs gave the woman the haughty look she cultivated. Today, Fox wore a soft white dress, slit to her knees. Platinum necklace, earrings, and matching watch.

"What you need, Doc?"

"The production values, Tony. It's always the production values."

"You sound great," said Nipper, not taking a seat.

Using her fingers, Jean ticked off the following: "I've got an engineer, a screener, and a gopher. It's not working. Kyle is strung so tight, I think he's going to explode."

Nipper shrugged. "He looks okay to me."

"His wife is worried about him."

"Don't worry about the wives. They're always complaining about something." Nipper saw the look on his talent's face. "But I'll check into it. Actually, Doc, I've been worried about you."

"Why is that?"

"You seem a little tense. Anything on your mind? I'm always here to talk to. Nothing leaves the room."

Jean smiled. "Would you like to address some wedding invitations?"

Nipper's hands came up in surrender. "I wouldn't be any good at that. You've seen my handwriting."

"Thanks for being so concerned, but just check on the extra engineer. And this time, while you're looking, see if you can find a woman."

"But you've only got one guy on your team now. You don't want us called sexist, do you?"

"My show's the only one with two women working in support."

"Three with you," Nipper said with a smile.

"But I'm not support, am I?"

"You're sure not. You're sure not." Nipper headed for the door. "I'll look into it for you."

"Thank you, Tony."

"Always glad to be of service."

After Nipper left, Jean sat there, staring at the desktop. She finally opened the center drawer and took out a folded sheet of paper. With trembling hands, she read her attorney's well-known scrawl.

Jean,

> *Raymond Lister has been paroled and will leave prison Wednesday of next week.*

Take care,
Harry

The letter had been written a week ago. Today was Wednesday. Jean tore up the letter and threw it in her wastebasket.

No! I won't be intimidated by that man. I was victimized by him once before but never again.

Over the intercom came the voice of a young woman. "Vernon Pinckney is ready. And Peggy has picked out another dress. She wants you to stop by after you have lunch with Vernon. You're to give her a call." The voice laughed. "What number dress is this?"

"Don't ask." Jean felt a smile fill her face. Yes, she could handle this, as she had everything else. Raymond Lister belonged to the past and there Raymond Lister would remain.

two

*F*rom the editorial page of *The Coventry Journal:*
Justice is done!

After six days of testimony a verdict has been reached in Coventry County vs. Raymond Lister. The Alamo Animal will spend the rest of his life in jail for the brutal rape of one of our city's young ladies. Whether to manor born or the lowest rungs of society's ladder makes no difference, a woman's honor must be upheld, and mindful of that, Judge Clements slapped the Alamo Animal with the stiffest possible penalty. According to Judge Clements this verdict reaffirms that our streets are safe to walk, and men such as Raymond Lister have been put on notice that Coventry County will not tolerate such vile and disgusting behavior. In rendering his decision, Judge Clements said . . . .

From the *Alamo Observer:*

Have men lost their rights as women gain theirs? In preaching from the bench regarding the Lister case, Judge Clements, who has three daughters, came down on the side of feminism. This paper agrees a woman has a basic right not to be molested. But when women dress as provocatively as this woman did, accept rides from a stranger, and drink from that man's bottle, it makes one wonder whether it was men's rights that were violated or the young woman's. (Contributions to the Lister Appeal Fund can be mailed to the Observer or dropped off at our office on Bennett Street.)

It seemed to this reporter, observing each day's testimony, that the young woman in question was. . . .

Calvin Burdett sat in his Cadillac on the main drag of Alamo, smoking a cigarette and contemplating a run down to Miami but knowing he didn't have the muscle to pull off the deal. Not since Manny Gonzales had gotten himself locked up for public drunkenness, disturbing the peace, and generally making an ass of himself. Calvin peered down the street. Was that Raymond Lister headed his way?

Couldn't be. Lister had been put away for life. Calvin could still remember Raymond shouting that he'd find that bitch and even things up, but only after the sentence had been passed and the bailiff said "all rise" and old Judge Clements left for his chambers.

The judge had stopped and stared at Raymond as if considering a return to his chair, then thought better of it and left Raymond standing there, shouting at the old fart for giving him life for raping some whore. Maybe the judge had seen those fists Ray sported, enough to make anyone think twice about tangling with someone Raymond Lister's size. Calvin had met those fists before, up close and personal, but then he and Ray had learned they had more in common than reason to fight. Suddenly, Calvin realized he'd accepted this middle-aged fellow in the short-sleeved white shirt and dark tie, sporting an out-of-date haircut, as Raymond Lister.

Lowering his car window, Calvin flipped out his cigarette, then leaned out the window. The heat hit him like a blast furnace. "Ray—that you?"

The man stopped and squinted at him. Over the arm carrying a suitcase was a coat that matched his brown pants. "Cal?"

Burdett turned off the engine and climbed out. He wore jeans and a striped polo shirt that couldn't restrain the extra pounds he'd put on in the last few years. "What you doing here?"

"I live here, remember?"

"Remember? Hell, I'm the one climbed the water tower with you and painted 'Alamo Sucks!'"

"Then why're you still here, if the place sucks?" Raymond looked down Main Street. Things had certainly changed while he'd been in the joint. The drug store, hardware, and furniture store were all closed.

"It sucks more than ever."

Burdett plopped his rump on the side of his car. Perspiration broke out under his arms. It was damn hot out here. "Just bought Kirby's Bar and Grill." He slapped the Cadillac. "Doing pretty good, if you don't mind my saying so. And I don't mind saying so."

Lister put down his suitcase. "What you selling? Must be something brings in a good bit of money."

"This and that."

"And Alamo's a good place to lie low."

Burdett came off the car. He didn't have to take this shit off Raymond Lister. After all, who was driving and who was walking? "What you saying, that I'm into something crooked?"

"Did time, didn't you?"

Cal wanted to say he didn't have to force himself on a woman to get a piece of ass, but he remembered he was in the market for some muscle, and if there was one thing Raymond Lister had it was muscle. Those shoulders looked bigger than when his friend had been sent away. And if he remembered correctly, Ray had been a pretty good thinker, if you gave him time to sort things out. Twenty years in the slammer, Raymond had probably sorted out a good number of things.

A sheen of sweat made Lister's face shine, but Calvin was sweating like a horse. He wiped the moisture away with a finger and flung it onto the sidewalk. That done, Burdett leaned against the Caddy again. "Why'd you come back? There's got to be millions of places better than Alamo."

"Come to see my sister. She's holding money for me."

"Not if her old man knows about it."

"Lamar still on the sauce?"

"Worse than that. Wrecked your pickup right after you went to the joint."

Raymond felt a chill run through him. Gladys was supposed to have sold the pickup. She'd wrote him it was a done deal.

"Ran through the wooden railing on the bridge crossing the railroad tracks. Going so fast he smashed into the wall on the far side. These days Lamar uses a wheelchair to get around."

Raymond looked in the direction of his sister's house. She damned well have better sold the rest of his gear and have his money waiting or she'd join her husband in that fucking wheelchair.

"Got anything planned?" Burdett asked as casually as possible, sweat running down the inside of his shirt, soaking the spot across his belly.

"Yeah, I got plans."

"Then they'd better be out of this town. Since the sawmill and the glass factory closed, everybody drives to Coventry for work." He studied Raymond for a moment. "I've got something working if you're interested."

Lister shook his head.

Burdett nodded. "I know how it is. When I first got out I didn't want anything to do with ex-cons. Thought there was a probation officer on every corner. Well, all the pussy's over in Coventry. Guess you heard, women changed while you were in the joint. Damn if they don't hit on you like we used to do to them. Like to hop a few bars tonight? Man just out of the joint probably wants to get laid, and not even my place can compete with what's in Coventry."

"Got things to do, Cal."

"Need a ride?"

"Nah," said Raymond, blotting his forehead with a short sleeve of his shirt. He picked up his suitcase and looked down the street in the direction of where the Army/Navy store had once been. "Think I'll take in the sights."

"Know where Gladys lives? The old Robinson place. I don't mind giving you a ride."

"I'll be fine, Cal. I've just got something to take care of and it's personal."

Burdett wiped more sweat away as he reached inside his car and pulled out his Marlboro hard pack. He lit a cigarette as he leaned against the Cadillac again. "You wouldn't be thinking of finding that woman and evening things out, would you?"

Raymond had started away. Now he stopped and turned around. "Why would you say that?"

Burdett sucked smoke into his lungs and let out a breath. "Because I remember what you said in the courthouse that day. Want some advice?"

Raymond said nothing.

"Whatever you do, make sure you do it elsewhere. Johnny Mack's the sheriff nowadays."

"Old chop-block Johnny?"

"That's the one."

"He oughta be in jail himself, all the shit he pulled when he was a kid."

"Alamo's gone downhill, Ray. Sawmill closed up. Lost

a lot of jobs there, then the glass factory was bought out. Over three hundred jobs in one fell swoop. My folks drive over to Coventry. Ma's working for Burger King. Pa's fixing cars at the Chevy dealership. Dottie's married. Moved to Coventry where she and her husband run a store together. I'm backing them."

"Why you telling me all this, Cal?"

"One, because Johnny Mack cracks heads of whoever he's told to crack. He's in Judge Clements' pocket. And, two," said Burdett, taking another drag off his cigarette, "I ain't planning on taking no job working at some McDonald's or being a damn fixer like my old man. I'm running down to Miami and picking up a load, and I need some muscle. Somebody good with a gun, and you, Ray, you could shoot the eyes out of a rabbit. I've got a kit to check the purity, but I need somebody to watch my backside. Want the job?"

"Like I said, I've got something to take care of."

"Pays twenty grand. Down and back the same night."

Raymond shook his head again and started away.

Burdett came off the car. "What you want out of this woman? What you think you can get?"

"Justice. All I want is a little justice."

"Justice!" snorted Burdett. "Where's the justice in the glass factory closing down, the sawmill going bankrupt, and your pa being killed by them logs rolling off that truck? There ain't no justice in life, Ray. You oughta know that by now."

"Wrong, Cal," said Raymond, facing his friend again. "There is justice and I'm the delivery man."

❖   ❖   ❖

The main dining room of the Magnolia Club was a step back in time: black men in tails waiting on tables, Jean Fox the only woman in the room, and men hunched over tables, most with gray in their thinning hair. The only sound was hushed conversation and the occasional clinking of glass and silverware. The walls of the huge room displayed oversized paintings of hunting scenes: men in red jackets and gold riding breeches astride horses, leaping fences in pursuit of their prey. At the far end of the long room stood a raised platform where a small orchestra might perform—when women were allowed inside the building.

If Jean was uncomfortable with her presence in this all-male club, her host had other ideas. Vernon Pinckney was proud to be seen with this woman. Jean Fox was quite a looker for a woman who'd just turned forty, and Pinckney never understood why she'd never remarried. Besides those incredible legs, Jean Fox had good breasts, and, as far as he could tell, no extra pounds around the middle. And he would've been in the hunt for this woman if he didn't believe you never got your honey where you got your money.

Smartest move he'd ever made, offering her a job solving people's problems on the radio—though Fox was no shrink. She was a therapist—someone who could talk to the Average Joe and not become bogged down in jargon, detailed explanations of neuroses, or prescribe medication. Of course, it was made clear that the opinions of Dr. Jean Fox did not reflect the network or its affiliates. Neither was Jean Fox an attorney, nor was she actually counseling anyone over the radio. Still, they had the lawsuits, mostly from men who thought they were being picked on by this woman sitting across the table from him. Pinckney knew the feeling. He had two divorces behind him and wanted to kill anyone who coached his ex-wives in their lawsuits against him.

"So what do you need, Jean?"

His major talent flashed a warm smile. "It's been taken care of. I need another engineer. Tony said he'd get on it."

The conversation stopped as a waiter poured water into their glasses.

Pinckney drank from his glass before asking, "Have you given any more thought to the idea of taking the show to Atlanta? Stations are bidding for the opportunity to originate your show. They don't understand why you don't want to make the move. It'd make connections to your speaking engagements a lot easier."

"I don't know, Vernon. Columbia's been good to me."

"There's a lot of perks associated with those stations in Atlanta."

"Perhaps after the wedding."

"And the radio awards?"

Jean dismissed the awards with a wave of the hand. "Not important."

"It is if you want to move to Atlanta."

Not to mention it would be more money in each of their pockets if Pinckney could get Jean off the dime. Leave the nest would be more accurate. In Columbia,

Jean had become too comfortable. She said she needed a second engineer. What was up with that? But whatever his major talent asked for, she always got—after Tony Nipper ran it past him.

Pinckney noticed Jean staring across the room. Sometimes men could be caught glancing in Jean's direction, but now, only Harry Hartner was looking at them. Hartner was the attorney who handled Jean's affairs and Hartner was staring at his luncheon partner. What could be the problem? There was Ruth, the grandmother, and Peggy, the about-to-be-married daughter—and nobody else. Hell, Pinckney didn't think Jean even dated. Pinckney nodded to one of the waiters, who disappeared into the kitchen, and across the room Harry Hartner broke off his stare when reminded to order his lunch.

Tony Nipper had told him he thought something was distracting their major talent, said he could hear something in Jean's voice. After the new engineer was hired, Pinckney would see if Nipper could still hear anything in their major talent's voice.

three

Raymond's sister lived in a two-story structure, a dull white house with a screened porch running its width, cars parked in the front yard. The screens had holes in them and most corners had slipped loose from the molding and curled inward. The screened door stood ajar, the stairs up to the porch tilted, and boxes of aluminum cans were stacked on the porch. Strung across a corner of the porch hung a hammock made of plastic beads.

One of the cars in the yard Raymond recognized. Parked under an old oak was his light blue Galaxy XL 500 convertible, faded black top riddled with holes, rust spots behind each wheel. Raymond was getting a bad feeling about the money his sister was supposed to have invested for him. He climbed the few steps to the porch, pushed the screened door out of the way, and knocked on the front door.

No answer.

Sounds of a TV game show came from a room over the porch. Raymond knocked again, this time hard enough to chip paint off the door. The front door opened, but only inches. A security chain pulled tight between him and a black-haired woman. He could see dark skin and darker eyes.

A spic! His sister lived with spics! Gladys had told him nothing about this. It was one thing to put up with them in the joint, but in your own home?

"Gladys Dockery live here?"

"Upstairs."

A man in a wheelchair lived upstairs? "Upstairs?"

"Yeah," said the thick lips through the crack in the door. "What are you—an echo?"

It took all his self-control for Raymond to back away instead of kicking in the door, ripping the chain from the wall, and taking the bitch by the throat . . . .

Get a hold of yourself. You knew there would be people who wouldn't give a damn about what you wanted. Finding The Woman is the only thing that's important. Not any woman, and certainly not any spic.

"How do . . . how do I get there?"

The woman studied him, then shut the door.

The goddamn spic had shut the door in his face! Raymond was about to hammer on the door again—actually had his hand raised—when the chain slipped off and flopped against the wall on the other side. When the door opened, the woman stood before him, filling the door and filling out a pair of jeans and a blouse pretty good, too. She had a nice set of tits but was a little wide at the hips. In her hand was a cigarette.

She let out a smoke-filled breath. "You the brother?"

Behind the dark-skinned woman, he could see that a hallway led to a kitchen. To one side appeared to be a living room, and through an archway Raymond saw a bedroom. He picked up his suitcase. "Do I come inside?"

"Hardly," said the woman, still studying him.

There was an arrogance about this woman; Raymond could feel himself heating up. In the old days, he would've slapped the hell out of her, then gone about his business. But today he had other things on his mind.

The woman jerked a thumb toward the corner of the porch. "You have to go around back."

Without another word, Raymond turned and went down the stairs.

She followed him. "Plan on staying a while?"

"I don't see that's any of your business."

"That's what you think."

Raymond looked up. "What the hell you talking about?"

"Your nephew and niece, they holler pretty good. Having their uncle around might stir them up even more." She gestured behind her. "I keep brooms handy so I can thump on the ceiling. I've got plenty of holes in my ceiling from your family's screaming or the TV or stereo blasting."

"So move."

The dark-skinned woman slouched against the doorway of the screened-in porch. "And maybe I was waiting around to check out the brother."

"And maybe you're full of shit." Suitcase in hand, Raymond headed for the corner of the house.

She followed him, trailing him down the porch. "Some women like having a real man around, not a wimp like Lamar. Drop around and have a beer. Name's Donna Diaz. I've got air conditioning."

Turning the corner, Raymond still said nothing.

"What's the problem, Ray? Just out of the joint and don't want to party? I know the joint does funny things to people. My first husband—he was right as rain before going in . . . ."

Raymond didn't hear any more, didn't want to hear any more. Why couldn't people just leave him the hell alone? Didn't they realize he had a job to do?

Behind the house an old wrought-iron staircase doubled back, climbing to a small porch in front of a screened door. More wrought iron ran around the small porch. In the window was a fan, and stretching from one corner of the porch to a pine tree hung the family laundry. Under the stairs sat a pair of battered trash cans and, farther away, a rusted drum for burning trash.

Raymond climbed the stairs and discovered they swayed under his weight. Like the rest of the house, the upstairs screened door needed some work. Flies came and went through a hole in the screen where someone had once poked something through to unlock the latch. His rapping on the door had to compete with the game show on TV.

No one seemed to hear him over the sound of the fan and the game show. When he pounded on the screened door, he heard the TV cut off and a man's voice—Lamar's voice—shouting for Gladys to get the door, that he couldn't do it, and would Gladys show him the same consideration she showed the children.

Raymond remembered Lamar Dockery. The boy had been faster than any nigger and there'd been talk of scholarships, but Lamar's grades weren't good enough, even for junior college. Now that *was* dumb.

The woman who came to the screened door had thick arms and a chubby face. She wore a brown-and-white uniform dotted with grease, and sturdy work shoes. Her hair was pulled back in a ponytail. Gladys' hair had turned gray shortly after Raymond had gone off to prison. Gladys had written him, telling him if he wanted to know what she looked like, it was like their mother in her old photographs.

Gladys peered through the screen. "Raymond—that you?"

"Yeah, it's me."

His sister pushed the screened door out of the way and Raymond came through, holding the suitcase in front of him. That didn't stop his sister. Gladys dodged the suitcase and grabbed him, giving him a hug he didn't return. She even gave him a kiss on his cheek before he slipped away.

"Here—let me take that," she said, reaching for the suitcase.

She slid the bag between a trash can and a table jammed up against the wall. The dinette set had four chairs, a shiny one trapped against the wall, three others with peeling vinyl and padding sticking out the corners. The window fan created a nice breeze through the kitchen, and even Raymond wasn't immune to that.

A voice from the bedroom yelled, "Well, if you don't want me to know who's there, just stay in there then."

Gladys leaned toward her brother. "I wrote you about Lamar's accident. He can't get around so well."

Raymond stepped back. "But you didn't write me about him wrecking my truck."

Gladys straightened up. "I didn't want to worry you none. There was nothing you could do about it. I'll pay you back when we get a little ahead."

"You should've sold the pickup before Lamar wrecked it. And what's my car doing out front? I thought you were going to sell it, too."

"Raymond, I have to have some way to get around."

"What about Lamar's car? He's not using it."

Gladys glanced at the bedroom. "They—they repossessed it when we couldn't make the payments on account of Lamar losing his job."

Raymond was becoming more than a little pissed, but he had the good sense to keep his voice down, at least below the level of the fan. He wouldn't get far with Lamar sticking his nose in where it didn't belong. "The guns and stereo—what happened to them?"

"I wanted to sell the stereo, but the kids really liked listening to it."

Raymond's hands flexed at his sides, but his sister didn't seem to notice. "You didn't do anything you told me you'd do. What was this about the hope I was supposed to have in the joint? Every damn letter you wrote me was filled with that."

"Well, things have been kind of tough since they closed down the glass factory."

"Gladys, I wasn't put on this earth to take care of your family, that's Lamar's job. I'll take my stereo to the pawn shop and hock it. I suppose the TV Lamar's watching is that new color set I bought before they sent me away." Twenty thousand dollars—hell, he'd be lucky to end up with twenty cents.

"About the stereo, the kids have been driving it pretty hard. There's a rattle in one of the—"

"Woman! Are you coming in here or do I have to drag myself out of this bed and come in there after you?"

Gladys tugged on her brother's arm. "Come on, Raymond. Come in and see Lamar."

He threw her off. "What about the guns? I doubt your kids could've busted up a shotgun and rifle."

"Gladys, get your butt in here! And bring me a beer."

Gladys' face brightened as she moved toward the refrigerator. "How about a beer?"

"My guns? Where are they?"

Hand on the refrigerator, his sister looked at the floor. "People have to eat, and you were gone an awfully long time."

"You sold my guns for food? Nobody sells guns for food."

"All but the rifle."

"What happened to the rifle?" It seemed like the question to ask.

"Lamar liked to tote it around in the pickup and—"

"It was stolen? My rifle was stole out of the pickup!" Raymond felt The Woman slipping away. This wasn't the way he'd planned it at all. He had to have some walking around money; otherwise he'd have to take a job, and that would get him nowhere closer to Her.

"Gladys," said the voice from the bedroom, "if it's that bitch from downstairs, I don't care to see her. You two stay in there and yack."

"It weren't Lamar's fault." Gladys bit her lip. "Somebody stole the rifle after he run off the bridge. He was unconscious—"

"Lamar wrecked my truck! It's his fault the rifle was stolen."

"Kids done it. They ran him off the road."

"I'll bet."

"Johnny Mack told me. Johnny Mack's the sheriff these days."

"And your husband's drinking buddy before that." A thought hit Raymond. "Insurance. There has to be insurance money." He saw Gladys staring at the floor again. "Oh, shit, don't tell me the insurance didn't pay off."

His sister shook her head.

"Why not? It cost plenty, but I always paid my insurance on time."

"We—we couldn't afford it."

"You couldn't afford the insurance on my truck?"

Gladys shook her head.

"Then there's nothing?"

A sudden firmness came into his sister's voice as she lifted her head. "I've got two young'uns to raise."

"That's what jobs are for, so you won't steal other folks' property."

Tears started down his sister's cheeks. "It's all I had and I had a family to feed."

"It's all *I* had and you stole it."

"I—I didn't know any other way. I work two jobs and all they pay is minimum wage. Every job worth having is over in Coventry, and I couldn't take care of Lamar if I worked there."

"Get Lamar's folks to help out."

From the other room came her husband's voice. "That don't sound like no woman. That some kind of bill collector you got in there? Well, bring him in here. He'll see why we're behind. What else they want? They're already garnishing your check and the bastards took out the cable. Now I ain't got nothing to watch but regular TV. Don't hide that bill collector from me. You bring him in here and I'll tell him what's what."

Gladys looked from the bedroom to her brother—who was heading for the door with his suitcase. "Aren't you going in to see Lamar? He's been looking forward to seeing you. The kids will be home in a while and they'll want to meet their uncle. You've never seen them, you know."

At the door Raymond turned and held out his hand. "Give me the keys, Gladys."

His sister glanced at the top of the refrigerator where a purse lay.

"Now don't tell me something's wrong with the car."

"It's just that sometimes I have trouble starting it." She took her purse down from the refrigerator, pulled the keys out, and handed them to him. "You'll be back in time for supper, won't you? I bought a ham."

Raymond slipped off a couple of keys and returned the ring. "I ain't never coming back." And he was out the door and heading for the stairs.

Gladys followed him as far as the porch. Raising her voice over the sound of the fan, she asked, "What you mean you're not coming back?"

Making the turn on the wrought-iron stairs, Raymond looked up. "I'm quits with the lot of you. I ain't having nothing to do with thieves and idlers."

"But the buses—they don't run anymore, not with the factory closed down. I won't have any way to work."

"Then walk. I walked here, now I'm driving back. In my car."

Gladys wiped tears away as she watched her brother finish the stairs and disappear around the corner of the house. Raymond wasn't a bad man. He just didn't understand what it took to raise a family, and it took a lot. Maybe, wherever he was headed, he'd meet a woman, settle down, and then he'd be back, bringing his kids, and there'd be picnics like there'd been with Ma and Pa while they'd been growing up. That's what Raymond needed. He needed a woman to make him understand how important family was. Then he'd understand why she'd had to do what she'd done with all his property.

Peggy swept out of the dressing room wearing yet another dress. Not at all timid and shy as she'd been when trying on the first gown. Odd to see Peggy so child-like again, thought her mother. Jean and her mother-in-law sat on a padded bench, taking in the swirling girl and her choice of gowns.

"It's not to dance in," said her mother.

Peggy flashed a smile. These days her daughter was all smiles. "Yes, it is, Mother, and I plan to dance the night away."

Jean didn't think so. Dancing wasn't what Elliot had had on his mind, nor had Jean been able to afford even a decent dress. Her wedding wouldn't come close to what Peggy would experience, but wasn't that what all parents wanted, for their child to have better than they had?

A justice of the peace had married Jean and Elliot, but her daughter would be married by the bishop of the lower diocese of the state of South Carolina, with hundreds of guests in attendance. The wife of the justice of the peace had been Jean's only guest; witness, too, and Jean had worn a mini-skirt, the best she could come up with on short notice. But Elliot wanted them married before he went overseas, wedding dress or not. Returning from his first sortie, his plane had crashed in the mountains of Afghanistan. Angry, confused, and all alone—her parents had died years before—Jean had fled to South Carolina and met her mother-in-law for the first time.

Peggy stood still long enough for the boutique owner to straighten out the bodice, then fluff up the lace. She smiled brightly. "What do you think?"

"Much nicer than before."

"Mother! The natural one was absolutely gorgeous!"

"Peggy," asked Ruth Fox, "were you seriously considering buying natural—something that would look dingy the first time you put it on."

"Actually," said her granddaughter, tossing her loose tresses, "the only color that goes with this color hair is black."

Ruth Fox coughed into her hand. The girl certainly had a mind of her own, and it made Ruth look forward to Peggy settling down. Peggy might continue her painting, but those beatnik friends would have to go.

"And pray tell," asked Ruth, "what color is that you're wearing?"

"Pearl." The girl looked at her mother. "It was a compromise. Mother wanted white."

"There's not enough lace across the top."

Peggy glanced at her bosom. You could hardly see anything. "Nana, I have to look good. I'm getting married."

"If anyone's there for any reason other than your wedding, they've come for the wrong reason."

"Yes, ma'am." Peggy lowered her eyes.

Jean had to smile. Peggy played them off against each other, and along the way, had doubled the wedding's budget. What could a mother do? It was hard to turn down your only child on her wedding day.

Peggy was looking in the mirrors. One straight ahead, two others at forty-five-degree angles. A carbon copy of her mother, the girl had the same narrow face and deep blue eyes, but where Jean's hair was black with a peppering of gray, her daughter's hair had turned gray only a couple of years ago. With the exception of the prematurely gray hair that Peggy refused to color—take me as I am—Jean considered Peggy to be a beautiful young woman. High breasts and long legs, with just enough bottom to make clothes fall properly.

Yes, Wesley Calhoun had chosen well. And so had Peggy. The Calhouns were some of the bluest blood in South Carolina; Peggy, too, through her father, not her mother. No, never through her mother, and for some reason, that gave Jean a certain sense of pride.

"We really must be going," Ruth said.

"Yes. I have to get back to the station." To the boutique owner, Jean said, "It's that one."

Ruth opened her purse. "I'll pay for it."

"Nonsense. I'll take care of it."

The older woman rummaged around, pulling out her checkbook. "How much is it?"

The boutique owner glanced at Jean, but said to Ruth, "Mrs. Fox, really, I don't think—"

"Well, speak up. I can certainly pay for my granddaughter's wedding dress."

Jean patted her mother-in-law's hand. "What she's trying to tell you is the gown's already paid for."

"Paid for? You've paid for a dress we just saw?"

"Peggy and I narrowed it down to one or the other. But we still wanted your opinion."

Ruth jammed the checkbook into her purse. "If it was a choice between white and natural, then there was no choice at all and I don't know why I was even invited."

Peggy beat a hasty retreat into the dressing room,

the boutique owner right behind her. Jean said nothing, only sat there, filled with an empty sense of victory.

"The least you could do is let me help out every once in a while."

"Ruth, you've done enough. You paid for my education and took care of my child while I was in school."

"Elliot would have done so himself—if he'd lived." She stared at the door of the dressing room, then said, "Sooner or later you're going to have to tell her."

Jean was staring at the dressing room, thinking of the present, not the past. "Tell her what?"

"You know very well what I'm talking about."

"We don't have to tell her anything."

"You don't think the child can handle it?"

"I don't think Peggy has to know."

"What about children? It's something any woman should know, if she wants to bring children into the world."

"Peggy is healthy as a horse—I had her tested for every conceivable disease while she was a child. Besides, she's not even twenty-one."

"You should've used that argument when Wesley asked for Peggy's hand."

Jean laughed. "I wouldn't've had a leg to stand on."

"Rushing Elliot to the altar like that."

Jean's laughter faded. "The way I remember it, Elliot was doing all the rushing."

"Good thing he's not here to defend himself."

Jean stared at the woman sitting alongside her. "What's wrong, Ruth? What's this really about?"

Her mother-in-law looked away. On the other side of the boutique a young woman sat at a table, flipping through pages of wedding invitations. When the girl came to one she liked, she showed it to her mother. The mother shook her head and they moved on.

Jean took Ruth's hand. "You don't want to lose her any more than I do, do you? We're not losing her. She'll soon be back in our lives, asking for cooking tips."

The older woman said nothing, only stared at the dressing room door.

"Ruth, I don't know if I could stand it if Peggy were to say I should've told her who her father was years ago. Years ago, she was only fourteen or fifteen, and going through a stage."

"One of many, if I remember correctly."

Jean squeezed the elderly woman's hand. "We don't have to test Peggy's capacity for forgiveness. It can wait. Let her have her day. There's no rush. Something like that can always wait."

Ruth looked at the dressing room where laughter cascaded through the curtain. "And the man? Her father?"

"Forgotten forever."

Ruth shuddered. "I don't see how someone who went through what you did could ever forget . . . . On TV the other day I heard some lawyer say what happened to you was no worse than someone breaking into your house and stealing your VCR."

"Well, based on my experience, I'd rather have my VCR stolen."

Tears started down Ruth's cheeks. "When I see Peggy,

I wish she was my granddaughter. She's everything I would want in a granddaughter."

Jean patted the older woman's hand. "She is your granddaughter, and I'd say we made the best of a bad situation."

Peggy burst out of the dressing room wearing jeans, a yellow cropped top, and running shoes. "Nana, you're crying."

The old woman dabbed at her eyes with a tissue. "Tears of joy, my dear, tears of joy. I'm sure you and Wesley will be very, very happy."

four

On the front yard of his sister's house, Raymond Lister sat in his old Galaxy XL 500, door open to let some air in, unable to reminisce while surrounded by the candy wrappers, fast food containers, and empty drink cups cluttering the front seat and floorboard. The ashtray overflowed with ashes and butts, and children's handprints marked every window. Across the back seat, a rip ran from one side of the car to the other. And the odor!—moisture trapped inside a car with a leaky roof.

Once this had been a real monstermobile: souped-up engine, four-barrel carburetor, four-on-the-floor, heavy duty shocks, and duel exhausts. Now, it was good only for that final trip to the boneyard. Raymond wasn't sure if he even wanted to try the key.

The door of the house opened and Donna Diaz came down the steps. She sauntered over to the car, took a cigarette from her lipsticked mouth, and put an arm on the window. Seeing his suitcase in the back seat, she asked, "Leaving already?"

"Leaving now." But when Raymond turned the key nothing happened. He tried again.

Nothing. Not even a whine.

Diaz dropped her cigarette to the ground and snubbed it out. "I'll have to jump it off."

No shit, thought Raymond. Maybe the faulty terminals on the taxi's battery had been an omen. Maybe he was supposed to have walked right back into that damn prison and let them shut him up forever.

Raymond brought his fists down on the steering wheel with a thump, and cracks appeared at ten and two. He stared at the cracks.

Shit! What next?

The woman was opening the door of some rice burner parked alongside him. Diaz moved with a litheness he hadn't seen in years, with the exception of queers in the joint. She saw Raymond staring at her, flashed an easy smile, and then cranked her engine. The engine of the rice burner turned over, purring away like a kitten.

Shit! Shit! Shit!

Diaz wheeled around and nosed her car up to the Ford. With the engine running, she slipped out of the car and popped the hood while Raymond bent to open his own. They bumped bottoms raising their respective hoods; Diaz nodding shyly, but Raymond only asking, "You got jumper cables?"

"They're in your trunk. It's not the first time I've done this for Gladys."

"You're not doing this for Gladys. This is my car."

Raymond reached through the window, pulled the

keys from his ignition, and walked around to the trunk. This was the first time he'd ever used jumper cables on his own car. In the past, jump-offs had been for losers or running a game on women, once you had them out in the country.

In the trunk was the spare, which, of course, was flat, some of the tools Raymond had left behind before going off to prison, and a pair of jumper cables lying across an empty donut box. Rings of chocolate clung to the bottom of the donut box, as did a line of ants.

Raymond shook the ants off the cables and returned to the front of the car. Once his terminals were connected to Diaz's, he returned to his car and cranked the engine. It fired up, and it wasn't long before Diaz was leaning on his window again, the sill this time. All four windows were down now, to let the spring heat blow through; but he didn't dare lower the top. What if it got stuck halfway down? Shit, he'd have to order a new one.

"How about that beer now?"

There was a lush, indolent look about this woman. Thick lashes under bangs reaching for a pair of dark, brown eyes, lipstick smeared across her mouth, meaty arms, and large breasts. She was a woman to be used and she would enjoy every minute.

"Got to drive around and recharge the battery."

"I'll go with you." Diaz rolled off the door. "Should I bring along some money or do you have some?"

"Bring money."

Diaz nodded and hurried off into the house.

Raymond watched her go and remembered how long

it took any woman to dress. He'd be long gone before this bitch pulled herself away from her mirror.

He got out of his car and listened to the engine. Satisfied, he jerked the cables loose, put the hood down, and walked around to the back of the car, where he threw the jumpers into the trunk. For a moment he stared at the flat, the trash, the few tools, and the damned jumper cables, then slammed the lid down and returned to the front of the car. There, he stopped, hand on the door, the other on the roof, staring at the other car with its hood still up. The rice burner's engine was still running.

He didn't want to be responsible for someone stealing the woman's fucking car. No, that wouldn't get him any closer to his goal. Diaz might even set the cops on him.

Raymond slammed the hood of the other car, then reached inside and turned the key, ready to drop it to the floorboard and be out of there. When he turned it, the engine shut off, but the key wouldn't come loose. He twisted the key one way, then the other, and the damn thing still wouldn't budge. There must be a trick to it.

What was it?

There had been an article in *Car and Driver* about keys locking down the steering column so cars couldn't be stolen. What had the article said? He pulled his head out of the car to study the situation and almost ran into the woman. He quickly stepped aside so Diaz could reach inside and twist the key out of the lock.

"There's this little button you have to push."

Raymond stared at the keys the woman slipped into a pocket of her jeans. Damn Nips! Who'd want to steal one of their fucking cars in the first place? No size, no power, no style—damn! He climbed back in his Ford, trying to think of a reason why Diaz shouldn't come along. Problem was he couldn't think of any reason. He hadn't planned for this. He needed time to think.

Diaz brushed candy wrappers off the seat and slid in on the passenger side, kicked a plastic pop bottle aside, and lit another cigarette. After her initial drag, she dropped off her sandals and put her feet up on the dash.

Now that was something Raymond never would've allowed—if the damn car had been in decent shape. But it didn't make sense to complain about feet on the dash with pop bottles, cigarette butts, and candy wrappers strewn across the floorboard. Hell, Diaz probably thought the dashboard was cleaner, and she was probably right.

"Where we headed?" asked the woman.

"Into the country."

Diaz sat up and her feet came off the dash. "Want me to get a blanket?"

Raymond shook his head and shifted the four-on-the-floor. God, did it feel good to have that chrome ball back in his hand, to feel the chassis shudder, about to shake off the dust of Alamo. That is, if he could come up with some damn money. If he hadn't spent all the money he'd earned in the prison laundry . . . but a man couldn't do a lifetime stretch without smokes.

"We're not stopping. Just recharging the battery."

"Well, don't take long. I want something to eat."

He shot a glance at the woman as she returned her feet to the dash. Then he backed into the street, drove a few blocks, and took a couple of well-remembered turns. But driving out of town, Raymond couldn't find his favorite radio station. All the stations did was talk, like the woman alongside him. Most of those on the radio yapped about what was wrong with the world and why the radio host was the one to solve the world's, or person's, problems. They all sounded like jailhouse lawyers.

Raymond ignored Diaz as she rambled on about what a bum her husband was and how she'd finally had to kick him out. He was always in jail or smoking dope. But wherever the bum was, he was always spending their money. That didn't mean she was sour on marriage, just that particular guy. What a jerk he'd turned out to be.

Raymond wasn't listening. He was twisting the radio dial. When would they play some damn music? He found a country music station that didn't come in worth a shit, then a preacher preaching in the middle of the week. Why couldn't they leave people alone until Sunday? And some Big Band crap, but no music.

"Damn!"

"What's the problem?" asked Diaz, breaking off her complaint about an abusive stepfather and a mother who'd enjoyed her new husband's rough little games.

"I'll have to buy a converter."

The woman glanced at the radio. "Nah. FM comes in all the new cars."

Raymond glared at her before stomping on the accelerator. Here he was down to his last few bucks and this bitch was talking about his buying a new car. Shit for brains, that's what she had. Well, what'd you expect from a woman?

Now they were out of town, running past Worm's Garage where Raymond had worked before being sent to prison. He wanted to wind out the engine and see what it could do, but it was knocking. A valve gone, maybe two. How much would that cost? Prices had gone through the roof while he'd been away. He could do the labor—Worm would let him use his tools—but the parts had to come from somewhere. Even junkyards wanted cash on the barrelhead.

Damn! His sister had screwed him but good. Raymond snapped off the radio in the middle of a woman yapping about another bitch's problems. God, but the number of whiners had increased while he'd been away.

"Hey, that was Dr. Fox you turned off. I listen to her every day."

"Shut up." He had to think.

"Raymond, something wrong?"

"There will be if you don't shut up."

"Raymond, what's . . . ?"

When he raised his hand, the bitch finally shut up. Where could he get some damn money?

It took a few minutes, but it finally came to him. Turning to the woman, he asked, "You hungry?"

"Yeah, but there's nothing out here." Diaz gestured at a countryside planted in orange trees. Ahead of them an old man sold vegetables and fruits at a roadside stand. "Unless you want me to cook. Did I tell you I was a fantastic cook? One time I was at the beach with these four guys and we . . . ."

Raymond didn't hear her. He was pulling into the roadside stand. Dust and gravel flew, and the old man went from smiling to frowning as Raymond whipped in and out of the parking lot. In seconds, they were roaring back toward town. Damn, thought Raymond, the old girl still has a kick to her, even with a valve or two on the fritz.

"Ever hear of a place called 'Kirby's'?"

"Yeah, but you don't want to go there. Why don't we eat at Alexander's? They serve supper, and you can get your veggies," she added with a smile.

"I want to try Kirby's."

"But all they got is hot dogs and hamburgers."

"Then I'll drop you off at the house."

Diaz shook her head, hair flying in the breeze from the open window. "I'm game if you are. Sometimes it gets a little rough in there, but I'll feel safe if I'm with you."

Then the woman went off in a tirade about how she hadn't thought they would hit it off when Raymond first knocked on her door, but she was glad things were working out. And it was true, she'd planned to move to Coventry, but Gladys had made Raymond sound—what was the word? Intriguing, maybe that was it. She'd heard that word on soap operas. So she'd waited around to meet the brother.

Raymond was thinking he'd been wrong to leave this woman behind. When they showed up at Kirby's, Calvin

Burdett was sure to approach him about the drug run again, and with the woman along, it would look more like a date than cutting a deal. He smiled, and Diaz thought the smile was meant for her. She scooted toward him, but Raymond didn't put his arm around her. He didn't even notice her. All that was on his mind was how close twenty grand would bring him to another woman.

The family sat across from each other in the dining room. The furniture was mahogany, the cushions matched the velvet drapes, and above the chair railing was the faint outline of wallpaper picking up the colors in the drapes and cornices. Wesley Calhoun wore a dark blue suit, light blue shirt, and paisley tie. His fiancée's dress was a short, black thing, which, when she sat down, scooted well up her thighs. Her grandmother wore a belted pink dress that drew out her complexion, and her mother wore a royal blue A-line dress with a pearl necklace and matching earrings.

Plates appeared and disappeared as they finished each course. Ruth and Jean on one side of the table; Wesley and Peggy on the other, and, from where she sat, it appeared to Jean that the young people were holding hands. Hattie, the black maid, seemed to think so, too. She smiled as she picked up the dishes from the young people's side of the table, then disappeared into the kitchen for after-dinner coffee.

This was how it should be, thought Jean, not your husband dying a few days after you've been married and being raped within hours of his death. Jean could see in Wesley and Peggy her own joy and foolishness, which must've been evident to older and wiser heads around MacDill Air Force Base.

Elliot had told her she was the most unique girl he'd ever met. Boy oh boy, had that made her young heart throb! The two of them made no other plans than for Jean to continue working and attending junior college and wait for Elliot's return. It had not escaped Jean's notice that her new husband hadn't told his mother about their marriage. Then Elliot died and the Air Force notified Ruth of her son's death—about the same time Jean began fighting her way through the indifference of her local police and the skepticism of the Air Force. The letter about their marriage, written but never mailed, had sat on the table in the hall, taunting Jean to send it off. She would not, nor did she have to. She had benefits from the Air Force. Until she missed her period. After that, all bets were off.

Years earlier, Jean's parents had been killed by a drunk driver and she'd been reluctantly taken in by grandparents. After she'd been raped, those grandparents would have nothing to do with her. They knew what the Good Book preached about harlots. Surely their granddaughter must've led that Raymond Lister on. Hadn't she given them trouble in the past, staying out late, not attending church, and even smoking cigarettes? And the Air Force Jean had come to depend on—all the Air Force could do was give her a stack of forms to fill out and a sympathetic clerk to tell the frightened, soon-to-be mother where her new mother-in-law lived. On the plus side, there was a military base in Columbia, with a commissary and free medical care. She would begin life anew in South Carolina.

Ruth Fox's reaction was quite different. Who was this hysterical girl standing on her stoop and what would the neighbors think? The last thought remarkable in itself, since the Fox home sat on three acres and behind hedges. It took several days to sort everything out; Jean hysterical and defensive, only breaking down when Ruth wouldn't allow the girl to sleep with her.

Sleep with her! For God's sake, girl, grow up! You're twenty years old.

Jean finally told her mother-in-law why she was afraid to sleep alone. *He* might come again. *He* might come again and rape her again. Anyone could come and rape her. The following day Jean was given a complete physical and the pregnancy confirmed.

Oh, God, yes! Jean cried out in shame, she and Elliot had done *It* over and over again before he had flown overseas. They had practically lived in bed, using room service, and frolicking around, innocent of what any future might hold. Jean swore she would never, ever, do *It* again.

And she never had.

Then came the child. Elliot's child, or so Ruth thought until Peggy's hair grayed before the girl turned sixteen. No one in Ruth's or her husband's family grayed prematurely. Pressing Jean on the issue, Ruth learned no one in the Murphy family grayed prematurely either, and Ruth suspected the worst. The child she had accepted into her home, the child she had introduced to her circle as her dead son's daughter, wasn't his child at all. Peggy Fox was the daughter of the rapist, Raymond Lister.

Ruth had collapsed and taken to her bed. Thank God her husband hadn't lived to see this day. But tonight, almost on the eve of the child's wedding, gazing across the table, Ruth realized Peggy was her grandchild, the only grandchild she had ever known or wanted. Maybe there was something to what Jean said on her radio show, that your parents are the people who take the time to raise you.

Peggy was asking something. ". . . do you remember where, Nana?"

"What did you say, my dear? I'm afraid I was daydreaming." Glancing at her coffee cup, Ruth realized it had been refilled.

"I asked where you honeymooned?"

"Your grandfather and I took a car trip to Florida. Florida wasn't what it is these days. No Disney World, Sea World, or Cape Kennedy."

"Cape Canaveral," corrected Jean when she saw the puzzled looks on the young people's faces. "They changed the name back to Cape Canaveral."

"Well, I wish they could make up their minds."

"And you, Mrs. Fox, where did you honeymoon?" Wesley's boyish grin quickly changed to pain. He turned on his fiancée. "What'd you kick me for, Peg?"

Jean smiled, and as Wesley reached down and rubbed his ankle, he realized he really liked that smile, really liked his future mother-in-law. There was something steady about Peggy's mother, a trait Wesley hoped would surface in his wife-to-be, if she ever grew up.

"Peggy is embarrassed that her father and I ran off and got married. But the answer's Florida, Wesley, same as Nana's."

"Mother, I didn't mean—"

"If you're embarrassed, think of how I felt," said Ruth, chiming in. "I had to live in this town."

Everyone laughed.

"I bet you were madder than hell, Nana."

"Don't use that language in this house, child. Cursing doesn't become you."

"I'm sorry," said Peggy, hanging her head.

"Really, Mrs. Fox, people our age hear that language everywhere, in the movies, on the street"—Wesley smiled—"even in the better homes in Columbia."

"Well, you won't hear it in this house."

"How long do you plan to be gone?" asked Jean, changing the subject.

Her daughter's head came up and she clapped her hands together. "A whole week! Imagine, a whole week in the Bahamas. I'll come back with the coolest tan."

"Your grandfather and I were away a whole month."

"A whole month, really?"

"Yes, but I'll have to admit things moved at a slower pace back in those days."

"Elliot and I had three days together before he went overseas," said Jean, more to herself than anyone else.

"To Afghanistan," stated Wesley.

"Yes."

"What was he doing over there?"

"We were paying back the Soviet Union."

"Paying them back for what?"

"They supported the rebels against us in Vietnam; we returned the favor in Afghanistan. Elliot was flying Stinger missiles into Pakistan for the Afghan rebels."

"Vietnam—that wasn't a good war, was it?"

"People shouldn't have to kill each other to settle their differences. They should be able to work them out."

"Even when someone's bullying you?"

"Trying to kill you?" asked Peggy. "Trying to kill your friends like they did mine in Kuwait?"

Jean considered the question; not the one about Kuwait but how it might pertain to Raymond Lister. At this point, she could consider the question dispassionately. After she'd been raped, she'd wanted Lister dead. But now? Jean didn't think so. That was all behind her. "No, my dear, we should try to work things out."

"Even if they killed a member of your family?" asked her daughter, leaning forward.

A surge of anger rushed through Jean, but instead of saying anything, she reached for her coffee. It was something she had taught herself: how the simplest act can distance you from your emotions and give you an opportunity to think. Or go on the attack.

Jean arched an eyebrow in Wesley Calhoun's direction. "I think I remember someone telling me your maternal grandparents eloped."

Peggy turned on her fiancé. "Is that true?"

The young man flushed. "Yes, but Mama doesn't allow us to talk about it."

"And the way your mother acts when I tease her we might run off and get married."

"Then there's your answer," said Jean, putting down her coffee cup. "Mrs. Calhoun prefers church weddings."

"How did you meet, Mrs. Fox?" asked Wesley, looking for safer ground. "Your—your husband, I mean."

"Please call me 'Jean.' You can reserve 'Mrs. Fox' for Ruth. I was attending junior college near MacDill Air Force Base. Pilots used to drive through the campus and ogle us girls."

"Elliot's father and I had hoped our son would get this flying bug out of his head . . . ." Ruth looked into her coffee cup. Someone had drunk all her coffee.

Jean was lost in her own thoughts, remembering having shot a bird at the cute young man in the red sports car, but once he climbed out . . . in that uniform. And this guy flew over her school every day. It was a heady experience to be courted by a pilot.

"How did it make you feel to lose your husband so soon after marrying him?"

"Wesley, how could you ask such a thing?"

"Don't let Peggy bother you," said Jean. "She has a tendency to romanticize her father."

"But Jean and I don't," spoke up Ruth. "Elliot was a real person to us. Flesh and blood."

"Nana, you know I—"

"Peggy," Jean said, "let's not have any secrets. That's the worst way to start a marriage. With lies." She glanced at her mother-in-law, who was openly staring at her. Both women's lives had been built on a lie, but a lie that worked. "Ruth suffered more than any of us. It's not right for children to predecease their parents."

Her mother-in-law was silent, staring into her empty cup. Hattie moved in, pouring more coffee. Why were these young people fascinated with the past? It was Peggy's desire to know everything about her father. The girl had pictures of him all over her room and tried Ruth's patience with questions about Elliot when her son hadn't even been her father. Would she have the same questions about Raymond Lister?

Looking up, Ruth saw the answer in the girl's eyes. Yes. This bright and inquisitive child would want to know everything about the man. Where he came from, what he was like, and why he would rape anyone. But could Peggy handle being the daughter of a rapist? Ruth didn't think so, not after elevating Elliot to almost deity. Perhaps Jean was right . . . let the past remain in the past.

Wesley was saying something . . . . Really, to keep drifting off like this . . . . Something she was doing more and more these days. Was it old age or the fact that in a few years she might become a great-grandmother, even if the child wouldn't be her great-grandchild. Still, she would treat the baby as if it were.

"What did you say, Wesley?"

"Drift off again, Nana?" asked Peggy with a chuckle.

"Probably too much talk about Elliot."

"That's who I was talking about," said the young man. "I said Peggy might romanticize her father, but I think Mrs. Fox, I mean Jean, might've done the same, otherwise, why hasn't she remarried?"

five

Down the street from the old glass factory stood
Kirby's Bar and Grill. The glass factory had been
in the Hastings family for generations, until one of the
later generations sold the plant to some very sharp operators out of New York. Now the sharp operators
bragged that one out of every two glass containers
manufactured in the United States was manufactured
by their company, but not in Alamo, Florida. The Alamo
facility had been closed as part of a consolidation
project. The people in Alamo knew better. Their jobs
had been eliminated to force people to buy one out of
every two glass containers from some very sharp operators in New York.

Kirby's Bar and Grill had been inherited by Kirby's
son, and although Kirby's father was regularly busted
for illegal card and dice games, Sheriff Johnny Mack
left well enough alone. The sheriff learned the hard
way that a little drinking, fighting, and gambling kept

the natives from being too restless during this long period of economic readjustment.

Raymond pulled into a practically empty gravel parking lot sprouting weeds around its edges. A couple of pickups displayed rifles across their rear windows. Raymond cursed and Diaz glanced at him. Maybe one of those rifles had once belonged to him. The vehicles were similar to what he drove: out-of-date and noisy. Raymond slammed the door of his car, not taking time even to lock up. Hell, do me a favor and steal the sumbitch. As he started across the parking lot, Diaz slipped her hand through his arm.

Kirby's was a cavernous room with a bar running practically the length of the building and a smattering of tables. To the rear was an open dance floor in front of a jukebox. The tables had few patrons, and the ones drinking, drank alone. A man stood behind the bar, drying glasses. He nodded as Raymond and Diaz came through the door, though Raymond figured the bartender was nodding at the opening door. The light had to have blinded him, the room was that dark. Mounted over the ends of the bar hung a pair of lifeless TVs. Booths ran the length of the opposite wall. But the place was cool and they were out of that oven-like heat.

Raymond took a seat after Diaz slid into one of the booths. The place hadn't changed much, just deader than a doornail. The jukebox was new, but the same pictures hung over the bar, pictures of Kirby with governors, sports heroes, and hometown folks, whenever the latter did something to get their picture in the paper. There was even a picture of Raymond up there, not from the trial, but from a game when he'd crashed through the line to nail the quarterback for a safety that won the Bronze Boot that year.

The Bronze Boot came about after Alamo High beat Coventry so many times that one of the Quail supporters was heard to say, as he left the stadium, that they'd been given the boot by Alamo again. This was picked up by the Alamo boosters, who promptly bronzed an old boot and paraded it around the sidelines before the following year's game played on Coventry's home turf. The embarrassed Quails promptly kicked Alamo's collective butts, and after the game demanded the boot, which Alamo would not yield. When a lawsuit was threatened, Alamo turned over the boot—but only until the following year when Alamo pounded the poor Quails again.

Those battles, a part of Raymond's past, had become less spectacular with the loss of so many jobs in Alamo. As the locals would say, these days Alamo couldn't win a game with so many of the boys having to play both ways. The kids were just plain worn out. Kirby's Bar and Grill suffered a similar malaise. Wags said cannonballs could be shot through the cavernous bar without hitting anyone.

A tired-looking woman wandered over from the doorway of a room where four or five men, down on their knees, laughed and cursed, all in good fun. She pulled out a pad and a pencil.

"Something to eat?" she asked, as though she'd be surprised if anyone took her up on her proposition.

Raymond looked at Diaz. "You brought money?"

"In my purse."

"Couple of burgers and a couple of beers." The waitress was staring at him, breaking off her stare only long enough to write down the order.

"You wouldn't happen to be Raymond Lister, would you?" she asked.

Raymond nodded.

The woman brushed back her hair. "I'm Doris Gentry. Pete's older sister. You played football with Pete. I was two years ahead of you in school." The waitress turned and hollered at the bar. "Kirby, this here's Raymond Lister."

Drunken heads lifted off tables and looked in his direction. The bartender nodded but said nothing.

"How about a beer for him and his friend? He just got out of the joint—that right, Ray?"

When Raymond nodded again, Diaz slipped a hand through his arm.

The bartender glanced in the direction of the door where all the laughing and cursing came from, then said, "One. For Raymond."

The waitress patted his arm. "Don't worry, Ray. I'll get your whole meal on the house." She winked at Diaz. "Save your money, honey. Had a cousin who did a stretch at Raiford. Maybe you knew him. Name's Billy Alford."

Raymond shook his head. Women could go on and on.

"Well, Raiford's a big place. For what it's worth, girl shakes her ass at a guy, deserves what she gets," said the waitress smiling at Diaz, "present company excluded, of course. Anything I can get beside the burgers? Fries? Onion rings? How about a half and half? I'll put it on the order with the burgers." With a nod she left to put in the order and pick up their beers.

Donna leaned over. "Did you know her?"

"Too old for me."

"Maybe she was more than a couple of years ahead of you in school." She squeezed his arm. "Looks closer to fifty if she's a day."

"You're not from around here, are you?"

"Coventry. I was a Quail." Diaz took out her cigarettes. "That bother you?"

"Nah. That was years ago."

Raymond took the cigarettes from Diaz before she could slip them back into her purse, then shook one out, stuck the pack in his shirt pocket, and pulled out a lighter. He lit his cigarette, then the woman's.

"What made you come to Kirby's?" she asked.

Raymond looked around. The drunks had returned to their beers, the bartender was cleaning his glasses again, and from the back room came more laughter and a few good-natured groans.

"I was told this was where the action was."

"You were told wrong. Coventry's got topless bars, the whole nine yards."

Calvin Burdett strolled out of the room where all the noise was coming from, a couple of guys trailing in his wake. Through the doorway, men could be seen on their hands and knees throwing dice against a corner. Burdett asked for a beer, turned his back to the bar, and slipped a foot up on the foot railing. He leaned back where he could survey the place. Seeing Lister in the booth across the room, Burdett left the hangers-on and sauntered over. Only when he was closer to the booth did he see the woman in the darkness.

"Raymond," he said.

"Hey, Cal, what you doing here?"

Burdett took a chair and whirled it around, sitting on it backwards. "Remember, I own this place."

"Well, I'm here—for the action."

Burdett jerked a thumb toward the back room. "In there for Alamo." He glanced at Diaz. "But you seem to have found your own."

Raymond put his arm around Diaz. "Donna lives under Gladys."

"Yeah. Seems I remember that." He looked back at Lister. "So what you doing?"

"Came in for a couple of burgers."

"They'll be free or I'll kick Kirby's ass."

"You kept Kirby on after buying out his daddy?"

"Where else would he go?" Burdett glanced at the bartender still cleaning glasses. "Kirby hasn't got his daddy's personality, but he's hell on them glasses. So, you're going to eat here, then—"

"Thought we'd take in Coventry." Raymond rubbed Diaz's arm and the woman snuggled up against him.

"Well," said Burdett, getting to his feet, "have what you want. It's on the house. I don't want you cracking that roll your sister held for you." He glanced at the men waiting at the bar. They were watching Burdett closely. "Well, back to work."

"So you found somebody."

"Like hell I did. They're all pussies. Sorry, ma'am," Burdett said to Diaz. "None of them have the balls." With another glance at Diaz, Burdett said, "Well, see you around."

"Yeah. See you."

Once Burdett left, Raymond took his hand off Diaz. But the woman was having none of that. She put her hand on his arm and held it tight. "You know that guy?"

"From years ago."

"I don't know what he was doing when you left town, but nowadays he deals in dope."

Raymond took a drag off his cigarette. "That's what I figured."

"You aren't going to have anything to do with him, are you?"

"What are you—my mother?"

Her hand slid off his arm. "I just didn't want you to get mixed up with something that'd send you back to prison."

"What's it to you?"

Diaz smiled. "Well, I kind of thought you were interested in me."

"Don't get any screwy ideas, Diaz. I've got a job to do."

After dinner, Jean returned to her condo. Wesley would drop off Peggy later. Then again, Peggy might have her fiancé return her to Ruth's, where, tomorrow morning, she could wheedle and cajole her grandmother into buying something else for the wedding. Peggy always kept clothes at Ruth's, at first because Ruth missed the girls when they moved out, then when Peggy needed her so-called space, and now, with more predatory interests in mind.

Jean's condo was in a fourteen-story structure which had been completed during a time when the state capital became overbuilt with condos. Very quickly the locals ran out of prospective tenants, then money. The bank repossessed the building, and there it sat, half finished, until the bank was approached by a group of Yankees interested in investing in a part of the country apparently impervious to recessions, but not to overbuilding. The men from up north named their latest acquisition Columbiana Towers, and moved several units at extremely low prices to some very high-profiled people in the city. Then, after the proper donations were made to the right political races, the Columbiana was allowed a variance and those high-profile people began to move in, before the building was completed. One of those people was Jean Fox.

Columbiana Towers had a twenty-two percent occupancy rate, most on the lower floors. The Yankees weren't stupid. They weren't going to sell the higher units at those cheaper prices. Jean, sensing a bargain, made up the difference and moved in on the eleventh floor. Sheets of plastic had been hung on the unfinished floors to keep out the spring thunderstorms.

Did it always rain this much in South Carolina, asked the Yankees. Yes, said the man selling the sheeting, and sold them even more plastic.

Most comings and goings were through the garage.

The front door was locked at night and a guard was stationed in the kiosk twenty-four hours a day. This was important to Jean. Being on the radio, she was not recognized on the street by many people, but the more adoring fans could become rather troublesome. They seemed to think Dr. Fox was on call whenever they ran into her. Or tracked her down.

A storm was passing through as a chubby young man wearing the brown uniform of a security guard stepped out of the kiosk of the Columbiana. He smiled as Jean's white BMW rolled down the ramp and out of the rain. The gate was down, preventing Jean from entering the garage.

"Evening, Mrs. Fox. Have a nice time at your mother-in-law's?"

Jean frowned. How did this guy know—Peggy! She'd have to speak to the girl about telling everyone where they were. Peggy would talk to anyone—which was frightening in itself. "I'm an artist, Mother," her daughter would say. "I have to know how people think." Well, that didn't include telling people what the family was up to every minute of their lives.

"Very pleasant, Jamie. Now would you raise the gate?"

The chubby young man smiled. "I've got a new girlfriend and I wanted to ask you a question."

Jean sighed. Stubbs always had a new girlfriend, and none of them were real. "What's the problem this time?"

"She's on Prozac—"

"Jamie, you don't need the hassle."

"But she needs me."

"Jamie, if you want to spend your life jousting with windmills, that's fine with me, but I've had a long day." She raised a finger off the steering column. "Now, if you don't mind."

"But, Dr. Fox—"

"We've talked about this before. You can't save these women. Now raise the gate."

"But, Dr. Fox—"

"Jamie, I have packages to carry upstairs, it's late, and I'd like to get to bed. Now, would you please raise the gate?"

Stubbs only stood there, shifting around and staring at his feet.

She was going to have to talk to someone about this fruitcake. Yeah, right, and who brings out the fruit in these cakes? "Jamie?"

Nodding as he continued to stare at his feet, the security guard finally stepped into the kiosk and punched a button on the counter.

Jean didn't even look at him as her car rolled into the garage. Very quickly she drove to her space near the elevator and got out. She closed the front door of the car and opened the back one. Using her remote, she set the locks, then started taking gifts out of the back seat. One of the boxes fell to the ground and Jean cursed. Where was Peggy when she needed her? Out dancing the night away while good old mom toted all the wedding gifts home.

Jean put down the packages and started her stack again. Finished, she closed the car door with her hip.

When she turned around she saw Jamie Stubbs headed in her direction. Not again! There was just so much she could take, and when she'd suggested Jamie enter therapy, the young man said he didn't have the money. He lived at home and had a mother to care for. Jean offered to pay for the first session, even recommend a psychotherapist, but Jamie could never seem to make the appointments.

Jean hurried to the elevator and punched the button with a corner of a gift. The elevator lurched into action, but before it arrived, Stubbs was at her side, taking several packages off her stack.

"Give you a hand there, Dr. Fox."

"No, no, I've got them," she said, twisting away.

The packages fell to the ground just as the elevator doors opened.

"Shit," muttered Jean.

Jamie looked up from where he had bent over to pick up the packages. His mouth had fallen open.

"Sorry for my language. Just restack them in my arms and get back to work."

Instead, Stubbs scooped up the remaining packages and stacked them against his chest. "No problem. It's slow this time of night."

"And if Wesley and Peggy are right behind me?"

"Not a chance," said the security guard with a smile. "They always go dancing."

Jean sighed and stepped on the elevator with Stubbs.

six

After finishing her burger, Donna excused herself. Before the door of the ladies' room closed behind her, Burdett walked over to the booth. He took a seat as the waitress poured another cup of coffee and tried to make small talk with Raymond. When Burdett sat down, the waitress disappeared into the grill.

"I still need that muscle, Ray."

"I don't know . . ." Raymond glanced at the ladies room. "I think I'm going to get lucky tonight." He grinned. "Maybe the whole week."

"Hell, Ray, pussy's pussy, but this is money—ten grand and I can't wait."

Raymond sipped from his coffee before saying, "I've got almost twenty."

"It couldn't've done that well in any damn bank."

"You forget, I was in jail during the Eighties. Sometimes my money earned more than ten percent." He looked around the bar and grill. "My money might've been used to finance this place."

"The hell you say! I paid cash, and that's what we're talking about. Cash."

"And maybe that's what this is all about—cash."

Burdett stared at Raymond. "I thought you were hot to get after that woman who put you away."

"I just got out of jail, Cal. Pussy's not just pussy."

"That's not what you said this afternoon."

"This afternoon I hadn't met Donna."

"Okay. Fifteen thousand."

Raymond took another sip of coffee.

"Twenty thousand and that's my last offer."

Raymond put down the cup. "When do we leave?"

Burdett glanced at Diaz who was coming out of the ladies room. "I guess when you're finished with her."

"I am finished with her."

Burdett shook his head. "You are a bastard, aren't you?"

"If you had all the money you needed, would you take a chance on going back to the joint for a measly ten grand?"

The men both got to their feet as Diaz returned to the table. She looked from one man to the other. "Time to go?"

Raymond handed her the keys to the Ford. "Take the car back to the house, Donna."

"Take the car back to the house?" She glanced at Burdett. "What do you mean 'take the car back to the house?' Where are you going?"

"That's none of your business."

"Raymond, I thought you and I were—"

"Take the car back to the house, Donna!"

The woman threw the keys at him. "You can drive your own damn car back to the house." She whirled around to go.

Lister fielded the key with one hand and grabbed the woman with the other, whipping her around to face him. Before she could bring her hands up to defend herself, one of the keys slashed across her face. When the woman screamed, heads turned and looked in their direction. The bartender stopped drying glasses, then started drying again. The waitress came out of the grill, saw what was happening, and disappeared into the grill again.

Diaz pulled a hand away from her cheek and saw the blood. "You bastard, you've ruined my face."

"Are you going to take the car back to the house or would you like matching cheeks?"

Donna shuddered, then nodded. Tears mixed with blood dripped across her blouse. Calvin Burdett pulled a wad of napkins out of the holder and handed them to her. Diaz pressed the napkins against her cheek, and as she did, winced in pain.

"Donna, you were thinking of leaving town—I think it's time you do. Give her some money, Cal."

"Give her some money! What the hell for? You're the one with all the money."

Burdett saw the look on Raymond's face, shook his head, and pulled out a roll of bills. He plopped part of the wad into Diaz's hand. The woman stood there, holding the money and keys in one hand, the wad of napkins against her cheek with the other.

As the two men left the bar, Burdett said, "I'll have Johnny Mack stop by and make sure she moves along."

The silence of the elevator ride was broken by Stubbs. "I won't see Peggy again tonight. She won't come home until after I'm off duty."

Keeping her attention on the floor indicator, Jean said, "Well, young people don't want to be around old fogies."

"You're being too hard on yourself, Dr. Fox. You're still a good-looking woman."

Jean continued to stare at the floor indicator. Just a few more floors. Just a few more floors.

Just a few more floors? Get a grip! This is Jamie Stubbs and you aren't Elizabeth Hartner. You aren't about to be murdered in your own home, so get over it!

The bell rang, the doors opened, and Jean hustled out of the elevator and down the hall.

"Hey, Doc! Wait up!"

"I want to put these down. I've been carrying gifts home for days."

"And you didn't want me to help. Anytime you need my help, just let me know."

Jean fumbled with her purse as she hurried down the hall. She'd returned the keys to her purse when she'd needed both hands to carry all the packages. She almost muttered another vulgarity but remembered how the last one had affected Jamie.

The eleventh floor hallway was absent of carpet or

wallpaper, just a concrete floor and walls of sheetrock. Jean passed an open door, and from inside the unit came the rhythmical tapping of a hammer. Paper sacks from fast food restaurants littered the corridor, and here and there lay mashed butts or spittle from a chaw.

Jean pulled the keys out, fumbled to find the correct one, and inserted the key. Opening the door and pushing it back, Jean put her packages on a narrow table just inside the door. "You don't have to come in."

Stubbs pushed by her, down the short hallway, and into the living room. The door closed behind him on a piece of thick, dark paper used to protect the carpet from the work in the hallway. "It's no bother, Doc. Where do you want these things?"

Riding down the Florida Turnpike in his Cadillac, Burdett raised his voice over the music on the radio. "You hooked up with that woman pretty quick. She really lives under Gladys?"

Raymond nodded.

"Her husband gets out of the county lockup next month and he's a real hothead."

Raymond shrugged.

"Just thought you might want to know."

"Cal, I don't give a damn about that woman."

They drove along in silence until Burdett said, "Just enough to make me think you're not available."

Again Raymond said nothing.

"You conned me out of ten grand."

"You made the deal. Want to welch on it?"

"No. I want to renegotiate."

"Just another word for welching."

"Not exactly. I know where the Murphy woman is. What's that worth?"

Raymond thought about this for a moment. "How specific is your information?"

Calvin glanced at the radio. "I found out where her mother-in-law lives. Is that specific enough?"

Raymond settled back into his seat. "Now something like that, that would be worth at least five grand."

"How about ten?"

"Five, Cal. Five. Seems like I wasn't the only one running games on people this evening."

"And that's something you'd best remember: one man's game might be another man's gain." Calvin punched a button on the radio. When he did, the voice of Dr. Jean Fox filled the car.

"Aw, shit, Cal. You listen to that?"

"Her callers are a hoot and Fox really cracks on them. You wouldn't know there were so many losers in the world."

"Yeah, and one of them is driving this car."

"They didn't listen to her in the joint?"

"They tried, but I made them stay with Rush Limbaugh."

"So you don't know who this bitch is?"

Raymond shifted around in his seat and faced Burdett. "You don't know where Murphy is, do you?"

"Yeah, dumb-ass. She's on the radio, right in front of you."

Jean followed Stubbs from the front door but not into the living room. "Just put them on the table, Jamie." After Stubbs had, Jean said, "Thank you" and returned to the door.

Stubbs was smiling when he walked toward her. "You're all set." Stopping at the door, he asked, "You sure I shouldn't date this woman?"

"I'm sure." Jean held the door open for him.

"Well, if you think so." He smiled and went out the door. "Thanks for the advice, Doc."

"You're welcome."

The door closed as soon as she let it go, and Jean didn't notice the paper protecting her carpet kept the door from latching. While she was stacking gifts on the serving window between the kitchen and the dining room, a knock came at the door.

Jean gritted her teeth. What would it take to get rid of this guy? She slapped a gift on the stack and stomped back to the door. Would she need a restraining order against him, too?

"Jamie, I told you . . . ."

It wasn't Jamie Stubbs at the door but Ernie Kelly, fan extraordinaire.

Over the voice on the radio, Raymond asked, "How's she on this late? I thought she came on during the day."

"It's tape-delayed."

"What?"

"It's on during the day and later that night. They do the same thing with Rush Limbaugh. I listen to them while rolling down the highway at night." Burdett shrugged. "It passes the time."

Raymond returned his attention to the radio. Some girl had called in about an abortion. What was the big deal? Get rid of the kid and get on with your life.

". . . what do you think, Dr. Fox?"

Dr. Fox? Could the woman on the radio really be the Murphy girl from Coventry?

"My folks want me to give up the baby for adoption. My girlfriends say I should have an abortion."

"And what do you think?"

"I don't know. That's why I'm calling."

"Abby, I can't make up your mind about this. I have an opinion, but so do many others. How far along are you?"

"Six weeks. My parents say it's a sin to kill the child, but my friends say it's a fetus, not a baby."

"Do your parents have any other grandchildren?"

"I'm an only child. My folks were really good to me when I was growing up and I feel real bad about messing up."

"Were you raised in the church?"

"Went every Sunday."

"Have your parents talked to you about what it means to them for you to abort their first grandchild?"

"My father said I'd been a silly girl. Mama just cried."

"Aren't you old enough to have an abortion without your parents' consent?"

"Sure. I'm eighteen."

"So you didn't have to tell them."

"I guess not."

"Then why'd you do it?"

"I guess I wanted to know how they felt."

"Abby, you knew how they would feel. Why did you tell them?"

"I've always been able to go to them—oh, Dr. Fox, I didn't think I could get pregnant. It was only the first time Jimmy and I did it."

"Have any of your girlfriends had an abortion?"

"No."

"Would they tell you if they had?"

"I think so. I'm sure of it. Yeah. We're pretty tight."

"So, you have another group of people giving you advice who've never been through a similar experience?"

"I guess you could say that. I'm supposed to go off to college this fall. My folks saved up the money. I really don't have time to raise a baby."

"Then why don't you have the abortion? It's legal."

"I just don't feel right about it. I know it's not a baby—yet. My friends say it's not even as advanced as a bug."

"But what's growing inside your body isn't going to become a bug, is it?"

"What are you telling me, Dr. Fox?"

"I'm telling you there are a lot of people who aren't being completely truthful with you, meaning your parents and your girlfriends. You ask one shrink and they'll tell you the moral thing to do is to have the baby and put the child up for adoption. If you have to postpone school for a year, that's insignificant compared to destroying a life. You ask another shrink and the first thing out of that shrink's mouth is: It's your body and nobody has a right to tell you what to do with it. The fact you were raised in the church means little to that second shrink. Remember, Abby, you'll have to live with yourself and your family a lot longer than any set of girlfriends, especially these girls. They'll view you as being rather dense for not having an abortion."

"They're real good friends. I've known them ever since junior high."

"And not one of them encouraged you to carry this baby to term? I find that hard to believe and I worry about the people you hang with."

"Well, one girl did. At first."

"Until peer pressure got to her."

"Dr. Fox, what if I decided to have the abortion?"

"Then, my dear, there's nothing I could say that would change your mind."

Raymond stared at the radio. What the hell had been decided? What was the answer? He shook his head.

Burdett noticed this and laughed. "She's a little more than you expected, isn't she, Ray?"

The fan extraordinaire pushed his way past Jean, down the short hallway, and into the living room. Ernie Kelly was a pale-skinned man in his late twenties who wore black-rimmed glasses. A light paunch hung over the top of a pair of blue work pants. His shirt was damp and the cuffs of his pants and his shoes wet. He walked over to the glass wall and stared at the blurred lights across the river.

He wiped the glass clear. "Can't see my place."

"Ernie, how did you get in here?"

"Came in through the garage."

"You're in violation of the restraining order."

The young man smiled as he turned away from the window wall and crossed the room. When he reached the hallway, he put a hand on the wall behind Jean and leaned down to her. "What's the matter, Doc? You aren't scared of me, are you?"

"No, but you don't belong up here. Now, I want—"

"I don't belong up here!" Ernie pushed himself off the wall. "I ought to fix it so I could come up here any-time I want. I can do that, you know."

Jean had had enough of this foolishness. She stepped into the kitchen and reached for the phone.

"Now what are you doing?"

"I'm calling Security."

"The hell you are!" Ernie snatched the phone away, then glanced at the door that had closed behind him. "This is as good a time as any to fix you."

Jean backed into the kitchen. "I don't know what you're talking about and I don't care to know. I just want you out of my house."

Kelly hung up the phone and reached for her.

Retreating, Jean bumped into the stove. "Get out of here or I'll go down the hall and find someone who'll throw you out."

When he kept moving toward her, Jean threw her arms up and forced her way past him. As she stormed out of the kitchen, Kelly grabbed her by the hair, jerking her back. Jean screamed. He laughed.

"They'll never hear you, Doc, and this'll only take a minute. Then you'll always let me up here."

Kelly pulled her into the living room, pushing her ahead of him, and with his free hand, pulled down Jean's jacket, locking her arms alongside her. Forcing her to the floor, he straddled her before Jean could roll away.

Jean turned her face out of the carpet and tried to keep an evenness in her voice. "Stop this right now, Ernie. Peggy will be here any minute."

"Your daughter never comes home before midnight. I don't think she really likes you."

Jean screamed when Kelly pulled her dress up over her hips. "Scream your head off. In a minute, you'll belong to me." Kelly cursed when he saw the panty hose, grabbed a handful, and ripped them off.

Tears burned in Jean's eyes. Oh, God, don't let this happen again! She cleared her throat to say, "Don't do this, Ernie. You don't know what you're doing."

Kelly was on his knees, straddling her legs and unzipping his pants. "Oh, I know what I'm doing."

"Ernie, I won't tell . . . if you'll only go away." She screamed again as Kelly's hardness pressed against her buttocks.

He silenced her with a blow across the back of the head. "Shut up! This'll only take a minute, but you've got to open up to me." He forced her legs apart.

Jean pulled them together, and for her trouble, was slapped across the back of the head again. The room swam, the dining room set became a brown blur, and blood roared in her ears, drowning out Kelly's gasps. She felt an overwhelming urge to give in and get it over. She felt so tired . . . .

"Please," she moaned, then realized she hadn't been rolled over. Kelly wasn't going to rape her! *She was to be sodomized!* That's what he'd meant about her belonging to him. How could she tell anyone she'd been sodomized? Especially after being raped. Everyone would think she was an out-and-out tease.

Jean bucked and heaved and tried to throw him off. Impossible. Kelly weighed a ton and there was always that hand across the back of her head. Lights exploded when he hit her, then the room began to darken.

Down the hall, Avery McFarland put down his hammer and wiped his forehead. He ran the bandanna around his face, drying it along with his beard. His plaid shirt was damp, his jeans had sawdust in the lap. He surveyed the kitchen from where he sat on the floor. This unit was almost finished, then it would be up to the fourteenth floor, the top floor, but despite everything he did, people wanted everything done yesterday.

Damn Yankees! Didn't they do any hunting or fishing up north? Not by the way they were working his ass off. But the money, now the money, it was real good, as the construction supervisor pointed out.

"And Avery," the supervisor had said, "it may look screwy, this finishing a few units on each floor, but the publicity generated a forty-six percent increase—"

There was a scream, followed by a man's laughter. At least that's what Avery thought he heard. Another scream, this one cut off, then a man cursing. McFarland scrambled to his feet and hurried into the hall.

He studied the unfinished side of the building. Nothing but a plywood door securing the open space. It was supposed to keep the tenants from falling off the building, if they were foolish enough to go out there. Avery wandered down to the plywood door. Maybe some workman had lured his girlfriend up here for a little slap and tickle and it had gotten out of hand.

McFarland shook the lock. Nope. Locked up tight. He looked down the hall in the opposite direction. No one down there but the tight-assed woman who lived with her high-and-mighty daughter, then a couple of condos—

Another scream and McFarland was running down the hall to the woman's door. He tried to stop by grabbing the knob. His foot came down on a food wrapper covered with special sauce and his leg went out from under him.

McFarland slammed to the floor and the fall jarred him. Stunned, he lay there for a moment, then turned over and got to his hands and knees. He pushed back the door with his shoulder, bulling his way into the condo on all fours. The door hadn't closed because the thick paper had caught between the door and the jamb. The carpet inside the unit had even more paper on it, and where it flowed into the living room, he saw a woman's legs pushed apart. A pair of shoes and a hairy butt sat between those legs. Pantyhose clung to the bottom of her legs and her feet were upside down.

Sweet Jesus! The guy wasn't trying to rape her but cornhole her!

McFarland leaped to his feet and raced down the short hallway and slapped the asshole across the back of the head. "Get off her!"

The asshole jerked around. "What the hell?" was all he got out before McFarland swung at him. The blow missed the chin but connected with the young man's shoulder.

Kelly fell off, scooting away. Where'd this guy come from? Nobody was supposed to be up here, except for some screwball installing cabinets all hours of the night. But the carpenter was a loner, never having anything to do with anyone.

Kelly threw a foot at the carpenter to keep him at bay. Out of the corner of his eye, he saw Fox on her hands and knees, pulling her skirt down over those long white legs. Damn, he wanted some of that! And on a regular basis. But first this carpenter.

The workman launched a kick of his own, and Kelly rolled away, behind the couch, pulling up his pants and snapping the fly. He leaped to his feet and saw the carpenter on the other side of the sofa. The fool wore a workman's knife on his belt but wasn't using it. Dumb bastard.

Kelly leaped to the couch, ready to pounce on the bastard on the other side. But the carpenter was gone! He wasn't there! And Ernie was off balance and headed for the coffee table. He tried to steady himself, but his foot caught between the cushions, sucking the foot down and tripping him. Ernie threw his arms out to break his fall but ended up sprawling across the table and shattering the glass.

Jean got to her feet in time to watch the carpenter pick up Kelly by the back of his pants and his shirt collar. The carpenter didn't seem to notice the blood dripping from Kelly's face, now dripping across the carpet as he ran the young man against the glass wall overlooking the river. The glass shuddered but held. Using Kelly as a battering ram wouldn't necessarily break the glass wall, but it just might break Kelly's neck.

Jean dashed across the room, avoiding the smashed table, and when the carpenter swung back for another go, Jean grabbed one of Kelly's feet, throwing off the rhythm of the swing. She stumbled forward with the swing, and at the same time, felt something bite into her foot.

Glass! She was standing in glass! And glass dribbled from the face of Ernie Kelly as well as blood. Who made a table that could hurt people so? The carpenter tried to pull away, but Jean held on.

"It's okay, lady. I'll take care of the little son of a bitch."

"I'll call the cops if you don't put him down."

"But he was trying to—"

"I know what he was trying to do." Jean glanced at where the blood puddled up on the beige carpet under Ernie's face.

McFarland dropped Kelly to the floor and wiped his hands on his jeans. "Well, pardon me all to hell." He stepped over Kelly and started for the door.

"No, you can't leave . . . ." The room swam and Jean's legs felt like rubber.

At the entrance of the short hallway, the carpenter turned around. "And why the hell not?"

"You've got to . . . ."

Jean glanced at Kelly. He was moving—no! The room was moving. She looked at the carpenter. The man was out of focus and the room growing darker.

"You've got to call . . ." Her voice sounded very far away. " . . . nine . . . one . . . one," she managed to get out before collapsing to the floor among the blood and glass.

seven

*P*eggy opened the door and saw the lights on in the condominium.

"Mother, I'm home, so you can go to bed."

Crossing the thick paper protecting the carpet in the short hallway, Peggy saw the coffee table smashed and some stranger with a beard bending over a man lying on his back. The bearded man held a towel to the unconscious one's face, wedding gifts littered the floor, and a trail of blood ran from couch to wall where more blood smeared the glass wall overlooking the river.

"What's going on here?"

The bearded man looked up. "This boy's hurt himself."

"Hurt himself?" Peggy reached for the phone inside the kitchen door. "I'll call EMS."

"I've already done that."

Peggy looked around, frantically. "Where's my mother?"

"In the bedroom, lying down."

Peggy ran down the hall. "Mother!"

Jean stumbled out of the bedroom. Her blouse was smeared with blood. She appeared groggy.

Peggy grabbed her mother by the shoulders, then put an arm around her waist. "Are you all right?"

"I'm so glad to see you. I was so worried."

"Worried about me?" They returned to the living room. "What about you?" Peggy gestured at the smashed table, the blood, the gifts, and the carpenter holding the towel to the unconscious man's face. When the workman repositioned the towel, Peggy saw a face that looked like ten pounds of ground meat. Her arm slid off her mother's waist and Jean had to help her daughter stand. The girl's face was white. She let her mother help her to the sofa where they sat down.

"What—what happened?"

Jean glanced at the carpenter. He was looking at her as if to say, it's your call, lady.

"It's Ernie Kelly."

"The stalker?"

"He showed up at the door . . . ." Jean glanced at the carpenter again, hunched down among wedding gifts scattered across the floor.

McFarland said, "I was working down the hall when I heard your mother scream."

"You screamed? Mother, I don't remember you ever screaming, not even when I fell off my horse and broke both arms."

"Well, Peggy, there was so much . . . ."

"Blood," said the carpenter.

"I'm sorry, but I don't even know your name."

Avery McFarland introduced himself.

"Avery, this is my daughter. Peggy's to be married next month. That's what got us into this mess. All these gifts."

"Mother!"

Jean smiled, feeling her old self returning. She could do this. Yeah, she could handle this. "Mr. McFarland made me lie down and found a towel for Ernie's face."

"I think you should go in the bedroom and lie down."

"Your daughter's right, Mrs. Fox. At least until the police get here."

Jean stared at McFarland. They didn't need the police here. Not asking all those questions. What would she tell them? That she'd almost been . . . the papers would have a field day with that.

"Mother, do you need a blanket?"

"What? Why?"

"You shivered."

"A good stiff drink," said McFarland, from where he knelt on the floor. "Whiskey, if you've got it." He gestured at the unconscious Kelly. "I'd get it, but I'd have to let go of the boy here."

Peggy leaped from the couch and hurried over to the bar, where she splashed some whiskey into a glass, then brought the drink over to the sofa.

After a long swallow and a small gasp, Jean said, "I really don't think we need the police."

"Mrs. Fox, EMS usually calls them in situations like this."

"I don't know . . . ."

"That boy tripping across your table and dropping

all your daughter's gifts. It had to be quite a shock."

Jean scanned the room. None of the wedding gifts had initially been strewn across the floor, and yet here they were, scattered among the blood and glass. And she was missing her panty hose. She looked around. Where were her hose?

"Mother, if you won't go in the bedroom, would you please lie down?"

"Your daughter's right. You need to pull yourself together before the police arrive."

"Uh—okay." Jean took another swallow of the whiskey and let Peggy pick up her feet and put them on the sofa.

"Peggy," asked McFarland, "why don't you go down and make sure the paramedics can get inside? That front door's always locked and I don't remember if I told them about using the rear entrance."

"I'm not going anywhere unless my mother promises not to leave that sofa."

McFarland smiled. "I'll make sure she stays there, if I have to go over there and sit on top of her. And if I do, this fellow's sure to bleed to death."

When the paramedics arrived they put the unconscious Kelly on a stretcher, covered him with a blanket, and started an IV, hung from a thin metal pole. Moments later, two plainclothes policemen walked in. The white cop had tousled brown hair and a tired look on his face. Lt. Dan Stafford had more than one question for Jean Fox, and very quickly he learned he didn't like her answers.

Stafford was accompanied by John Greene, a bald black man who wore a beret. The first thing Greene did was take off his beret, walk over to the glass wall, and stare at the lights on the far side of the river. Or was he examining the blood caked on the glass?

As the stretcher was wheeled out, Jean glanced at the unconscious Kelly. "I guess I freaked out . . . seeing all that blood." Peggy sat alongside her on the sofa, holding her mother's hand.

"And you say Kelly tripped and fell into the table?"

"Yes."

"Had any trouble with Kelly before?"

"He has a restraining order to stay away from me."

"And your and his relationship was?"

"There is none, beyond the fact he's an overzealous fan."

"But you allowed him inside your condominium?"

"He wanted to help me with my daughter's wedding gifts."

"And you let him in?" asked Greene, joining Stafford at the sofa and skirting the coffee table, which had three of its legs collapsed and the center glass smashed.

"There was little I could do but humor him since he was already on the property."

"Does the guard in the kiosk know about the restraining order?" asked Greene.

"I'm sure he does."

The black man headed for the door, past Avery McFarland, who leaned against the wall. "I'll check with the guard and find out how that happened."

After his partner left, Stafford asked, "What's this

guard's name?"

"Jamie Stubbs, but I wouldn't want to get him into any more trouble."

"More trouble?" asked Stafford, looking up from his pad. "What other trouble has Stubbs been in?"

"Oh, Jamie helped me bring the packages upstairs."

"Then what did you need Kelly for?"

"I—I didn't. I opened the door because I thought it was Jamie. I thought we had dropped—"

"Mother, you opened the door without looking through the peephole? I don't know how many times you've warned me—"

"Once again, Mrs. Fox—"

"She's a psychotherapist and should be addressed as 'doctor.'"

"Very well. Did Kelly have any gifts in his hands?"

"Two."

"For you or your daughter?"

"For Peggy, of course."

"I just thought, if he was trying to see you, he might have had a gift for you."

"No," said Jean, shaking her head. "They were for Peggy."

"Then Kelly's accident was caused by him trying to place two boxes on the table?" Stafford scanned the packages on the floor. "Which ones were they?"

"I really don't know." Jean glanced at the floor. "Actually, there was a lot more to it than that."

Across the room Avery McFarland came off the wall. A worried look appeared on his face.

"A lot more of what?" asked Stafford.

"Well . . ." said Jean, almost smiling, "he did a little dance."

"A little dance?"

"He brushed past me at the door, came down the hall, and tossed the gifts on the table. After that, he strutted around, saying he was glad to finally be invited into my home."

"But you didn't invite him?"

"Not at all, and once he was in here, I threatened to call the police if he didn't leave. Before I could, Ernie had leaped on the sofa and was jumping around like a little kid, saying how happy he was to be here. He lost his footing, I guess, and fell on the glass."

"You guess? You're not sure how he hit the table?"

"Actually, I'm not. I had the phone in my hand—it's in the kitchen—and was dialing 911. The next thing I knew Ernie had smashed into the table. When I came out of the kitchen, he was stumbling around and bleeding badly. Before I could reach him, he ran into the wall." She gestured at the glass.

Across the room, Avery McFarland relaxed against the wall. This woman was good. Real good.

"Had Kelly come on to you before?"

"No more than approaching me on the street for advice. When he wouldn't stop, I asked for the restraining order. I didn't want to, but . . . does Ernie have some kind of record?"

"Not for sexual assault, he doesn't."

Peggy gaped at the detective. "Sexual assault?"

"But that wasn't what I asked," Jean said.

"And just what did you ask, Dr. Fox?"

"I—I just wanted to make sure . . . ." Jean cleared her throat. "I think the owners would like to know how people gain access to this building. There's a lock on the front door and the rear entrance has a security guard."

"Is that what you really wanted to know?"

Jean straightened up on the sofa. "I wouldn't want Ernie getting away with anything."

The policeman glanced at the blood-covered floor with its coppery smell, which even the air conditioning couldn't remove. "I don't think he did."

McFarland rolled off the wall. "Lieutenant, if you're saying this happened any other way than what the lady's said, then spit it out."

"I'm not saying anything. But I would like to hear Mr. Kelly's side of the story. If he survives."

"Survives?" McFarland almost shouted. "You make it sound like Mrs. Fox tried to kill the little fool."

Peggy gripped her mother's hand again.

"And why would you call him a little fool?"

"Because the dummy nearly killed himself when he hit that table."

The detective glanced at the glass wall overlooking the river. "Then got to his feet and ran into that wall."

"Yeah—like a chicken with his head cut off."

"How would you know? Were you here when it happened?"

McFarland looked puzzled. "I was down the hall."

"Then how would you know what happened?"

"Any fool can see what happened. Anybody but a cop." McFarland headed for the door. "I have a kitchen to finish. If you have any more questions, you can ask them while I'm getting my work done."

Once he was gone, Peggy asked, "You don't really think my mother tried to kill Mr. Kelly, do you, Lieutenant?"

"What I think doesn't matter, Miss Fox. It's the facts that count. Men who hit their faces on tabletops hard enough to smash the glass don't usually get up and walk around, much less run into a wall."

"He could've been disoriented, like Mr. McFarland said."

"Anything's possible."

"But you're hinting that my mother and Mr. McFarland colluded to kill Mr. Kelly."

"I'm just saying your mother's and Mr. McFarland's story doesn't make sense. Dr. Fox, you say you've never met McFarland before tonight?"

"I may have seen him coming or going. This was the first time I've ever spoken with him."

"Well, I hope you're not holding out on me. Ernie Kelly has no record, but your friend has. McFarland's been in jail more than once." He gestured at the table and all the blood. "And this is something Avery McFarland could've easily done."

"But why?" asked Peggy, leaning forward, desperate to understand. "Why would Mr. McFarland want to kill someone for my mother?"

Stafford looked at Jean. "That's a question your mother will have to answer."

❖   ❖   ❖

Raymond and Calvin were to meet the drug dealers at a crossroads where an abandoned Texaco stood. Up and down both blacktops nothing lay but miles and miles of beans; no trees, no power lines, no other structures, just acres and acres of beans. It was a good place to hold a meet. The former service station was an old cinder block building with boarded-up windows and a narrow porch, where empty fertilizer sacks and newspapers had blown into its corners.

Three drug dealers stood at the edge of the crossroads in front of a red pimpmobile. Parked across from them, in a corner of one of the fields, another man sat in an old Chevy with a souped-up engine, ready to do any blocking and ramming if the deal went sour.

As Burdett's car approached the intersection, Raymond said, "Pull through the intersection and stop in front of the Chevy. A hard turn and that Chevy just might bury its front end in the loose dirt."

Burdett nodded and pulled through the intersection and parked his Caddy in front of the Chevy. The three black men in front of the car that looked like a pimpmobile watched them stop, as did the driver of the Chevy.

"When we get out of the car, stay at least ten feet away from me. If they want to back-shoot us, they'll have to chance hitting one of their own men."

After climbing out of the car, Burdett grinned across its top. "You and I should do more business. We work real good together."

"Like I told you, I've got other business."

"Yeah," said Burdett, losing his smile, "and like I told you, revenge don't pay as well as dealing drugs."

"You're not the one who wants the revenge."

"You've got that right. All I've ever wanted is the money."

Raymond was staring at the three drug dealers, black men who wore flashy clothes and lightweight jackets. "I don't want to blow your quality control, but the sooner we're out of here, the better."

Burdett faced the black men. As he did, he gripped a nine millimeter, the briefcase in his other hand. The fields seemed to go on forever and a light fog obscured anything more than a hundred yards away. Still, there was a decent moon and you could make out the features of the four men. The one in the Chevy appeared to be a Chicano.

"Burdett?" asked the man in the middle of the three standing across the road. He was a short fellow and spoke with a squeaky voice.

"It's me, Cricket."

Raymond joined Burdett on the other side of the car. Behind them, the Chicano got out of the Chevy. Glancing over his shoulder, Raymond saw the Chicano leave the door open and the engine running.

"You got the money?" asked the squeaky-voiced man. He, like the other two black men, wore flashy, baggy clothing and jackets. Behind Raymond and Calvin, the driver of the ramming car walked into the road.

"I don't like the looks of this," murmured Raymond.

"It's only security. They do it all the time."

Raymond glanced at the Chicano again, then studied the colored guys alongside the guy doing the talking. As Raymond watched, the bodyguards stepped away from the squeaky-voiced dealer.

"Cal, if I didn't know better, I'd say we were about to be ambushed and robbed."

Burdett glanced at him. "What the hell you talking about? They need us as much as we need them."

"As much as you need them," corrected Raymond, noticing the Chicano now stood at an angle where he could shoot them without hitting any of the three across the crossroads. Raymond stepped away from Burdett, putting himself closer to the service station.

"I said," asked the squeaky-voiced man, "do you have the money?"

Calvin held up the briefcase. "I've got the money. You got the product?"

The man with the squeaky voice reached under his jacket and jerked out a pistol. "You don't need the product this time!"

Raymond brought up the shotgun, and without aiming, fired. The blast caught Cricket in the chest, lifting him up and throwing him across the hood. Cricket hit the windshield and lay there, arms extended, gun no longer in his hand.

The back-shooter was looking for an angle on Raymond. Seeing that was impossible, he took a shot at Burdett. Cal clutched his side and dropped the briefcase, which landed on its corner and popped open. Money scattered across the blacktop.

After firing his first blast, Raymond threw himself to

the ground, rolling for the porch of the service station. The first time he rolled over, he jacked a round in the breech. The second time he came up, he fired at the closest bodyguard. Though his aim was high, some of the shot caught the bodyguard across the face. The man screamed, dropped his pistol, and clutched his face. Raymond jacked another round into the breech and fired again as he rolled onto the porch. Newspaper and fertilizer sacks crunched under him as he came to a stop behind one of the narrow brick columns.

Cricket's other bodyguard didn't know who to shoot. He'd been told to take the man on Burdett's right. Now that man was Burdett. But Burdett had been shot by Pedro, who was scrambling for his Chevy. When the white man with the shotgun let loose with his second blast, Freddie Noyles ducked behind the pimpmobile without ever firing a shot.

Burdett lay in the road near the spilled money and did not move. Neither did the man who'd once spoken with a squeaky voice. Cricket lay on the hood, above the bodyguard who had caught some shot in the face. The bodyguard was screaming that he couldn't see.

On the other side of the crossroads, the Chicano jammed gears and roared out of the field, wheels spinning and dirt flying. The Chevy sideswiped Burdett's Cadillac, bounced off it, and then fishedtailed away, along the same road Raymond and Calvin had used in approaching the rendezvous.

The crossroads was quiet but for the bodyguard moaning for help. He was quickly silenced when Freddie Noyles popped up for a moment to take a shot at

Raymond and missed, blowing off a piece of the injured man's skull instead. Bullets slammed into the column Raymond scrunched behind. After that, the bean fields fell silent again.

From behind the column, Raymond reloaded the shotgun. As he did, he heard a door open on the far side of the pimpmobile. Raymond wheeled around the brick column and put several shots through the near side of the car, producing a scream from the other side. Arms and legs could be heard scrambling away.

"You motherfucker!" screamed Noyles. "I'll kill you for that!"

Raymond didn't reply. He was wondering how in the hell he was going to get out of this. People had seen him leave Alamo with Burdett. Hell, even that bitch Diaz could rat him out. What to do?

"I was going to blow this place," said Noyles from the other side of the car, "but now I'm gonna stay and shoot it out with you."

"And wait around for the cops to arrive."

"They'll get you, too, motherfucker."

"Shut up, asshole." Raymond was thinking and he couldn't think with all this yammering.

The bean fields became silent once more and the fog drifted back in. The fog was joined by the smell of cordite. Money blew across the blacktop. In the distance, lightning crackled. A storm was moving their way.

From the far side of the pimpmobile, Noyles shouted, "Hey, man, we've got to get out of here."

"Why the ambush?"

"Why the ambush? What the hell's that got to do

with anything? We've got to get out of here."

"What was wrong with Burdett's money?"

"Hey, I'm talking about the cops grabbing your white ass."

"Then take off, nigger."

"I need the car."

"So do I," said Raymond, the outline of a plan forming in his head.

"There's two of them," said the voice on the other side of the pimpmobile, "how you want to do this thing?"

"I'll need them both."

"I just want out of here and you're trying to fuck with me." Silence, then, "We've got to get moving, man."

Raymond said nothing. He knew what must be done and he was sticking to his plan.

From the other side of the pimpmobile came, "Hey, you ain't gonna stay here all night, are you?"

"Depends on you."

"What you mean, depends on me?"

"You leave, then I'll leave."

"No way. You leave first. I don't trust you."

"Feeling's mutual, but there's no reason to leave without any money. I was promised a cut and I want it."

"You ain't gonna spend that money in no jail."

"You got money?" asked Raymond.

"In a bag in the back seat. We were blowing town."

"And taking our money."

"Hell, the mob don't like the brothers getting too big. Cricket said it'd be best to lie low for a while. Said the cops wouldn't be looking for folks who'd killed a couple of drug dealers." Noyles laughed. "They might even give us a going-away present. Pedro's headed for Brazil. He had all his stuff in his car; me, too."

"So get it and go."

"All I need's the bag. It's got my ticket and passport. You won't shoot old Freddie, will you?"

"Get it and go!"

"Shit, man! You'll shoot my ass."

"Not if you get it and go. Otherwise, I'm going to blow holes in that Caddy of yours until I get you. I brought along a box of twenty-four. I've used five and I ain't saving any for the cops."

From the other side of the car, Noyles asked, "You're saying I can walk away?"

"That's right, and as soon as you're gone, I'm taking that money and disappearing. But I'm leaving these two Caddies behind, with enough flat tires that you won't be interested in coming back and using one."

The black man was quiet for a moment. "So it'll look like some drug deal gone bad."

"Well, it did, didn't it?"

Noyles laughed. "Yeah, man, that's right."

"And you'll be out of the country. Make it a country that won't send you back."

"Hell, man, I'm on my way to Africa." Noyles laughed again. "To find my roots."

"Each to his own. You've got thirty seconds."

Noyles hustled into the car and jerked out his bag. After catching his breath, he said, "There's more in the trunk if you want it. Key's in Cricket's pants. Two big suitcases, one filled with money. We could split it."

Raymond's answer was to whip around the column

and blow out the windows of the pimpmobile, showering Noyles with glass.

"I'm going! I'm going!"

Raymond stopped firing long enough to listen to the bodyguard scurry into the field, then he rushed the car and took up a position against the near side. When he heard something rustling in the beans, Raymond stood up, leaned into the vehicle, and fired. Noyles sprang to his feet and tore out across the field, zigzagging and throwing shots over his shoulder. Raymond answered with a few of his own. By then, the bodyguard was well out of range, disappearing into the mist.

Raymond made sure the other men were dead, then scattered Burdett's money across the intersection, taking only the fifteen grand he'd been promised. "It's only right, Cal." The back shooter had hit his friend under the arm, the bullet running through into his heart.

"Shit, Reagan was luckier than that."

Raymond walked over to Burdett's Cadillac and threw some money inside, then tossed more money where the Chevy had been parked. Now there were two Caddies in the middle of the crossroads, waiting for some farmer to come along and find them. No way Farmer John wasn't going to help himself to some of that money. The civilians would muddy up the trail but good. Raymond hated to leave all that money behind, but he couldn't explain having it. And if the cops stopped him, he'd never find The Woman. But the cops would have a way to close this case and close it quick. There'd be some missing persons, but the county mounties wouldn't look too hard. They'd have three dead men, two cars, and more than enough money.

Before pulling his suitcase out of Burdett's car, Raymond picked up the gun of the squeaky-voiced man and stuck it into his belt, then he tossed Cricket and the shotgun on the narrow porch of the old Texaco. After that, he ripped a bean plant from the ground and dragged the bush behind him as he walked in the opposite direction from the one the black bodyguard had taken. Crossing the first creek, Raymond lost the pistol.

❖   ❖   ❖

"My husband hit me, Dr. Fox."

"Are there children there?"

"Yes."

"Why are you and your children still in the house?"

"It's only the second time he's done it. He's really a good man."

"Bonnie, get out of the house and take the kids with you."

"Dr. Fox, I want my marriage to work."

"Figure out how to make it work elsewhere. Get out of the house now."

"But, Dr. Fox—"

"No ifs or buts about it. Don't be there when he comes home tonight. Get into a shelter or go to your parents' house."

"My daughters need their father, and you've always said it's important to have an intact family unit."

"Bonnie! Are you listening to me? Get out of the house! Take the kids with you. Show your daughters how to handle a man who brutalizes women."

eight

The nurse stuck her head in Ernie Kelly's hospital room. "Visitor to see you," she announced with a bright smile.

Ernie opened his eyes. Christ! Even that hurt! There were bandages wrapped around his face and neck, an IV stuck in his arm, and his head had been shaved clean. But no one could see that because of the heavy bandaging.

The doctor said he'd been lucky. Very lucky indeed. A piece of glass had just missed the jugular vein. There was more than one stitch in his lips, and the inside of his mouth was cut from several broken teeth. They'd busted him up but good.

"What happened, Mr. Kelly?" asked the detective admitted to see him. Dan Stafford didn't take a seat but stood near the head of the bed.

"I—I don't remember . . . ."

"Do you remember being in Dr. Fox's condominium?"

"I don't think so." Ernie almost shook his head before remembering he couldn't. His head was practically immobilized.

"Whether you remember or not, we've established that you were in the Fox condominium. Why were you there?"

"I'm her number one fan."

"How do you know that?"

"By the way she talks to me on the radio."

"You talk to her every day?"

"Yes, I do," said Ernie, getting into the swing of the conversation.

"Let me see if I have this clear. Dr. Fox talks to you on her radio program every day?"

"Yes."

"And no one else?"

"Well, there are those other people, but Dr. Fox gets rid of them so we can spend more time together. She knows I have lots of self-doubts and she's helping me work my way through them."

"How did you injure yourself?"

Kelly looked at the sheet covering his body. Blood dotted its whiteness where fluid oozed down from his neck, and he wore a nightie and no underpants. His arms were strapped down. "At the warehouse?"

"What warehouse?"

"The one where I work."

"And where is that?"

Kelly told him. An industrial park on the interstate. At least that part of this conversation was real.

"Do you remember tripping over something and smashing your face?"

"No."

"Then, getting to your feet and running into a wall and collapsing where an Avery McFarland—do you know Avery McFarland?"

"Er—no. I don't think so."

"Avery McFarland works in the building where you were injured, installing cabinets. Are you sure he didn't let you in so you could see Dr. Fox?"

"I came through the garage. Dr. Fox told the guard to let me in."

"The guard did, did he?" Jamie Stubbs was already history, but not before Stafford had interrogated him. "Are you aware of the restraining order Dr. Fox had issued against you?"

Ernie smiled—well, the best the stitches would let him smile. "Oh, that doesn't mean anything. Dr. Fox had to do that so her other fans wouldn't be jealous."

"Is that so?"

"Yes, and you can tell Dr. Fox that I understand."

"Understand what?"

"Why she had the restraining order issued."

"Mr. Kelly, do you know Jamie Stubbs?"

"Is he a fan? I might have met him in a chat room."

"So none of your friends is named Jamie Stubbs?"

"I . . . really don't have a lot of friends. I don't connect with people well. Dr. Fox understands. She can explain everything."

Stafford stood there, staring down at the man. "Does Dr. Fox have any friends of her own?"

Another painful smile. "Just me."

"Excuse me, I thought Dr. Fox was getting married."

"What? Oh, no. I haven't asked her. It wouldn't be appropriate."

"Why is that?"

"It's a busy time in her life. We'll have more time together when Peggy's out of the house."

Stafford let out a breath. "You said Dr. Fox told the guard to let you in the garage. I guess you took the elevator upstairs?"

"I used the stairs."

"To the eleventh floor?"

"I needed the exercise. Dr. Fox doesn't like fat people. I was pretty overweight when I started listening to her show, but I've lost a few pounds."

"How many?"

"Sixty-two," Kelly said proudly.

"Sounds like you've found the right diet."

Another smile. "Well, there's nothing like being in love."

"Have you ever forced your attentions on Dr. Fox?"

"Of course not. I wouldn't do such a thing."

"They why the restraining order?"

"You know, the jealousy of the other fans."

"Then you've never put a hand on her?"

"Oh, no." Ernie raised a finger and wagged it. "That's a no-no."

"A no-no?"

"Inappropriate touching. One of the first lessons I learned from Dr. Fox."

"So, if she's busy, how do you see her? I don't mean on the radio, but to be with her?"

"If she's real busy I'm content to watch her from my

place across the river."

"And how do you do that?"

"I have a telescope. Just like the one Dr. Fox has to look at me."

"She has a telescope?"

"Sure. Why else would she have those glass walls in her building?"

Dan Stafford left the room, shaking his head. He wouldn't be a celebrity for all the money in the world.

"Here you are, Mr. Kelly." The nurse placed a lunch tray on the swing-out table and elevated his bed. "Looks like a good one. Chicken broth. Take your time and use the straw. If you're up to it, you have another visitor. This one's not a policeman, but a friend asked him to stop by and check on you."

"Who's the friend?"

"Jean Fox. He has another man with him, a colored man. But I told him only one visitor at a time. Want me to send him in, after your meal?"

Ernie smiled, stretching the limits of his stitches. "Oh, yes, please send them both in."

The old colored guy came in first. He wore a brown suit with a yellow tie and a no-nonsense look on his face. Once inside, the old colored guy didn't acknowledge Ernie but took a small metal box from his inside coat pocket and ran it around the room.

"What are you doing?"

The old colored man put a finger to his lips and continued to run the box up one side of the horseshoe-shaped space hollowed out by Ernie's bed, then the other side.

"Get out of here! I don't think Dr. Fox sent you."

The old colored guy put his hand over Ernie's nose and mouth and Ernie passed out. He came to as a tall, silver-haired gent entered the hospital room.

"What . . . was that all about?"

"Security, Mr. Kelly. Security." This guy, and he was white, wore a pinstriped suit, white shirt, and a dull red tie. He carried a briefcase. "Things have changed since I graduated from law school. Nowadays, you can't hold a decent conversation without expecting to be overheard. I, myself, have my office swept daily." The silver-haired gent moved across the room to the chair between Ernie's bed and the window. "You don't mind if I sit down, do you? Of course not or you wouldn't have invited me in." He sat down.

"Just who the hell are you?"

"I'm Dr. Fox's attorney. Actually, I've been her attorney since she moved to town, the family's attorney before that. It was thought at one time that young Elliot would come into the firm after his stint in the military, but you wouldn't be interested in that. Simply stated, Mr. Kelly, I handle Dr. Fox's legal affairs. Now I'm to handle yours." The old coot looked down his nose at him, and even though he sat in a chair lower than Ernie's bed, the old coot brought it off.

"But I don't know you."

"Sorry to be so ill-mannered, but I'm overly acquainted with your case. I'm Harry Hartner, Jr."

"I'm not interested in talking with you."

"I know. You're interested in talking with Dr. Fox. You appear to be very interested in talking with her."

"That's right." Ernie glanced at the door but only saw the back of the old colored guy who had caused him to pass out. "Where is she? I know she wants to talk to me."

Harry Hartner took a pair of funny-looking glasses from his briefcase and perched them on his nose. That was followed by some papers from his briefcase. He looked over the glasses at Ernie. "You'll never see her again, Mr. Kelly. It's part of the terms of your treatment."

Ernie tried to sit up, but the straps, then the pain caught him, forcing him to lie down. Sweat erupted from every pore in his body. Tears ran down his cheeks. "You . . . you can't do this to me. I'm a fan. Probably her biggest fan."

"From what we found in your apartment, that's not something anyone could dispute in a court of law. Where did you get all those pictures?" Hartner waved off any response. "I really don't want to know. It's evident some of them were shot through windows."

"You've been in my apartment? Is that legal?"

"It will be after I leave. This power of attorney has been backdated for that purpose. Now, let's discuss the terms of your resettlement to the West Coast—"

"But Dr. Fox lives in a high-rise. How could I have taken her picture?"

"Oh, don't go simple on me. You're a rather smart fellow, shooting all those pictures. The ones your attorney would feature in your trial would be the ones shot through the windows of Ruth Fox's residence. If I were handling this for Ruth, you'd be in jail instead of in the Bull Street facility."

Bull Street. Anyone who lived in the state of South Carolina knew what facility was on Bull Street, and for the first time, Ernie noticed there were bars on the windows. "What am I doing here?"

"Why, we're treating you, Mr. Kelly. You need treatment for an unhealthy fixation and you're going to get it."

"You've got this all wrong. I'm Dr. Fox's biggest fan. That's why I have all the photographs."

"Yes. Amazing little machines you own, and to the untrained eye, it could fool anyone. I am one of those untrained eyes. I never did accept the teachings of Sigmund Freud." Hartner leaned toward the bed and smiled. "Actually, I deal more with frauds. Now I have some papers for you to sign. They'll enable us to conclude your affairs in Columbia: sell your automobile, close out your bank accounts, pay your bills, the normal run of things."

"I'll sign nothing."

"Would you rather I ask Melvin to join us?"

"Who?"

"The man who preceded me into the room."

"The old colored guy?"

"He prefers to be referred to as 'Mr. Ott,'" said Harry Hartner, raising his voice.

And with that, the old colored man returned to the room, closing the door behind him. He took up a position near the head of Ernie's bed.

"I demand to see Dr. Fox."

The attorney shook his head. "Sorry. Your only options are Melvin or myself."

"But Dr. Fox will want to deal with me."

"Please get your language straight. Say what you mean. You want a deal from Dr. Fox, right?"

Ernie stared at the old man, and for the first time a sense of dread filled his heart. "You know?"

"Of course, we know."

"I'll scream for the nurse."

The old colored guy put his hand over Ernie's mouth, clamping down hard. No scream was heard, nor could Ernie's sore jaw move. When the old colored guy used the fingers of his free hand to close Ernie's nose, there was no air. Ernie thrashed around, ignoring the pain. Strong guttural sounds came from deep inside his throat, then a sort of keening. The room swam, spots appeared before his eyes, then there only darkness.

Ernie opened his eyes. He blinked, then looked from one man to the other. "What happened?"

"You passed out," said Harry Hartner.

Ernie stared at the old colored guy who was bending over him, waiting for him to try to scream again. Ernie did.

Ernie opened his eyes. Again he looked from one man to the other. "Who are you people?"

"Friends of Dr. Fox."

"I'm a friend . . . ." Ernie's voice trailed off as he saw those two black hands moving toward him. "No," he said with a shudder. "Please not again." Tears ran down his cheeks. He felt himself wet the bed. "What do you want me to do?"

"Just sign these papers, Mr. Kelly, and Melvin will notarize them."

"And if I don't, you'll kill me."

"Hardly the humane thing to do to such a sick mind."

"But—but I'm not sick. You know that."

"Of course, but that won't prevent you from getting the treatment you so rightly deserve."

nine

One evening, several days after the attack, Jean was waiting for the elevator in the building that housed her radio network when Tony Nipper walked down the hall.

"Hey, Doc, what you doing leaving so late?"

"Had those affiliate promos to do, plus the newsletter."

"How's the new engineer working out?"

"Just fine."

"Didn't I tell you I'd take care of you?"

"You always do." Jean watched Nipper go. It had been a good week: Harry Hartner had Ernie Kelly hospitalized and under treatment on the West Coast, the condo was cleaned up, and the Columbiana Towers Corporation was installing new carpeting at no cost to her. It had been a week of surprises. Dan Stafford invited her out for lunch, but Jean brushed him off.

Who'd he think he was kidding? He only wanted to

grill her about the Kelly incident, and Jean could see the pride in the lean, tired-looking man with the unruly hair. The Kelly incident had happened on his watch, and Stafford was anxious to learn what kind of game she was running on him. No, it couldn't be that the detective was actually interested in her. Not that at all. But she had to admit the guy was kind of cute.

Kind of cute. Where had that come from? Perhaps the empty nest syndrome was telling her to move on.

The bell rang and the elevator doors opened.

Anyway, how could you have a relationship with someone you'd begun that relationship with by lying to them? She'd have a better chance with Avery McFarland, if she wanted a relationship at all.

The night Kelly had attacked her, a knot had swollen up on the back of Avery's head. Jean didn't know about it until Avery returned and asked for some ice, this after Dan Stafford had left and Peggy headed for bed. It seems Avery had slipped and fallen, racing down the hall to her rescue, and the two of them had shared a drink and some quiet conversation.

Avery apologized for trying to throw Kelly through the glass wall. "If I hadn't, we wouldn't be in this fix."

"Oh, I don't think there's much of a fix. I can't see Kelly talking about what you did to him."

Jean suddenly realized she was sitting in her total disaster of a living room with a real roughneck, and she wasn't the least bit concerned. On the contrary, she wanted to know more about this man, not only out of a sense of gratitude, but because she wasn't afraid of him.

Peggy protested when sent off to bed. "Me—what about you, Mother?"

"Mr. McFarland and I are talking it out."

"Then why can't I stay up? I'm no kid. I'm a woman and about to be married."

"And quite a good-looking woman, too," said McFarland from a barstool at the serving window between the kitchen and dining area.

"I don't like being patronized, no matter who's doing the patronizing."

"Even by Wesley?" asked Jean with a smile.

"That's different."

"And this is different," said Jean, inclining her head toward McFarland. "Hit the sack."

Her daughter got the message. "If I'm not old enough to stay up, then come tuck me in."

The carpenter slid off his stool. "Dr. Fox, I'll be moving along. It's been a long night and I appreciate the ice."

"You stay right here."

The tone of her voice held him, another thing she had learned from her mother-in-law. Jean slipped into a pair of flats while Peggy pulled on some pink cotton pajamas. When her daughter crawled into bed, Jean was there to pull the covers up over her. The bedroom suite was the one Peggy had picked out as a teen: white oak, now stained dark cherry. And the ruffles were gone, replaced by matching drawn drapes. Several paintings hung on the wall, dating back to when Peggy's talent had first emerged at age eight.

"How long's he going to be here?" she asked.

"I don't know."

"He's not going to spend the night, is he? I read somewhere when people's lives are threatened, all they want to do is make love. It doesn't matter who with."

Jean took a seat on the edge of the bed. "Peggy, what are you talking about? My life wasn't threatened."

"Lieutenant Stafford seemed to think so."

"Policemen tend to see trouble where there's not any."

"Whatever you do, just remember I'm here, and not about to leave, at least not for a few more weeks."

Jean squeezed her daughter's shoulder. "I'm glad to hear you say that. Sometimes I think you can't wait to leave."

Peggy sat up. She hugged her mother and Jean hugged back. "Maybe I should've waited a while before getting married. I'm giving up my childhood awfully fast."

Jean eased her back into the bed. "Not much faster than I, and you're getting a fine young man, just like I did."

"I only hope my marriage lasts longer than yours."

"What's this? Cold feet?"

"Maybe."

"Happens to the best of us."

"Even you?"

"I was the one who wanted to wait until your father returned from overseas."

"You and I—we don't talk about him—Daddy, I mean. At the table with Nana and Wesley was the most. You know, Wesley's mother won't let me call him 'Wes.' Mrs. Calhoun says it sounds *sooo* common. I thought I was getting away from all that stuffiness when we moved out of Nana's."

"Actually, you gave the impression you didn't want to leave."

Peggy smiled. "Well, I didn't want to give up without a fight."

"Maybe your marriage will give us some breathing room. And the reason you and I don't talk about your father is because you think you'll hurt my feelings. Your father died over twenty years ago. I'm not saying it didn't upset me—for a short time I was a basket case and Nana had to take care of me—but that was twenty years ago." *Actually the rape was what did me in. Elliot's death only compounded it.* "Twenty years softens a lot of pain, like it did when I lost my parents." *I've even forgiven Raymond Lister.*

Peggy scooted up against her pillow. "I'm lucky to be here, aren't I?"

"Pardon?"

"I'm lucky you were thrown clear from the wreck when that drunk driver hit your parents, and lucky Daddy got you pregnant before he went overseas."

Jean rubbed her daughter's shoulders. "Nothing's going to happen, Peggy. You and Wesley will make each other very happy."

"And this from a woman who never remarried."

"Well," Jean said with a smile, "if you don't care for my advice, you can always ask advice from your new mother-in-law."

"Ugh!" said Peggy, her face twisting into a frown. "Mrs. Calhoun still doesn't like me, and Wesley and

I've been dating for three years."

"Neither did Nana like me."

"At least you and I have that in common."

Jean settled the covers over her daughter again and Peggy snuggled under them.

"Well, I'm looking forward to your marriage, even if you aren't. And if you have any second thoughts, we'll talk about them in the morning."

Peggy glanced at her bedroom door. "He'll be gone by then, won't he?"

"Sooner than you think."

"Good, because I want you all to myself these last few weeks—is that so wrong?"

"And I want to spend those last few weeks with you before you begin your new life."

McFarland sat on the barstool and held the ice pack against the back of his head. He looked morose.

"Having a bit of a letdown?" Jean asked softly.

"I guess so, and I have to tell you I don't remember the last time that happened."

"A fight or the feeling?"

McFarland smiled. "The feeling."

Jean took a seat on another barstool at the serving window and tried to ignore the mess. Separating them from glass, blood, and broken coffee table were the table, chairs, and sideboard of a formal dining area. Beyond that, sofa and overstuffed chairs sported flecks of blood on their fabric. Against the far wall stood an antique hutch with an oil painting by Peggy over it, the first thing Jean had checked before the police had arrived.

"Lieutenant Stafford seemed to know all about you."

"A few fights, that's all. People who lost, complaining."

Jean picked up her drink, a Tom Collins. "And you threw the losers through a window like you tried to do tonight?"

McFarland nodded.

Jean almost dropped her drink. "My God, Avery, I was only kidding."

He shrugged. "When you fight in a bar, it's like the place belongs to you. You fight to defend it."

"Like in John Wayne movies."

"Just like that."

"What starts the fighting?"

"Women, drinking, cards, whatever."

She shook her head. "Another world."

"You've got that right, and I forgot I was across the river. Now I'm gonna have that cop on my case until he pins something on me."

"I don't know about that. Stafford didn't seem to be that kind of guy. But do you really like this, this knocking of heads?"

McFarland stood up. "You and me, Dr. Fox, we come from different sides of the tracks. Now, if you don't mind, I'll be taking this beer with me."

Jean came off her stool and took his arm, then pulled her hand back. "Avery, I'm no snob. At least I'd like to think I'm not. I have a mother-in-law with that problem." She gestured at the living room. "That's why I live here and not with her. All I meant was, if you keep up all this fighting, aren't you endangering your life?"

radio secrets

McFarland grinned. "Dr. Fox, some of us fellows do just fine on our own, and I know that riles you gals, but you take me, I work long and hard during the week, then I'm gone, doing what I want: hunting, fishing, drinking. A woman like you, a real lady, you need a man comes home every night. I'm too wild. But if that Kelly fellow ever bothers you again, I'll take care of him. You don't have to worry about him none."

"There's no need. He's just a fan."

"A fan?"

"A listener to my radio program."

McFarland stared at her. "You're the one who gives advice on the radio? My mother listens to you every day."

"Thank her for me."

McFarland's face reddened. "Well, I guess I really goofed, didn't I?"

"How's that?"

"Telling you what I was going to do if Kelly came sniffing around."

"Ernie Kelly is mentally ill. He needs treatment, not incarceration."

"I just can't believe you can feel sorry for that sumbitch. Sorry about my French."

"I'm the one who made the mistake, not Ernie Kelly."

"How's that?"

"I opened the door without looking through the peep-hole."

McFarland smiled. "So shrinks can be wrong?"

"I've been wrong before and I'm sure I'll be wrong again, but I try to give people like your mother a window onto the real world."

120

"My mom tells me sometimes I'm not living in the real world. She got that from you."

"I imagine she did."

McFarland slid off the stool again. "Would you like to see some of my work?"

Jean took her keys off the serving window as she stood up. "Just don't keep me out too late or Peggy will worry."

McFarland chuckled. "Dr. Fox, I don't know enough about cabinet-making to keep you out that late."

As they went down the entrance hallway, Jean asked, "What about my cabinets? What do you think?"

"Store-bought. Came with the unit, didn't they?"

"Yes?"

"You can do better."

"And you'd like to make them for me?"

"Can't get to you until next year."

"Must be nice to be so busy."

McFarland grinned as he opened the door for her. "Oh, your business, the radio business, it's not the kind where you can tell customers to go jump?"

"Not hardly," answered Jean with a smile, "but I must admit, sometimes it's tempting."

And they went down the hall to where McFarland was working and where Jean found she enjoyed being with this man. That might've been the reason that she ordered a set of new cabinets.

The elevator doors opened and Jean strode across the lobby of the building housing her syndicated program. When walking alone, it was important to walk

with a purpose, as if you knew where you were going-
and expected to get there. She pushed back the door
to the parking area. Near the door was a space Jean
paid good money for, a spot supposedly safer than most.
That hardly seemed to have mattered. Her BMW stood
under the light and near the door, its windows smashed
and tires slashed.

Two patrolmen and some slick-looking guy were in
Jean Fox's office when Dan Stafford arrived. Stafford
nodded to the patrolmen. They left, having other calls
to handle and wondering why a detective asked to be
called in on a simple case of vandalism.

Stafford looked around, taking in the odd furniture
and the paintings that didn't make much sense. That
seemed apropos. The woman behind the desk didn't
make sense either. Jean Fox looked the same as last
time: face white and body limp, leaning into her chair,
arms dangling off armrests, a blank look in her eyes—
until she recognized him. In contrast, the slick-looking young man was agitated, hands fiddling one with
each other.

"Dr. Fox?" asked Stafford.

He saw a small smile cross the woman's face. She
sat up, brushing back that intriguing salt-and-pepper
hair, readying herself for the next lie. But why did she
have to lie? Fox had moved here from Florida when her
husband was killed overseas, earned her degree, and
raised her only child at her mother-in-law's until moving out, first to an apartment, then a condo at the
Columbiana. And her ratings had steadily grown, ac-

cording to a local DJ he had talked to.

"Twice in one week . . . ." Stafford let the thought hang in the air.

The slick-looking fellow asked, "Twice in one week? Doc, what's he talking about? This happened before?"

"Lieutenant Stafford caught the call when Ernie Kelly injured himself in my condo."

"Wow! What a coincidence."

"I'd like to talk with Dr. Fox alone."

"I'm cool with that." The slick-looking fellow left the room.

"You okay?" Stafford asked her.

"I'm fine, really."

"Good."

"One of the patrolmen said there was someone who wanted to ask me a few additional questions."

"The offer still stands. I can't take you to dinner this week because I'm working nights."

"Thank you, but no thank you."

"Okay. Do you want me to find out which one of Ernie Kelly's friends did this to your car?"

"I thought the patrolmen would take care of that."

"They will."

"Then why don't we let well enough alone?"

"I thought you were a therapist."

"I am."

"Every day you advise folks to seek professional help whenever they need it, right?"

"Lieutenant, it's a mere case of vandalism."

"Is that all it is?"

"I think you're making more of this than there is."

"And I think you're out of touch with the real world."

Jean smiled. "Lieutenant, are you a listener?"

"In the last few days. I find it strange that people call in and talk about their most intimate problems."

"I'm a psychotherapist."

"But on the radio?"

"On the radio."

"It doesn't sound like anything I'd do."

"Not everyone is as self-sufficient as you are."

"Yes, but I don't hear anything they couldn't learn from a priest."

"Many people don't belong to a church."

"But they could talk out their problems with a priest. How could a priest turn them away?"

"Agreed, but it appears there are a good number of people who like to pick up the phone and call. No appointment, no fees, and no face-to-face. Why did you come by tonight?"

Stafford took out a card and laid it at the edge of her desk. "I want you to know that the police are here to help you. No matter what you may have to divulge, if you ever need my help, just give me a call."

Fox glanced at the card but didn't pick it up. "I don't think that'll be necessary, but thanks for the offer."

Stafford started for the door. There he stopped and turned around. "By the way, do you need a ride home?"

The woman was still behind her desk. "Thank you, but Tony said he'd give me a lift."

Stafford said his good-byes, then headed back to the precinct station where he made a phone call to the state of Florida. He asked a friend from a training session at the FBI Academy to make a trip over to Coventry and learn what he could about a certain Jean Fox, formerly Jean Murphy. The friend said he couldn't get to it right away, and Stafford said there was no great rush.

Stafford hung up and stared at the phone long enough to make his partner ask what the hell was bugging him. What was bugging Stafford was the torn pair of panty hose he had found in a dumpster at Jean Fox's condominium. There had been blood on those pantyhose. Blood that matched Ernie Kelly's DNA.

It hadn't been all that difficult for Stafford to scrape up a bit of blood and take it along from the Kelly interview in the hospital. Nor to come by Jean Fox's genetic material while wandering around the crime scene. You couldn't use such evidence in a court of law, but it could point you in the right direction.

"You're on the air with Dr. Jean Fox. Raymond . . ." Jean's voice tightened. "Welcome to the real world."

"I have a bone to pick with you, Dr. Fox."

Jean swallowed. She looked at Kyle, who was staring at the instruments on the board. Sitting alongside him was the new engineer, Ashley, a heavy girl in her twenties. Through the window, Jean saw Beverly grilling another caller, trying to learn if the caller could make his or her problem clear to the audience. Not everyone who called got on the air. Some were incoherent because of rage or genetic makeup. Many were asked to call later when Dr. Fox could make out what their problem was. That generally took up another hour of Jean's day.

"You have a bone to pick with me? I don't think I understand."

Now Kyle was on the case, his eyes flashing concern and ready to cut off the caller. With ten-second delay, there was no way Raymond Lister would be able to cause an incident.

Raymond Lister! What was she thinking? Raymond Lister was in Florida. A sentence typed in by her screener told her that Raymond wanted to talk about getting help for his girlfriend's drinking problem.

"Dr. Fox, you say women are responsible for the morals in our society."

"You misquote me."

"How's that?"

"I said that women have more of a stake in the morals of any society. Women generally spend more time raising society's children."

Silence on the other end of the line. This relieved Jean. Raymond Lister would not be so cowed. She remembered Lister as being more dominating, a bully, very physical. Yes, very, very physical . . . . She could still feel Lister's hands pushing her down in the front seat of his car, the back of her head hitting the door handle as she went down, the smell of whiskey on his breath. Lister forcing her legs apart . . . .

The voice in her headphones was speaking to her. Jean saw Kyle and Ashley staring at her. Even her screener, Beverly, was staring through the soundproof glass window. Perspiration formed inside her blouse.

"Pardon me, Raymond, but what did you say?"

"Dr. Fox, why is that women dress as they do?"

"Dress . . . the way they do?"

"You see how women dress these days. They hardly wear any clothes. No wonder they're raped."

Jean cut off her mike, cleared her voice, and then returned to the air. "The number of rapes have increased because of a new category called 'date rape.' I don't believe anyone is ever date-raped but simply raped. It's playing semantics with women's lives."

"Semantics?"

"Word games."

"Uh-huh. Well, I don't think women should dress so provocatively."

"Raymond, is there a question here?"

"Yeah. Why are men to blame when it's women shaking their asses at them?"

"Women in our society should be able to wear what they wish and not be subjected to attack. Raymond, this is so obvious, why did you call?"

"I wanted to know if you were once Jean Murphy, a girl I knew from Florida."

"I don't usually talk about my personal life. It's far too ordinary." Jean forced a laugh. "Of course, nowadays all listeners would hear would be me whining about my daughter's impending wedding."

She made a cutting motion across her throat and that was the end of Raymond whoever-the-hell-he-had-been. "I'm Dr. Jean Fox and the phone number is 1-800-555-2000. I'll be right back." She punched a button. "Beverly, what the hell was that all about?"

The slim woman on the other side of the glass made a helpless motion with her hands. "I don't know, Jean. I haven't had anyone jerk me around like that in a long time. He out-and-out lied to me. That call had nothing to do with anybody's drinking problem."

"So I learned . . . the hard way."

"I'm sorry. It won't happen again."

"Yes, it will, and it won't be your fault." Jean punched another button. "Kyle, where are we going next?"

"I've got Claire . . . from LA."

"Hmm. Got up early for the show, did she?"

"They love you out there, Dr. Fox," said the young woman sitting alongside Kyle. The new engineer was still going through a stage of hero-worshipping. Well, thought Jean, after she burped or passed gas more than once, the young woman would come down to earth.

"How much time do I have?"

"I went to music after dumping that jerk. The news is up next."

Jean pulled off her headphones and pushed her chair back. "I'll be right back."

In the hallway, she met Tony Nipper. The station manager glanced at his watch. "Problem, Doc?"

"Not at all. Just making a potty run."

As Jean continued down the hall, he said, "Anything you need, you let me know."

Oh, is that so? Can you find Raymond Lister? Is he in Florida or South Carolina? And damn him for being able to intrude in her life again. And damn her for allowing it to happen.

In the rest room, Jean's secretary was sneaking a smoke, about to drop the cigarette in the toilet before closing the door of the stall.

"Let me have one of those, please."

Merle stared at her boss. "Jean, I've never seen you smoke before."

"There's a first time for everything."

The secretary passed over the cigarette. "Have mine. Next time I'm caught, Tony's going to write me up."

"As well he should."

"Oh, moralizing by the sinful, is this?"

"Absolutely."

"Is it Peggy again?" asked Merle.

Letting out a smoke-filled breath, Jean finally smiled. Not everyone knew about the attack by Ernie Kelly and that was good.

"You can do it, Jean. Remember what you told me before we were able to get the sexual harassment stopped around here. Don't let the bastards get you down."

"Thank you, Merle. I appreciate that."

Merle smiled, then left Jean alone with her thoughts.

Obviously Lister was intent on getting on her nerves. But there was little he could do to hurt her. Embarrass her, yes, but actually hurt her? Lister didn't want to go back to jail, did he? Did he? Maybe all those years behind bars had driven him nuts.

But calling the station. That was nowhere close to being crazy. That was clever. How had he found her? What did he want? And where was the son of a bitch right now?

Beverly walked through the door of the rest room

with a portable phone. "Jean, it's your mother-in-law."

"Calling now? In the middle of a show?"

Beverly nodded and turned over the phone. Going out the door, she threw over her shoulder, "Kyle says you've got two minutes."

"Thanks, Bev." Into the phone, she said, "Yes, Ruth, what is it? I'm in the middle of my show."

"I wouldn't bother you, but I felt you should know."

A chill ran through Jean. "Know what?"

"He was here today."

"Er—who was?" But Jean didn't have to be told who had been there.

"Peggy's father."

"Pardon me?"

"Raymond Lister. You don't think I couldn't see the resemblance? That hair, those eyes. It's Peggy's father for sure. Did you know Peggy's father was in town?"

"What did he want?"

"Why, he said he'd been going door-to-door, asking for jobs cutting grass. I swear I had to have a glass of sherry after he left and I never drink before noon. Goodness gracious. Imagine, Peggy's father in town."

"Elliot is Peggy's father and always will be." Jean snubbed out the cigarette in the wash basin. "I'll be right there."

"There's no reason. I'm perfectly safe. Hattie's in the house and Washington has boys working in the yard."

"No. I'm coming out."

"What about your show?"

"They can put on a tape. I'm not leaving you alone with Raymond Lister in town."

ten

*P*eggy looked over her shoulder at her fiancé skiing behind the Chris Craft. Wesley looked terrific. He looked gorgeous. Good shoulders, narrow hips, and strong legs. She giggled. Marriage was doing something to her. Yes, making it possible to enjoy their lovemaking. Soon there'd be no more worries, no more fears, and no more condoms.

Wesley flashed an obscene gesture from the slalom, and Peggy giggled again, then laughed out loud when he went spinning out of control, pinwheeling across the surface of the water. She wheeled the boat around, saw him surface—he was okay—and brought the boat alongside, then leaned over to comment about his skiing ability. For her trouble, she caught a pair of swim trunks in the face.

Peggy yelped and jumped back. The trunks fell to the deck of the boat. "What a dirty trick!"

"It's not a trick," said her fiancé, wet hair hanging

over his forehead. "It's an invitation."

Peggy looked around. Lake Murray was quiet. There was no one out here. Why should there be? It was the middle of the week. Now Peggy understood what Wesley had in mind, inviting her to go for a ride to get away from the house. He'd wanted to make it back at the lake house, but Peggy wouldn't have any part of that. Wesley's mother didn't approve of their marriage, and Peggy didn't need the old bitch upset about something else, the worst possible something else; proof positive they were only marrying to jump into bed, which translated into Peggy using her body to take Mrs. Calhoun's baby away. But Wesley was no baby. Peggy could attest to that by the way he responded to her.

"What if someone sees us?"

"Let them see what they're missing. I'm going to marry the best-looking girl in the state." Wesley threw his arms up, almost submerging himself. "The best-looking girl in the whole, wide world!"

Peggy tingled all over. And she was going to marry the sweetest boy in the whole, wide world. But Wesley wouldn't get off lightly. He should be taught a lesson.

She picked up the wet trunks. "What if I left you out here to fend for yourself, to ward off the creatures of the deep with only that little stick of yours."

"Little?"

"Okay. Bigger than little."

"You said that stick belonged to you, and the best way to protect it was to keep it sheathed."

Peggy trembled with excitement. Was this what love did to you? If so, it was glorious. But still, skinny-dipping in front of God and everybody. She scanned the lake again. At this point, Lake Murray was over a mile wide and they sat in the middle of that mile. The shoreline was dotted with houses, but if anyone was home she couldn't see them—which meant they couldn't see her. And they'd hear anyone coming, wouldn't they?

"Hurry up, Peggy, or I'll use up all my strength treading water."

"Close your eyes first."

"Close my eyes! Are you kidding? I've seen you naked before."

"And turn around."

"This is silly," said Wesley, shifting around in the water.

When his back was turned, Peggy undid her top and tossed it into the bottom of the boat. She was shimming out of her bottoms when Wesley said, "You'd better hurry or—"

Peggy jerked up her bottoms and slapped a hand across her breasts. "Don't you dare turn around!"

"I'm not . . . I'm not."

"What about the boat? Do I throw out the anchor or what?"

"Just get in the water, Peg. I've been thinking about this all day."

She slipped out of her bottoms and jumped into the water, making a big splash. Very quickly Wesley's arms were around her and he was kissing her, running his hands all over her. Wesley was ready. Peggy could tell that.

"Why didn't you tell me . . . what you had in mind? I

would've enjoyed . . . anticipating it."

Wesley kissed her, his tongue searching her mouth, his penis searching for where her legs came together. "I thought you wouldn't approve. I mean, we are out in the middle of the lake."

"I'm no prude, darling." To make that point, Peggy reached down and fitted Wesley inside her.

There was a small, pleasant gasp she couldn't help but make, then, "Oh, that's ever so nice." And she began to move.

"Prudish mother," said her fiancé, "likewise daughter."

Her eyes opened. "What do you mean . . . ." But that was all she got out. It felt *sooo* good to have him inside her again. After they got married, they'd do it every night. Sometimes in the mornings . . . before Wesley went off to work. That'd give him something to . . . .

They sank beneath the surface, and by the time they resurfaced, both were gasping for air and bucking against each other, trying to find any point of leverage.

The boat drifted away, and when they were finished, they had to swim for it. Peggy made Wesley go. "After all, this was your idea."

Wesley was about ten yards away when Peggy heard something behind her. She shifted around in the water to see an outboard headed in their direction. A man stood behind the controls, looking over the bow. He was coming right at her! Did he see her? Did he even see their boat?

Frozen in place, Peggy could only tread water and watch that bow bear down on her. As the boat came closer, it slowed down, but Peggy continued to shake. Caught naked as a jaybird in the middle of the lake! How could this have happened?

Now the stranger was running at an angle that would put his boat between Wesley and her. What was this guy doing? Avoiding them or trying to cut them off? Oh, God, why'd she ever let Wesley talk her into this?

Peggy covered herself with her hands and tried to move away, using her feet. The awkward motion made her tip over and her hands fall away from her body. That was enough to make her give up trying to move away and to concentrate on screening herself with her hands.

The engine shut off and the boat slid to a stop alongside her. This guy was going to see her completely bareass! And she'd always thought her mother a bit oversensitive about her being molested, but now . . . .

"Ahoy, there!" said the man, a burly guy with a gray flattop and wearing work clothes: blue short-sleeved shirt, same color pants. His arms were sunburned, and when he rested one of those forearms across a knee, Peggy saw they were enormous.

"Ahoy, yourself." Peggy felt herself heat up, blushing from head to toes.

"Need any help?"

From the other side of the boat, she heard Wesley shouting, and shouting at this man. The stranger paid absolutely no attention to her fiancé but continued to stare at her.

Peggy flushed again and focused her anger on controlling her voice. "No help needed. My fiancé and I were just swimming."

The man grinned. "Skinny-dipping from where I'm standing."

"And if you don't mind," said Peggy, using the tone she'd heard her mother use when putting men in their place, "we'd like to be left alone."

Wesley stopped yelling. Maybe he was swimming for their boat. Maybe he was swimming for this man's boat. Peggy didn't think that was such a good idea. Had Wesley seen this guy's arms?

The water moved slowly in the middle of the lake, but still it moved. It flowed in the direction of a dam five or six miles away. Maybe she could use that motion to see what Wesley was doing. She kicked her feet ever so slowly. She damned well wasn't going to fall over again. Not in front of this man!

"Look," said the stranger, "it's not safe for you to be out here fooling around. You were fooling around, weren't you?"

"Really, I don't think that's any of your business."

The man was obviously puzzled. "Women don't save themselves for their husbands anymore? Things have really changed—"

"Nowadays women make decisions what to do or not to do with their bodies." Peggy couldn't believe she was discussing biological politics with some stranger in the middle of Lake Murray. And in the nude!

"Don't you worry about what people will think?"

"Like I said, Mister, what I was doing was none of your business. Now, if you don't mind—"

"You're Jean Fox's daughter, aren't you?"

"Er—yes." Oh, my God, this guy was going to rat on her to her mother.

"That surprises me. Your mother's kind of a tight-ass, isn't she?"

Would this never end? Peggy kicked with her feet, propelling herself toward the stern. She had to see what Wesley was doing, if he was doing anything at all. What kind of fiancé was he, not taking up for her?

While moving along, she said, "My mother may be a little stiff at times. It comes from people approaching her on the street, asking advice about their personal lives." She couldn't see around the boat. Her legs wouldn't give her enough propulsion to move around the boat's stern. The stranger's boat was drifting, too, blocking her view. And the stranger? He just stood there, staring at her. Who was this guy anyway?

"How do you know my mother?"

"Oh, we go back a ways."

Peggy didn't think her mother knew anyone like this guy. "If you want to do my mother a favor, help my fiancé catch our boat. I'm getting pretty tired."

"Here," said the man, extending one of his huge arms, "let me give you a hand."

"No!" screamed Peggy, throwing up her hands and not caring what anyone saw. "You stay away from me!" She pushed away, using her hands, then turned her back on him.

The stranger straightened up. "Well, I guess you wouldn't even want your daddy to see you like this, would you?"

But Peggy didn't hear him. She was swimming for

the stern of his boat, despite the fact that the stranger could see her ass.

"I'll get the boat for you, Peggy."

She stopped and recovered herself. "Thank you."

The stranger cranked the engine, put his boat in gear, and waved at her as he left. And Peggy, forgetting her predicament, waved back, but only for a second, then jerked her hand down. The stranger laughed and Peggy flushed. If she ever got out of this, she was going to fix Wesley Calhoun and fix him good.

With the man's boat no longer blocking her view, she could see her fiancé struggling in the direction of their boat. The stranger beat him to it, reaching out and grabbing the bow line, then pulling the boat away. Wesley waved his arms and screamed bloody murder. The man still didn't stop. Terror cut through Peggy like an ax.

He was going to leave them out here!

Peggy joined Wesley in screaming and waving her arms over her head. A joke was a joke, but they might drown if left out here.

The stranger made a wide turn, sweeping around, and as he approached her, cut the power to his engine. The two boats slowed down and drifted toward her, pushing their wakes ahead of them.

He was grinning. "Your boyfriend's pretty mad, but I figured you were madder—him talking you into skinny-dipping."

"Right." Voice hoarse, Peggy crossed her chest with one hand and paddled toward the boat with the other.

The man glanced in their boat. "That your bathing suit?" he asked.

"Yes. I'll get into it after you leave."

Lashing the two boats together, he stepped over into her boat and picked up the bikini

"No!" shouted Peggy, throwing up a hand. "Don't throw it to me."

The stranger held up the suit. "There's nothing to it."

"It's enough . . . ." Peggy cleared her throat. If the son of a bitch dropped the thing . . . . He was holding it over the water. Oh, God, what had she gotten herself into? "It's enough to cover me."

He looked from her to the brightly-covered cloth. "It don't seem right for a girl to be going around dressed this way. People could get the wrong kind of idea."

It was all Peggy could do to force back the tears. "Please, Mister . . . ."

He glanced at her. "It seems little better than what you've got on."

"Mister . . . ."

"Lister. Raymond Lister."

"Mr. Lister—"

"You can call me 'Ray.'"

"Okay, Ray . . . ." Peggy cleared her throat, barely keeping the tears at bay. "If you don't mind, I'd like to get dressed. I'm—I'm getting cold out here."

Lister glanced at her fiancé struggling to close the distance between himself and their boat. Lister dropped the bikini in the bottom of their boat and stepped back into his. Once the engine was started, he shouted, "Well, see you around." With a flick of the wrist, his engine responded, and Raymond Lister was gone, leaving their boat only a few feet away.

Wesley hollered for her to run the boat over to him. Peggy looked in the direction of the marina, the direction Raymond Lister was taking, then, with heavy arms, she finished her swim to the boat. The jerk hadn't approved of what she'd been doing, and she really didn't give a damn. Still, she was left with the impression Raymond Lister would never let himself or his woman be caught in such a compromising situation.

Peggy glanced at Wesley, floating on his back and looking up at the sky. And what became of women who married boys who put them in such situations? She stopped at the ladder and marshaled her strength before climbing over the side. She'd better keep a tight rein on Mister Wesley Calhoun, until he showed signs of growing up.

Skinny-dipping in the middle of Lake Murray. How adolescent!

eleven

Peggy put on her cover-up before maneuvering the boat over to where Wesley treaded water. As Wesley climbed over the side, he asked, "What was that all about?"

"What do you mean?"

"Well, you talked to him—"

"Wesley!"

"I just thought—"

"Why are you fussing at me?"

"I'm not fussing." He found his swim trunks.

"Yes, you are."

"Okay, okay." Wesley pulled on his trunks. "Who was that guy anyway?"

"Raymond Lister."

"You know him?"

"He knows my mother."

"Well, who is he?"

Peggy put her hands on her hips. "Wesley, how

should I know? Can we just go back now?"

"What's the problem, Peg?"

"What's the problem! I was totally humiliated in front of some man I don't even know, but you"—her voice turned sarcastic—"you think I'm supposed to know who he is, what kind of work he does, his social security number . . . ." Peggy moved to the bow and sat down, turning her back on him. She drew a towel around her. "That's all you care about, who the guy was, not how humiliated I might've been. What if he'd showed up while we were doing it." She felt the boat move, saw a shadow fall across the bow, and threw a hand up without turning around. "No! Stay away from me! I just want to go in!"

"But, honey, nothing happened."

Peggy gritted her teeth. "That's right. Nothing happened. Could we just go back?"

Her fiancé stared at her for a moment, then shrugged and stepped back to the controls. He turned over the engine, shifted the boat into gear, and slowly opened up the engine.

When Wesley didn't immediately head for the lake house, Peggy whirled around. "Now where are we going?"

"I told you we had to gas up before going in. That was our excuse for coming out here in the first place."

Peggy turned her back to him. "Just make it quick!"

Wesley throttled back on the engine, shifting into neutral and letting it idle. "Darling, don't you think—"

"Wesley, if you don't get this damn boat moving, I'm going to come back there and drive it myself."

Minutes later, Peggy's worst fear was confirmed. Raymond Lister was there, moored at the far end of the pier. After Wesley gassed up and disappeared inside the marina, Lister ambled over. God, but he was big, much bigger than Wesley. Lister had arms Peggy hadn't seen since dating football players, or such a haircut. His short hair appeared to be gray, but Lister didn't look all that old.

What kind of work did he do to develop such arms? Lister didn't look like the type to work out at any gym. She glanced at the marina. Wesley was taking his own sweet time coming back. Probably bragging about how he got a little out in the middle of the lake. Peggy gritted her teeth as Lister stopped where their boat was moored alongside a gas pump.

"Miss Fox?"

Peggy wished she could crawl under the bow and hide. Unfortunately, it was a tiny place, only suitable for children. So she lifted her chin and looked the bastard right in the eye. She'd seen her mother handle men like Raymond Lister. She could do it, too.

"Yes, Mr. Lister."

"Ray."

"I don't think we know each other well enough to be on a first-name basis."

"I just wanted you to know . . . ." Lister glanced at the pier. "I just wanted to tell you . . . ."

"What'd you want to tell me? That you enjoyed the show?"

"Oh, no, it wasn't that. I just wanted you to know there wasn't much I could see, the water being so dark."

"Don't worry about what you saw. It comes with the territory, when you're trying to be one of the boys."

"A girl shouldn't be one of the boys. You should be a lady, not horsing around in the water with some guy."

"That guy, as you call him, Mr. Lister, is my fiancé. We're to be married next month, though, as I said, I don't think what we were doing is any of your business."

Lister stared at her for a long moment, then turned and walked away. He'd only gone a few steps before returning. "As far as I'm concerned I didn't even see you today. I won't mention it to your mother."

Wesley came out of the marina and saw his fiancée talking with the asshole who'd jerked them around in the middle of the lake. He hurried down the gangplank.

Peggy saw Wesley coming. "Mr. Lister?"

Raymond had turned to go again. "Yes?"

"Are you saying you're an honorable man?"

"I try to think so."

She stood up. "Then give me a hand."

Lister pulled Peggy to the dock as Wesley raced across the pier toward them. "What was that all about out there, Mister? We could've drowned."

Lister stared at Wesley, who was the same height but certainly not the same size.

Not the same size at all, thought Peggy. No, Raymond Lister was a grown man. "Would you give me a ride into town?"

Lister only looked at her.

"Peggy, what are you talking about? You don't know this man, and you saw how he treated us out on the water."

"He's a friend of my mother, and he's going to do me a favor. Isn't that right?"

Lister was staring at her fiancé, not her.

"But your clothes and purse—they're back at the house."

"Drop them off on your way into town. It ought to give your mother something else to talk about."

"But what will *your* mother say?"

"Wesley, I don't think—"

"Miss Fox," cut in Lister, "I wouldn't want to come between you and your mother. She's not the kind of woman a man would want mad at him."

"Mr. Lister, I'll be twenty-one in a few days. I think I can make my own decisions."

"Peggy, I won't let you do this."

"Wesley, I don't see where you have any say in the matter. You're not my keeper."

"And maybe you need one."

"I'm ready to go, Ray. That is, if you are."

"I am, Miss Fox, but I have to warn you, I haven't eaten all day and plan to stop for lunch."

"After that swim I'm ready for something to eat."

Lister set off, not waiting for her to follow him. As he headed for the parking lot, Wesley took Peggy's arm, holding her back. "Why are you doing this?"

"Take your hands off me."

"Honey, this is Wesley you're talking to, the man you're going to marry."

"Don't be so sure of that." And with that, Peggy jerked out of his grasp and left him on the dock.

❖   ❖   ❖

Jean pulled into the turnaround in front of her mother-in-law's house and leaped out of her rental car. She remembered to turn the engine off but left the door open. One of the gardeners stopped his pruning, put his clippers down, and walked over to the car as Jean disappeared into the house. The man closed the door and returned to his work. Things sure went crazy around a house when a white gal got married. They made all sorts of a fuss. His own daughter had tried that, but he'd put a stop to it and quick. But this Peggy, she called the tune around this house.

Inside, Jean rushed past the other member of the household staff. "Where is she, Hattie?"

"Miss Ruth," said the black woman, pointing in the direction of the Florida room, "is out yonder . . . and she's drinking."

Jean stopped and stared at the elderly woman.

"I ain't seen Miss Ruth drink like this since young Mister Fox died."

"Bring me a sherry, too." Jean disappeared into the study that led into the Florida room.

The black woman shook her head. "Bring me a drink, bring me a drink. A house surely is messed up when people start drinking this time of day."

Hattie knew that for a fact. She'd left her last post where both the husband and the wife drank, and after the lady of the house passed out, the master came upstairs and tried to have his way with her. Of course, there was no man around this house, which might be good or it might be bad. Hattie sure didn't like opening the door to strangers without no man around, especially the kind who'd come around this morning, asking for work. That white man had shore given her the willies.

In the kitchen, Hattie took the sherry from one of the cabinets and poured a drink for Miss Jean, then poured one for herself. Might as well get happy like everybody else.

Jean found her mother-in-law in the Florida room, surrounded by plants and flowers. She was staring through the glass at the backyard, drink in hand, and looking older than her years. The last time Jean had seen Ruth like this had been when Peggy told them she was getting married, before that, when Jean said she and her daughter were moving out.

Jean cleared her throat.

Ruth turned her head ever so slowly and looked at her. "Come in and sit, child."

Jean did and realized Ruth had called her "child"— a nickname she reserved exclusively for Peggy.

The two women sat in silence until Hattie arrived with Jean's drink. After the housekeeper left, Jean asked, "What did he say, Ruth?"

Her mother-in-law continued to stare through the glass wall. In the middle of the lawn sat a gazebo and behind the gazebo, a garage where the cars were housed. To their left lay the tennis court, to the right, a croquet court. There were no wickets on the grass now, only a black man moving back and forth with a mower, cutting grass without the advantage of a gas engine.

"You know, after I'm gone, all this will be yours."

"You aren't going anywhere, Ruth."

"I don't know about that. Sometimes the weight of living outweighs dying. Anyway, I want it all to be yours. You're my only daughter, Peggy my only grandchild. Sell it if you wish. I know you don't think much of this lifestyle, but the Foxes and the Marchbanks fought, not only in the War Between the States but also in the Revolutionary War, several Indian Wars before that, and we believe we deserve this place." For a moment Ruth was silent, then she went on. "Young people don't value the past. Only today's important, but, child, you live in the South, and the past won't go away."

"What did Raymond Lister say?"

Ruth faced Jean for the first time. "Just that he wanted to see if there was any work that needed to be done. I pointed out the boys in the yard and told him I had plenty of help."

"Did he leave?"

"Yes. After pulling out a piece of paper and scribbling down his phone number. It was your number, Jean. Your home telephone number. Now how did he get that?"

About to take a sip of her sherry, Jean stopped. If anyone had asked at that very moment, she would have said she felt nothing above her waist, only an emptiness where her chest had once been. "My—my number? But it's unlisted."

"That's when I knew for sure who he was. But Lister was gone by them. Why didn't you tell me he was in town, child?"

"I didn't know he was here until last night when my car was bashed in, and then I didn't know it was Lister that—"

"You smashed up your car? Were you hurt, my dear?"

"No, no. It wasn't a wreck. It happened outside the station. In the parking lot. Someone smashed the windows and slashed the tires. I didn't even tell Peggy. I thought it was the man who . . . ." Jean realized Ruth didn't know anything about Ernie Kelly, and she had forbidden Peggy to mention the attack to her grandmother. "It's a long story," said Jean, waving her off. "Lister called my program today. I think."

"You think?"

"I was coming to talk to you after my program, and with Peggy up at Lake Murray . . . ." Jean glanced at the floor of the room, algae trying to gain a foothold in the corners. "I'm sorry, Ruth. It won't happen again."

"What will you do, child?"

"I don't know yet."

"Call the police."

"And tell them what?"

"The truth about Raymond Lister. Where he comes from, who he is, and why you're frightened of him."

"I'm not scared of him."

"Call them for Peggy's sake." Ruth sat up. "She's his daughter. He wouldn't harm her, would he?"

"I don't know."

"Then what's he doing here? What does he want?"

It was a moment before Jean could speak. "I think Raymond Lister has come here to destroy me."

twelve

Raymond Lister drove an old blue convertible with a black top. Certainly not the kind of car to be found in the garage of the condo where she and her mother lived. Peggy stood back, legs apart, hands on hips, staring at the old car. The thing was so old, it was cool.

"What is it?"

"A Galaxy XL 500." When she looked perplexed, Raymond added, "Made by Ford."

"Yes, but will it make it back to Columbia?"

"It made it out here, didn't it?"

"That's no answer."

"And what do you drive?"

"A Honda."

Lister shook his head. "Another rice burner."

"What?"

"Made in Japan."

"I'll bet it gets better mileage than this old thing."

"So?"

"So, don't you want to do something about the environment?"

"Not if I have to drive around in a little box."

"Not exactly a socially correct attitude."

"Peggy, I doubt I've done anything socially correct in the last twenty years."

"And what have you been doing for the last twenty years?"

"Sure you can handle it?"

"I can handle it." And right there and then, Peggy decided it wasn't such a smart idea to catch a ride into town with this man. But when she opened her mouth to tell him that, she saw her fiancé crossing the parking lot. She vaulted over the door and plopped down into the passenger seat. "Tell me over lunch."

Lister opened the door and slid in behind the wheel. He started the engine, then punched in the lighter. When the lighter popped out, he had a big fat cigar waiting, a nasty thing, bigger than his thumb. He lit the cigar, jammed the lighter back into the holder, and shifted the car into gear, then put a hand on the seat behind her to back out of the parking lot. He stopped.

Behind them stood Wesley Calhoun.

Peggy grabbed the top of the windshield and the back of the front seat to raise up and turn around. "Wesley, what do you think you're doing?"

Her fiancé walked over to her side of the car. "I don't think this is such a good idea."

She glanced at Lister. The older man was leaning against his door, watching these two . . . kids! She felt the heat rush up the sides of her neck. "What I do is none of your business."

"Peggy, we're engaged to be married."

"That doesn't mean you own me."

"I didn't mean—"

"I know what you meant." Sliding to her knees on the front seat, she worked the diamond ring around on her finger. "You want this back, is that what you want?"

Her fiancé's hands came up in surrender. "No, no, that's not what I mean."

"Then what do you want?" she asked, jamming the ring down on her finger. She glanced at Lister again. The man hadn't moved, only sat there, puffing away on his cigar, watching them.

"What'll I tell your mother?"

"I'll probably see her before you do."

"But she's depending on me—"

"To what? Baby-sit me?" Peggy slid her legs out from under. "Ray, if you're ready for lunch, I know I am."

Lister flipped his cigar out of the car and it flew over Peggy's head, making Wesley duck. Lister put his hand on the back of her seat again to back out of the parking space. The car started moving, but Wesley wouldn't let go. He followed them by holding onto the side of the car.

"Peggy, I won't let you do this!"

"I am doing it, so get over it!"

Wesley reached inside the car and grabbed her arm.

Peggy fought to get free. "Wesley, stop! Stop this very instant!"

The car stopped and Lister reached over and gripped the young man's wrist. Peggy saw pain flash across her fiancé's face. Wesley let go and jerked away. He stared at Lister, who, once again, leaned back against his side of the car.

Wesley rubbed his wrist. "I'd better call your mother."

Peggy stared straight ahead. At any moment she was going to burst into tears. Why was Wesley doing this?

"You hear me. I'm calling your mother."

"Do that, and don't forget to tell her how you tried to force me to come with you."

"You ought to be coming with me. I'm your fiancé."

Wesley's breath came hard and fast. He was frightened. Peggy could see it in his eyes. Could he see the same fear in her eyes? And what were they afraid of? Raymond Lister? Peggy didn't think so. No. They'd glimpsed a side of each other never seen before. Was this what their future held? Wesley becoming physical whenever he couldn't have his way? Forcing himself on her when she didn't want him? There was something wrong here, something that needed to be fixed.

Peggy twisted around in her seat. "Wesley . . . ."

But her fiancé was gone, striding across the parking lot and heading for the marina.

"Want to chase after him?" asked Lister. "But I'll tell you, I ain't waiting for you."

Hot tears formed in Peggy's eyes as she faced the windshield again. It was all she could do not to wipe them away. "I don't have to see him. I don't ever have to see him again."

Lister said nothing, only lit another cigar, then drove

out of the parking lot, down the road to the gate, and turned onto the highway. And all the while, Peggy was thinking that if her grandmother were here she would be ragging her to kiss and make up. Nana believed couples should never go to bed mad, that's what ruined marriages. Her mother had nothing to add to the discussion. Never once had her mother gone to bed mad. Her mother's marriage hadn't lasted long enough.

Why hadn't her mother remarried? Was it true what Wesley said: That she wasn't the only one who idealized her dead father? Whatever it was, it'd be nice to have someone to talk to. All her friends were in school, none of them married; and as far as advice from Nana, she was much too old-fashioned. Women had rights. Maybe not in Nana's day, but things were different now. If Nana knew Wesley and she were sleeping together . . . .

"Have you ever been married, Mr. Lister?"

"Never had the chance." Lister didn't take his eyes off the road.

Peggy slumped down in her seat and fell into a funk as she watched the countryside fly by. It was a while before she realized that they hadn't taken the turnoff to the interstate. They passed a dilapidated building where produce was being sold and a cemetery filled with more weeds than headstones. The best hot dogs were up ahead, or so said a sign peppered with bullet holes.

She sat up. "We're not taking the interstate?"

Lister glanced at her. "That bother you?"

Peggy shook her head. "I should've known, your car not being up to it."

"This old heap could take that rice burner of yours any day of the week."

"You mean, like in drag racing?" She glanced at the floorboard. "I guess so. You've got a stick shift."

"It's good to see you know something about cars."

"Cars are only good for getting from point A to point B."

"Come again?"

"Transportation, Ray, that's all cars are good for."

Lister shook his head.

"My mother gave me that so-called rice burner when I graduated from high school. I was in the top ten percent of my class."

"Good to hear."

Peggy thought her interest in cars would start a conversation, but the man was strangely silent as they floated down the road, and float they did in this big boat of a car. A slight tapping noise came from the engine. Was there something wrong? Lister didn't seem worried. Matter-of-fact, Raymond Lister didn't seem to worry about much of anything.

"Don't think I've ever seen a car ride so smooth."

Lister said nothing.

"And the way its big old hood sticks out in front of us, like a big boat gliding across water."

"You worried about what your mother'll think—about me bringing you home?"

Peggy lifted her head. "I'm an artist, Ray. I can't afford to worry about what people think."

"Then what's with the crying back there?"

"I was . . . mad. Wesley always thinks he knows

what's best. I'm sick and tired of being treated like a child. He's only four years older than me. I don't want someone telling me what to do the rest of my life." She looked at Lister. "Is that why you never married?"

"I couldn't. I've been in prison the last twenty years."

Peggy felt a bubble of fear rise in her throat. "Pri— prison? What for?"

"Does it matter?"

She shook her head. "Not if you don't want to talk about it."

"I'll tell you. If you really want to know."

She shook her head again and her hands came palm down alongside her on the seat. "No, no, you don't have to say a thing. You really don't."

Lister glanced in the mirror, slowed down, and pulled off the road about a hundred yards from the hot dog stand Peggy thought they were heading for. Now she didn't know what they were heading for. She glanced up and down the road. The two-lane was empty. At the hot dog stand were parked two cars and a pickup. But it was a long way down there.

"Why—why are we stopping?"

"So I can tell you why I was in prison."

Peggy twisted up against the door. "No, no, Mr. Lister. Really, you don't have to tell me."

His cigar had gone out. He punched in the lighter again. "Nasty habit, smoking. Not much to do in prison. Once I got out, I rewarded myself with cigars."

Peggy could hardly hear him. Blood rushed through her head and her mind raced. Should she leap out of the car and run to the hot dog stand? Lister would certainly catch her. He had a car. Should she run into the woods? Peggy didn't think so. If Lister caught her, she'd be alone with him. In the woods. What had this man done to be in prison for so long?

The lighter popped out and Lister relit his cigar. After jamming the lighter into its holder, he said, "Rape."

Peggy's throat constricted with fear. She couldn't get her breath. She fumbled for the doorknob but couldn't find it. And Raymond Lister, well, he just sat there. But at any moment he would leap on her.

Where was Wesley? Peggy looked in the direction of the marina. Oh, God! What had she done? She'd gotten in the car with a rapist.

Peggy found the lever, opened the door, and fell out, landing on her butt. Her cover-up slid up her legs and she uttered a small 'oh!' as she hit the ground. For a second, the world went ajar, then back into focus. Yet Lister only reclined against the door and smoked his cigar while she sat on her butt, feet still in the car.

She scrambled to her feet and brushed down her cover-up.

"That's why I stopped. I didn't want you getting out while it was moving. You could've hurt yourself."

Peggy backed away, leaving the door open. All she wore were flip-flops, and the weeds scratched her legs. She looked toward the hot dog stand, and while she watched, the pickup from the parking lot drove toward them. Inside the cab were two guys, and as the pickup slowed, then stopped, the driver leaned out the window. He was a freckled-faced kid with red hair.

"Need any help, Miss?"

Peggy glanced at Lister. Lister never looked at the boys but continued to sit there, smoke his cigar, and study her. It was up to her if she was going to catch a ride with these boys. Lister wasn't going to make up her mind for her. He wasn't even threatening her. Wasn't stopping her from talking with these boys. Hadn't tried to stop her from getting out of the car. He'd even been considerate enough to stop so she could get out, knowing she'd be frightened when he told her about why he'd been sent to prison. Wesley would never think of such a thing. All Wesley could think of was sticking his thing inside her, and if that was Raymond Lister's plan, he sure had a funny way of going about it.

"Hey, lady," called the freckled-face boy again. "I said: You need a ride?"

She shook her head. "No, no. Everything's fine."

The young man gave Lister another look, then clunked his pickup into gear. "Okay then. Have a nice day."

As they started to drive away, Peggy heard the passenger ask, "What was that all about?"

"Some girl fighting with her old man, I reckon."

After they were gone, Lister scooted across the seat. Peggy backed away, tripping and catching herself by grabbing a small tree. One of the limbs stuck her in the back, another worked its way under her cover-up. Peggy never noticed. She was watching Lister. She only had eyes for Raymond Lister.

He pulled the door shut, then pointed down the road. "You see that place? I'll buy lunch like I said. But if I do, you have to promise one thing."

Peggy turned loose of the tree and brushed away the limb. "What—what's that?"

"Promise to listen to my story all the way through. If you won't listen to my story all the way through, then don't even sit at my table. I'll still pay for lunch." He returned to his side of the car, then looked up and down the two-lane. "You can wait here for another ride, but I think you oughta walk down there. It'll be safer and that'll be plenty of time to make up your mind whether you'll listen to what I have to say. And Peggy?"

"Yes?"

"If you don't listen to why I was sent to prison, I'd appreciate you never asking again. Just talk behind my back like everybody else does."

thirteen

Raymond Lister had a chili dog waiting for Peggy when she reached the hot dog stand. A glass of lemonade sat alongside it. By the time the girl reached the stand, she and Lister were its only customers. The restaurant operated out of a mobile home overlooking a redwood deck filled with tables and benches made of the same material. Overhead, a yellowish tarp provided shade, rustling when a breeze hit it. Through the serving window, a heavy woman watched Peggy take a seat.

"You can use the phone if you need to, honey."

"No, thank you. I think I'll eat lunch first."

"Well, do what you want, but Elrod and me, we're in here if you need us."

Peggy nodded, then asked, "How'd you know I liked chili dogs, Ray?"

"Just a lucky guess."

"And lemonade." She took a swallow of the tangy, ice-cold liquid. "I just love lemonade."

"But don't drink it because your friends would think you're still a kid."

"How'd you know?"

Lister chuckled. "I was a kid once, Peggy."

"Where'd you live?" she asked, picking up the hot dog and being careful not to allow the chili to drip on her cover-up. "When you were a kid?"

"Florida."

"So'd my mom. Is that where you know her from?"

"She's from Coventry. I lived in Alamo. We were cross-county rivals."

Lister smiled, and Peggy thought she knew that smile from somewhere. She just couldn't place where she'd seen it.

"Where'd you get that gray hair?" he asked.

Peggy reached up and tossed her drying hair. "It's a family curse."

"On whose side?"

"My mother's."

Lister nodded before taking a final bite from his hot dog and another sip of lemonade. "Well, if you're here, that means you want to know why a man would rape a woman, right?"

Peggy glanced at the table. "If you don't want to talk about it, Mr. Lister, that's all right with me."

"Ray, Peggy, Ray. You're old enough to call . . . to call me Ray or Raymond."

"I like Ray better." She took a bite of the chili dog and chewed it. After wiping chili off her mouth, she asked, "Why's it so important for me to know about the rape?"

"If you don't let me explain what happened, you'll never be able to relax around me."

"Then you'll be the only one not hitting on me."

Lister straightened up. "You let me know who they are and I'll make sure they don't ever bother you again."

"I can handle them."

"Including your fiancé?"

"Especially my fiancé."

"You didn't want to come with me, did you? You just wanted to get away from him."

Peggy stared at the table again. "Yes."

Lister reached across the table and lifted her face with his hand. "If anyone ever tries to hurt you—"

A ketchup bottle fell off the shelf as the heavy woman stuck her head through the serving window. "You take your hands off that girl, you hear me? Elrod's got a shotgun in here."

Peggy and Raymond looked at the woman. Pulling his hand away, Lister said, "Maybe we should get out of here."

"I'd like that." Peggy took another bite of the hot dog, threw the rest away, and brought along her lemonade.

As they went down the steps the woman continued to hang out the window. "You can use our phone to call your folks if you want to, honey."

Peggy smiled as she went down the stairs. "No, thank you."

The woman jotted down the tag number as the man opened the door for the girl. "Out-of-state—that figures. I'm of a good mind to call the sheriff." She pulled her head back through the window.

"What business is it of yours?" asked the man scraping the grill.

"And that's what's wrong with the world today, Elrod. Nobody looks out for their neighbor. Anybody with two eyes can see that girl's asking for trouble, going off with that man."

"And anybody with two eyes can see that girl just left here with her father."

Jean and Ruth sat in the Florida room, sipping sherry and considering ways out of their predicament.

"Maybe you should leave town for a few weeks," suggested Ruth.

"And go where?"

"What would it matter as long as that man didn't know where you were. Take Peggy with you."

"You'd leave, too?"

"It's not me he's after, dear."

"And you'd feel safe here? You've met him. He came to your door."

Ruth watched the young man pushing the mower back and forth across the backyard. He must be an awfully strong young man to move a mower across such a stretch of grass without the benefit of an engine, but the yard looked so good cut that way.

"Yes. I'd leave."

"And the wedding? My radio programs? I have responsibilities, obligations, something Raymond Lister doesn't have. I'm trapped here. If I were a man, I'd beat the hell out of him." Jean paused, remembering the size of Raymond Lister's arms, how they pushed her down, forcing her to submit, to open up for him . . . .

"Jean?" asked a voice.

She shivered, then shrugged it off. "If I can just hang on until the wedding's over, I could leave. And Lister would have to spend that time knowing I was off somewhere, enjoying myself. It might be enough to make him blow his stack, do something foolish, and end up in prison again."

"Or come after you."

"I could go around the world. Go up the Amazon. Lister doesn't have the resources. He's just out of prison, and when he went in, he was only a mechanic. Lister doesn't have money, and he'd have to have a passport. I doubt he could get one on such short notice."

"And what if he already has one, anticipating you'd do something like that? What if he has access to money? What if he decides to follow you? Or Peggy and Wesley?"

"He'd pay hell following me, and as for the children, I think I could get their plans changed. I could tell the Calhouns we've received threatening phone calls since the wedding announcement. I think they'd buy that and wouldn't tell people where the children were. They might even leave town themselves."

"Would Peggy go along?" asked Ruth, sipping from her sherry.

"I'd have to convince her Lister posed a threat, but I don't see any problem since he's an ex-con. It would be enough to make me leave town."

"But Peggy isn't you, my dear. You came up the hard way, earning everything you have. No parents to raise you, grandparents who did little better, a mother-in-law who didn't want—"

"Ruth!"

"No. This needs to be said. You didn't think I wanted you here when you first arrived and you were right. But you showed me what you were made of by putting your life back together, having Peggy, and going back to school. Even moving out. I didn't like that one little bit. All that room in this big old house. It didn't make any sense. Peggy hasn't faced any of those problems. Peggy Fox is spoiled rotten."

Jean tried to protest.

"Let me finish. I should know what I'm talking about. I was the one doing most of the spoiling. Worst of all, my granddaughter is bored. Children from well-to-do families get in trouble because they don't have enough to do. I've seen plenty at the country club. Peggy is so insulated from the real world, she's fascinated by anything deviating from the norm. Her paintings exhibit those traits, and don't argue with me, I asked an expert. I wouldn't be surprised if she thinks marriage is life's next great adventure. She has no idea marriage is a lifetime commitment, and sometimes can become a burden."

"I think Peggy is smart enough to understand the threat any rapist would pose."

"You'd tell her Lister was a rapist?"

"I'd make sure she learned about it . . . somehow."

"If you're willing to do that, why not go to the police?"

"And throw away everything I have? Everything I've worked for?"

"Jean, this . . . this thing that happened to you happens to women every day. And women come forward and they send the man to prison." Ruth gestured with her hand. "It happened over twenty years ago and Raymond Lister went to prison as he deserved. If he's come here to harass you, you have every right to go to the police for protection."

"And have people looking at me funny. Men approaching me with lewd suggestions, and this, right after . . . ." Jean bit her tongue at the memory of Ernie Kelly. Fortunately, Ernie had agreed to treatment. Why he'd chosen California, Jean didn't know. Perhaps family.

She went on to add, "And my boss would look at me like what kind of woman attracts so much trouble? And how will the Calhouns feel about their son marrying into a family where the mother of the bride was raped, not to mention Peggy being the son of an ex-con?"

"We'll buy him off, that's what we'll do. I have the money. I don't want her future ruined by that man."

"He'd only come back for more."

"And we'd give it to him. The money's not doing me any good in the bank."

"Sooner or later, Lister's going to get around to what he really wants—me!"

Her mother-in-law stared at her. "In . . . in a physical sense?"

Jean couldn't bear to meet her mother-in-law's eyes. The next question would be did she enjoy the rape?

Even Ruth wasn't immune to *that* question, a question asked more and more these days as women were supposed to enjoy the sex act.

"After twenty years in prison, I think Raymond Lister would get a perverse thrill out of dominating me."

"Do you think that would make him leave Peggy alone?"

Jean felt herself recoil. "Ruth, what are you suggesting?"

"We're women, you and I. We know what men want. It's all they ever want. If they didn't have that urge, we'd receive no attention at all."

Jean almost laughed. She'd never heard her mother-in-law speak so frankly about sex. "Ruth, this isn't the kind of attention any woman would want. Rape isn't anything akin to love."

"Nonetheless, it's a variation of an age-old game."

"What—what do you mean?"

"Face facts, child. You may have it in your power to rid us of this man forever."

"By sleeping with him."

"No, my dear, there wouldn't be any reason to spend the night." Ruth put down her sherry glass and looked out the window. Finished with the larger sections, the yardman was working the mower into the hard-to-get places around the flower beds. "You think you're the first woman to endure some unpleasantness to protect her chicks? Your father-in-law had his little trysts. My mother-in-law said it was the French side of the family, that the blood ran hotter on that side. In my anger and pride, I decided to put an end to . . . that part of our marriage. Nowadays, it's fashionable to throw your husband out, but where does that get you? Sometimes those husbands come back and murder you, like one did Harry Hartner's daughter."

Straightening up, she added, "I outlived my husband and his little trysts, and now I have a wonderful grand-daughter." She smiled. "A granddaughter I wouldn't have had if I had been in Florida when you were ro-mancing my son. I would've put a stop to that and very quickly. Some country girl—not for my son. Once again, my pride would've gotten in the way and I would've been left with nothing." Ruth glanced at the window again. "A woman who wouldn't let her husband come to her bed because he was running around on her. That woman came close to having nothing, my dear."

Jean felt as if her face were about to explode. The pressure around her eyes was intense. "So your advice is . . . ." She took a breath and started again, then found she couldn't swallow. Swallow what? Swallow her pride and give herself to Raymond Lister? "So your advice is to let Raymond Lister have his way with me." That sounded so ludicrous, but it kept her from burst-ing into tears. "In hopes that'll get rid of him."

"No, my dear. I'm telling you what an old woman has been thinking while sitting in this glass room of this big old house. You have to make your own decision. I can't make it for you, if I ever could. It's not me he wants. I'd give my life for Peggy and Wesley, and what they're about to have. All the joys, all the problems. Everything. They deserve their chance at happiness."

Jean gritted her teeth. "I'm going to fight him. I'm

going to fight and I'm going to win. Raymond Lister ruined my life once. I'm not going to let it happen again. And he's certainly not going to ruin Peggy's."

Ruth reached over and patted her knee. "I don't know what you plan to do, but remember, it only takes one word from Lister and my granddaughter's world will fall apart. The marriage won't happen and Peggy will wonder why you didn't tell her she was the daughter of a rapist in the first place."

"If I can hold out until they're married . . . ."

Hattie appeared at the door. "Telephone for you, Miss Jean. Mister Wesley calling."

"Wesley? Not Peggy?"

Ruth looked at her daughter-in-law. "I thought Peggy went to Lake Murray with Wesley's family."

But Jean was already out of her seat, plunking down her sherry glass as she went. "I did, too."

She rushed by Hattie, almost knocking the black woman aside. Ruth followed her to the phone on the desk in the study. Hattie followed, then saw the look on her mistress' face and left the study, closing the door behind her.

Whatever Wesley said on the phone, Ruth saw Jean's face turn white. The receiver slipped from her hand and thumped to the floor. She collapsed into the chair behind the desk as Wesley's voice continued to squawk from the phone.

"Jean," asked Ruth, "has there been an accident? Is Peggy all right?"

Her daughter-in-law looked up at her. "Raymond Lister has Peggy."

fourteen

*P*eggy leaned back in the passenger seat, sipped her lemonade, and let the air whip her hair around, making a total mess of her curls. She looked over at Raymond Lister, smoking another of those nasty cigars. Her fiancé was a child compared to this man.

What would her father have been like at this age? In control of his life like Raymond Lister, or a child like Wesley Calhoun? Probably more like Raymond Lister. But her father was no rapist. He had certainly never forced himself on any woman, of that, Peggy was certain. And her father had died in the service of his country.

"Ever been in the service, Ray?"

"I have a bum knee, like Joe Namath."

"Who?"

"Played football before you were born. I'm no rapist, Peggy."

"I didn't say you were."

"But you were thinking it."

"You don't act like a rapist. Giving me a chance to run away and buying me a chili dog"—Peggy held up her drink—"and a lemonade," she added with a smile.

"I moved here on your mother's say-so. If I run into you again, I want you to know you're safe around me. Twenty years ago, when I was coming home from Tampa, I picked up this girl—"

"How old was she?"

"Eighteen, nineteen, somewhere around there."

"Then she was no girl. The person you picked up was a young woman."

"Twenty years ago she was a girl, and twenty years ago she could accuse me of rape and send me to prison."

"My mother met my father in Tampa."

"That's what I heard."

"You seem to know a good deal about my family."

Lister shrugged. "People talk, and they talk about people from the old neighborhood, wondering how they made it, if they're crooked or not."

"She's not a crook, Ray."

"And they wonder how a woman could do as well as she's done."

"She didn't go down on anyone and I resent the—"

He looked at her. "Oh, questions about me are okay, but your mother, she's off-limits."

"You're the one who brought up the rape."

"Because I want you to know how women can twist the truth and ruin a man's life. Now, don't get me wrong, if you don't want to talk about your mother, that's fine."

"I'm not afraid to discuss my mom. Matter of fact,

I'm rather proud of what she's accomplished."

"There's not much I couldn't do with that kind of money behind me."

"She did it on her own."

"How do you know? You weren't around when she was making her decisions."

Peggy sat up. "And I think I made a poor decision getting in this car with you."

"Maybe you did. Why don't I drop you off where you can catch a cab back to your dream world. That woman back there, the one at the hot dog stand, she was pretty anxious to protect you from the real world."

"You're just jealous because you weren't brought up with the advantages I had."

"I'm not jealous, Peggy, because you're spoiled. And it's going to get you in trouble one day, trouble your mother won't be able to get you out of. Letting yourself be picked up by me, I could do anything I wanted and there's nothing you could do about it."

"And you'd go back to prison."

"And you'd be raped, maybe dead."

Peggy looked at the passing countryside, green and lush from so much rain this spring. There wasn't an adult alive who didn't try to turn around what she said. Adults didn't like children who could think for themselves. It meant they were no longer children.

"Your mother made a success of herself in spite of family money, is that what you're saying?"

Peggy whirled around. "Right! And my grandmother doesn't care for my mother's working either."

Lister finally looked at her. "Then why does she? With

all that money—"

"She wants to be her own person. Like I do. Like leaving my fiancé back there because he was acting like a jerk. Then ending up with another jerk." And Peggy wondered if it was smart to call a convicted rapist a jerk while riding in his car.

"Well, Peggy, you can get out my car anytime you want, but you won't be able to get out of marriage that easy."

"Now you sound like my grandmother."

Lister said nothing.

"I'd leave Wesley if he didn't treat me properly."

Lister was silent, smoking his cigar, hand hardly working the wheel as they floated down the road past an old service station where vegetables, fruits, and granite headstones were being sold.

"Oh, I'll bet you're from the old school. You think a woman should be subservient to her husband. You and Nana would get along just fine."

"It's only right. The husband should be the head of the family, and that's probably why your mother's never remarried. She's never found anyone to be the head of her household."

Peggy laughed. "'Man as the head of the household'— when women bring home, sometimes, just as much money. You really are out of touch. Then what do I do about Wesley?"

"Find another man."

Peggy twisted around in her seat. "I was joking, but you're serious, aren't you?"

Lister nodded.

"The invitations have been sent out, the wedding gifts have started to arrive. I've bought my dress."

Lister only puffed away on his cigar.

"You've nothing to say?"

"I've already had my say. You don't marry a boy, you marry a man."

"Someone like you, I would imagine?"

Lister looked at her. "Someone with the same kind of values."

"Same kind of values as me?"

Lister thumped his chest. "Same values as mine. Fathers like to see their daughters marrying the right man. I'm no different."

"I am marrying the right . . . . What do you mean 'fathers like to see their daughters marry the right man'?"

"You said I sounded like your grandmother—why couldn't I sound like your father?"

Peggy stared at him, then slumped into her seat. She'd never met this guy before today and here he was giving her advice like he was . . . her father. Or her best friend. Except friends would never tell her not to marry Wesley Calhoun. At the university, Wesley Calhoun was a catch *par excellence*. Even her mother admitted that. And this man sitting alongside her had a value system one hundred and eighty degrees from her own. Saying her mother had never remarried because she'd never found someone to lead her. The idea was preposterous.

"Ray, it's a new century. Women don't need someone to tell them what to do with their lives."

"Then why are you listening to me?"

Peggy threw away her cup and stared out her side of

the car. She didn't have to leap out because it wouldn't be long before they'd be in Columbia and she'd be rid of this guy, some guy who presumed to tell her what to do with her life. Who the hell did he think he was?

But Lister did have a point. Why was she listening to him? Why was she interested in his opinion? And why did she find Wesley's father so interesting? It might sound weird—to girls with fathers—but she was actually looking forward to being Mr. Calhoun's daughter-in-law. Maybe because she missed the daddy she'd never known. Or did she simply want a daddy? She'd been accused of that more than once by her mother.

Peggy didn't realize they'd entered the city, didn't see anything. The world around her blurred, and the only time she remembered feeling this disconnected was when she thought she was pregnant and scared to death to tell her mother. Her mother would've freaked out. Having sex at seventeen, and not even out of high school. Thank God, she'd only been late.

And Raymond Lister said a woman didn't marry a boy, she married a man. Peggy glanced at Lister as they crossed the bridge, heading into the capital. Chiseled features, ropy muscles, flat stomach, and a serious look. The look of a man who could take care of himself.

"Tell me about the rape, Ray."

"Like I said, it wasn't rape."

"Prove it. Prove it wasn't rape."

"I've only got my word."

"And I'll take it, until you say something that doesn't make sense."

"Like I said, I picked up this girl who wanted a ride into Coventry—"

"Coventry, did you say?" Peggy's breath caught in her throat. What was Lister trying to tell her? Where had this man come from? And why had he chosen this moment to drop in on her life?

Because he's been incarcerated for the last twenty years, you idiot.

Yes, but he knows my mother.

But how well does he know your mother?

"Same place your mom's from," added Lister.

Finally, Peggy could draw a breath. Evidently, Lister didn't mean what she suspected. I mean, after all, Ray's hair was the same color as hers. But Ray was old. Old enough to be her . . . father. Peggy shuddered. Lister was talking. Maybe she should be listening.

". . . came on to me. She propositioned me."

"The woman was a whore?"

"Not a very nice term for a woman, but that's what she was. When I wouldn't play along, she called me a rapist, and in front of a lot of people. I wasn't thinking. I ran. I knew what they did to rapists in my part of the country."

"What?" asked Peggy, holding her breath.

"You're a nice girl. I wouldn't—"

"They cut off their balls. Is that what they do?"

He stopped for a light. "Not very nice language for a young lady to use."

Peggy gestured at the Columbiana Towers, several blocks away. "Just trying to cut to the chase. I'm not going to invite you up, even if you did buy my lunch."

"Oh, I'm not good enough for you, except to play off against your fiancé?"

Now Peggy smiled. "If I invited you up, you might not think I was a lady."

The light changed, but Lister didn't notice, until the car behind him tooted. He glanced in the mirror, an angry scowl appearing on his face. He took a breath and let it out before continuing down the street.

"You're not in prison anymore, Ray. You can't go around kicking everyone's butt."

"Trying . . . trying to rehabilitate me?"

"I can help, if you want me to."

Lister seemed to consider her proposition. "I'd like that. If your mother doesn't mind."

"You're always bringing up my mother. What the hell does it matter what she thinks? I'm my own person, or do you have the same problem as Wesley?"

"Peggy, I wish you wouldn't use that kind of language. It may not bother you, but I don't like hearing my friends talk that way."

"I'll tell you what, Ray, I'll rehabilitate you and you rehabilitate my language. You didn't tell me what happened to the woman."

"Oh, when we got to court she told the judge I'd raped her and they took her word over mine."

"But there must've been some kind of test—to see if the woman had intercourse."

"You know, Peggy, I'm not sure I'm comfortable talking to you about this."

"Well, it's where we start," said the girl as she waved at the guard in the kiosk. "And while I'm at it, I'm going to change your attitude toward women."

Lister shook his head as he drove into the garage. "I don't think so. I don't think much of women and one of them in particular."

When Jean collapsed into a chair, it was left to Ruth to dig out the story from an angry and frustrated Wesley Calhoun. After Ruth talked with the boy, she talked with his mother, and planted seeds of doubt as to what her son might've done to irritate Peggy so. Otherwise why would a girl as intelligent as her granddaughter accept a ride with a total stranger, as Wesley's mother had called Raymond Lister.

Ruth put down the phone. "You'd think her son was God's gift to women. Sometimes I wonder how she can give him up. Now, Jean, why would Peggy get in the car with Raymond Lister?"

Her daughter-in-law held her head in her hands. "I have no idea, unless Lister told Peggy he's her father."

Ruth considered this as she picked up a pencil. "If he's toying with you, why tell Peggy anything?"

Jean sat up. "He's kidnapped her!" She reached for the phone. "I have to call the police."

Ruth tapped her daughter-in-law's hand with the pencil. "But from what you"—she gestured at the phone with the pencil—"and Wesley have told me, I think Lister has other plans."

"A ransom?"

"If so, we can only wait for his call."

"But Peggy could be with him, on some back road, where he's—"

"Doing the same to her as he did to her mother?"

Jean nodded, unable to speak.

"I don't think so. We have to assume he knows Peggy's his daughter. You said Lister's sister had the same gray hair when you ran into her in Coventry, just a few months after her brother was convicted?"

Jean nodded, remembering her return to Coventry when Lister's attorney had asked for a mistrial because of some inconsistency in her testimony. Jean hadn't recognized Gladys, the change having been that dramatic—until the young woman was in her face, screaming about what Jean had done to her brother. Jean retreated to Columbia, thinking the girl's hair had grayed because of what had happened to her brother. Then, Peggy's hair had grayed before her graduation from high school, just like Gladys Lister's.

Jean bit her lip. "By just sitting here, we become the ones toying with Peggy's life."

"As Raymond Lister is toying with us."

Jean opened a drawer. "I can't handle it. Not when it's my daughter. The attack—it's all coming back . . . ." She ran her hands around the drawer, finally opening a narrow one alongside the middle drawer. "Don't you have any cigarettes?"

"Jean, you haven't smoked in years."

Her daughter-in-law continued scrounging inside the drawers. "I thought maybe for guests."

Before she could find a cigarette, the phone rang again. Jean snatched it up. "Yes?"

"Mother?"

"Peggy? Peggy darling, is that you?"

"Yes, I wanted to tell you—"

"Where are you?"

"Where am I? I'm at home. I wanted you to know—"

"Who's with you?"

"No one's with me. That's why I called. I left Wesley at Lake Murray—"

"Yes—he's already called. Wesley said you left with Raymond Lister. Are you all right?"

"Ray gave me a ride home, that's all."

"Ray?"

"He's an okay guy. Just a little out-of-date."

"Did he do anything . . . to you?"

"He bought me a chili dog and lemonade. I was perfectly safe, Mother. I wouldn't've gotten into the car if I didn't think he was going to act like a perfect gentleman."

"A gentleman?"

"Yes, and guess what? Ray and I like chili dogs and lemonade—things you hate. Ray ordered them without—"

"Peggy, stay right where you are and lock the door."

"I've already locked it. You always tell me to lock it. For God's sake, Mother, I'm not some kid. Besides, there's no one up here but the workmen."

"Is Avery there?"

"I don't know. Why?"

"Then keep the door locked. I'll be right home."

"I don't understand why you're so upset. Is that what this is all about? Wesley called and scared the hell out of you? Just wait until I—"

"No, it wasn't Wesley. Do you know you got in the car with an ex-convict?"

"Yes, Mother," said Peggy, a tolerant tone appearing in her voice. "He was in prison for rape."

Jean gasped. "He told you that?"

"Did you know the girl accusing him was from your hometown? Did you know her?"

Jean looked around for help. But her mother-in-law was no longer in the room—because when Ruth hadn't been able to understand this one-way phone call, she had gone down the hall and picked up an extension. And she had to chase Hattie off that extension. Hattie knew when something was going on around this house.

"Accused him of rape?" asked Jean. "What do you mean 'accused him of rape'?"

"The girl made it all up and she was nothing more than a common whore. Don't you think that's terrible?"

Jean didn't know what to say, but she damn well knew by now her mother-in-law was listening on the extension, possibly even Hattie. "We'll have to see about that."

"Is it true you knew him in Florida?"

"You stay where you are. I'll be right there."

"I've got to get cleaned up. Wesley and I are going out, and boy, am I going to straighten him out about a few things."

After Peggy hung up, Jean sat there, never hearing Ruth hang up in the hall or Hattie in the kitchen. The phone was still in her hand when Ruth returned to the study, closing the door behind her.

Because of the vacant look on her daughter-in-law's

face, Ruth took the phone from her hand and cradled it.

"You all right, my dear?"

Jean's eyes focused on her. "I guess you heard. Now I'm a whore and a liar."

"Nonsense, dear, Peggy doesn't know the whole story."

"And Lister's counting on me telling her. That's why he's here."

"You don't know. Lister might want to do the telling himself."

Jean shook her head. "I think Lister wants me to defend myself. After he's poisoned her mind."

"You've been her mother a lot longer than Raymond Lister's been her father. Who do you think she'll believe? Why Peggy doesn't even know he's her father."

"Until Lister shows her a picture of his sister in Florida."

"Jean, you can't imagine Peggy is going to believe anything that man has to say."

"I think Lister is planting enough doubt in Peggy's mind that she'll question anything I say. Ruth, you can't tell me that when you heard Peggy say the woman accusing Lister of raping her was nothing more than a common whore, a flicker of doubt didn't cross your mind? For a moment, you doubted the verdict by the jury."

"Jean, I have never—"

Her daughter-in-law got to her feet. "You could've asked Harry Hartner for a copy of the transcript, but you never did. Why, Ruth? Were you afraid of what you might learn?"

"It wasn't any of my business."

Jean didn't appear to hear her. She was gazing toward the door of the Florida room. "Maybe it's time I started listening to things I haven't wanted to hear." She picked up the phone and dialed a number.

"Who are you calling, dear?"

"Harry Hartner. I'm siccing Melvin Ott on Raymond Lister."

"Jean, it's one thing to go to the police, but do you really think you should be telling family secrets? Melvin Ott is a colored man."

"Melvin's the one who tracked down Elizabeth Hartner's husband and brought him back to stand trial. Hello, this is Jean Fox. May I speak to Harry? He is? Would you have him call me? Try my car phone. Do you have that number? Good. Tell Harry I'm on my way home. If he misses me in the car, try there."

Jean said good-bye and put down the phone. "I'm going to find a way to protect my baby from that monster. He's not going to destroy her life like he destroyed mine." A thought crossed Jean's mind. She pulled a card from her purse and dialed again. After someone answered, she said, "Lieutenant Stafford, please."

Ruth's hand came to her throat. "You don't have to call the police, my dear. Peggy is safe. There's no reason to drag this out for all to see."

But Jean was talking into the phone. "Lieutenant Stafford, this is Jean Fox . . . . I'm sure you didn't think you'd hear from me . . . . No. I don't have anything to tell you. I have something to ask. Would you like to come over for dinner tomorrow night? . . . That'll be fine, and Lieutenant, when you come to the Columbiana, pull into the garage. The front is always locked after dark. I'll tell the guard to be expecting you."

Jean put down the phone and smiled for the first time since entering the house. "Dan Stafford doesn't know it, but he's my new boyfriend. That should be enough to make Lister think twice before pulling another stunt like the one he pulled this afternoon."

fifteen

A thunderstorm blew into downtown about the same time as Jean returned to the Columbiana. The guard, a young black man, hardly acknowledged her as she drove through the gate, and this, through a distorted windshield. Jean muttered to herself as she parked her car alongside a truck from Ethan Allen Galleries. Before getting out, she glanced at the kiosk. The guard hadn't moved. He was still reading his magazine. And the gate still up, as it had been when she'd driven in.

She got out of the car, locked the doors, and walked over to the elevator and punched the button. There, she turned around and watched the rain fall beyond the kiosk. The guard still hadn't moved. And she'd told Dan Stafford he might have to show some ID to get in here. What a laugh.

The elevator took its own sweet time coming down. She punched the button again. Why couldn't the thing be programmed to return to the garage, not the first floor, which wouldn't be open until fifty percent occupancy was achieved—something Jean considered a gimmick to keep the current residents promoting the virtues of life at the Columbiana.

Finally, the doors opened, and the men from Ethan Allen wheeled a dolly off. They nodded to her before Jean stepped on the elevator. A minute later, on the eleventh floor, the doors opened to the whine of an electric screwdriver. Peggy had said Avery wasn't here. The girl simply wasn't alert to the dangers, or resident saviors, around her. She would put an end to her daughter's naiveté this very evening.

Jean knocked on the door of the unit McFarland was working in. During their conversation after the Kelly incident, Avery told her what he hated most was not being able to hear people coming up from behind. Some fool would walk in while you were working and scare the bejesus out of you.

McFarland stood on a short ladder, working with an electric screwdriver inside one of the cabinets. "Oh, hello, Dr. Fox. Short day at the office?"

"No, actually . . . ." Jean thumped her head. "Thanks for reminding me. My boss and I were scheduled to have a chat. Sorry, I have to run."

He smiled. "Then I'm sorry I mentioned it."

"I did want to tell you I'm having that policeman, Dan Stafford, over for dinner tomorrow night."

McFarland stepped down from his ladder. "What for?"

Yes, Jean, why are you doing this? It made perfectly good sense at your mother-in-law's, but to Avery, how can you justify it? Are you going to tell him about Raymond Lister? You do that and it's the same as siccing Avery on Lister; not to mention, another battle royal in the Columbiana that would only draw attention to what you're doing.

"Stafford asked me out to lunch. I turned him down several times before I realized what he was up to."

"And what's that?" asked McFarland, leaning against the door, cordless drill across his chest, sawdust sprinkled through his graying beard.

"It's evident he thinks we're covering up something, so I'm going to throw him off the trail."

"By inviting him over for dinner? Dr. Fox, I don't think you should fool around with that guy. He didn't look like no dummy and I don't want to go to prison."

Jean was leaving the unit. "Don't worry. I can handle him."

He followed her into the hallway. "I hope so. By the way, I'm finishing up here tonight. I'll be on fourteen if you need me. I brought along my cell phone and left the number with Peggy."

"Thanks, Avery. You're a good friend. And keep your eyes open for strangers."

"I thought that's what they had that guard downstairs for."

"That guard may not be enough for the stranger I have in mind."

McFarland was at work again when the elevator doors opened and Raymond Lister stepped off. Lister walked down to the Fox condo, checked the door, then walked back past the condo McFarland was working in. Avery didn't see Lister go by the first time, but when he returned, Avery thought he saw something in the hall.

He walked out of the condo, hammer in hand. "Need something?" McFarland followed the stranger past the elevator, toward a plywood door.

"Checking out the place. Might buy a unit." The stranger continued into the unfinished part of the floor where another four condominiums were planned.

McFarland followed him through the plywood door as the stranger crossed the open space to stand at the edge of the building. He stared through the plastic sheeting as workmen sat around, smoking cigarettes and waiting for the rain to stop so they could finish seating glass into walls with the assistance of a crane and cherry picker. Wind rattled the sheeting as rain blew in from the west. Stacks of insulation, plywood, and sheetrock stood in the middle of the floor along with support beams, pipes, and wiring.

This floor couldn't be finished soon enough for McFarland. The sooner the units were finished, the sooner tenants would occupy them, and unlike up north, these tenants would likely get to know each other and look out for each other. McFarland joined the stranger at the edge of the open floor, just out of reach of the plastic billowing in their faces. There was nothing below them but the hill, falling away from the building, no setback, no porch, only the concrete sidewalk eleven floors straight down. Rain hit the sheeting like machine-gun fire.

Raising his voice, McFarland said, "Everybody I've seen up here had a real estate agent with them."

Now the stranger faced him and Avery could see this guy was a hard case. Not that he intimidated Avery, but he sure as hell wasn't any real estate prospect. The residents of the Columbiana were a congenial bunch, almost as if the gift of gab was a condition of ownership, as much as the humongous down payment.

"What's it to you?" asked the stranger.

"We're kinda touchy about who comes up here."

"Who's *we*?"

Gesturing toward the finished part of the building with his hammer, Avery said, "The tenants."

The stranger looked toward the river again. "You must be the guy saved Ernie Kelly's life."

Avery nodded, and if the guy wanted to see the nod, he'd have to face him again. He could be cool, too.

The stranger continued to stare across the river. "Kelly fell onto a table hard enough to smash it, then got up and ran into a wall—that the story?"

Avery regarded the man. Short-sleeved work shirt and matching pants with boots. And a gray flattop. It'd been a long time since Avery had seen anyone with a flattop or such huge forearms. Was it possible the cops had planted someone inside the Columbiana? And just as quickly, he dismissed the notion. No need. Fox was having that damn cop over for dinner, and this guy was no cop, undercover or otherwise.

"That's what the police say."

"Well, it's what the cops think that's important, isn't it, sport?"

Avery met him eye to eye, hammer thumping into his open palm. "And it's what I think when it comes to the Foxes, sport."

The stranger glanced at the hammer. "You the Foxes' protector?"

"You might say that."

A smile crossed the stranger's face. "Well, it gets better and better."

"Where you from?" asked Avery.

"Who says I'm not from around here?"

"You don't have the look."

"And what look do I have?"

"Not of a man buying real estate."

The stranger crossed in front of McFarland. "They needed out-of-town money to finish this place. Maybe that's what I am, out-of-town talent."

"I agree with the out-of-town part."

The stranger chuckled as he left the open space. Avery trailed him down the hall toward the elevator. When the doors opened, the construction supervisor stepped out.

The supervisor nodded to Lister. "See you found him."

"That I did," the stranger replied, before stepping on the elevator.

The supervisor met Avery as he came down the hall. "I thought you worked alone, just brought in day laborers to do the heavy lifting."

"I do."

"Then I take it you're not going to hire that guy?"

"Why would I?"

"He said he was here to talk to you about a job:

installing cabinets."

McFarland looked at the elevator. "He said that? He knew I was a cabinetmaker?"

"Sure. Why you think I sent him up?"

"Well, I'm sure as hell not going to hire him. And you don't have to send anyone up, especially that guy."

Peggy was drying her hair with a towel as she came out of the bathroom. "Your messages are by the phone." She wore panties and no bra, which revealed not only her tan but—when Peggy turned to go back into the bathroom—also the places she shouldn't have gotten any sun.

"Peggy, I want to talk to you." Skinny-dipping, with Raymond Lister lurking around! It was nuts! Crazier still, catching a ride home with him.

"In a moment."

"This is more important than your hair."

Peggy returned to the living room, leaned over, and shook out her hair. "Okay, but one of those messages is from Vernon Pinckney."

"Let me make this one call, then you and I need to talk."

"Always business before family," said Peggy, returning to the bathroom.

"And we'll talk about your attitude, too."

"Chill out, Mother. I won't be here much longer."

Jean followed her down the hall. "Marriage won't cure that attitude."

"That's not my only option," said Peggy, slamming the bathroom door.

"Peggy!"

But the hair dryer was going full blast. So was the music. Jean sighed and returned to the phone, where she called her office and found her secretary frantic.

"I've been trying to reach you all afternoon. Vernon Pinckney's here for your appointment."

Jean pulled a pack of cigarettes from her purse. "What can I tell you? Weddings make me frantic, especially when it's the only wedding I'll ever put on."

"Pinckney wants to talk to you, wedding or not."

Jean used a nail to slice open the cellophane on the pack. "Then put him on."

When she did, Pinckney demanded, "Where the hell are you? We had an appointment."

Jean tapped out a cigarette. "I forgot about our meeting and I apologize for any inconvenience I might've caused."

"You . . . forgot?"

"Yes. It appears I'm human after all." Jean lit the cigarette, sucked down the smoke, and let it burn through her lungs and clear her head. "Something on your mind, Vernon? You don't usually blow up at people."

"You weren't here. You weren't in the studio. They had to put a tape on because you left early. I didn't know what was going on."

"Vernon, you don't have anything to worry about but my going crazy before June seventeenth."

"Tomorrow then?"

Jean glanced in the direction of the hallway leading to the bedrooms. The music had stopped. The hair dryer was still going. Maybe there was hope yet. She snubbed out her cigarette. "Tomorrow it is."

Her mother was sitting on the sofa when Peggy came out of the bathroom. Peggy wore her hair in soft, loose curls and had on a green dressing gown. When her hair had grayed, her mother warned her that, if Peggy chose not to color it, the hair could be worn as any other young woman's, but only if the gray was never highlighted or frosted.

The windows her mother was staring through had fogged up from the rain, something people never consider when they purchase a house with glass walls. From the kitchen came the smell of dinner. Peggy didn't know how her mother did it. Time to work, time to keep house, time to fight with her daughter.

When her mother continued staring across the river and holding her drink casually in her hand, Peggy asked, "Is there a problem at work?"

"No problem."

"Mother, what are you not telling me?"

"Nothing."

"You're treating me like a child, not telling me what's going on in your life."

Now her mother looked at her. "Oh, and that was very adult, slamming the door in my face so you could go sulk in the bathroom?"

"I wasn't sulking."

"Blowing your brains out with that dryer and damaging your hearing with that music. I hope marriage will give us the necessary space so we can become friends."

"We *are* friends."

"Not when we can't talk. Friends always talk things out. It's families that let things fester."

"Mother, what's bothering you?"

"This afternoon you got into a car with Raymond Lister."

"Wesley made me mad, that's all."

"Lister's an ex-con."

"Yes, but are we going to hold that against him for the rest of his life? As women, why can't we be the first to forgive?"

Jean only stared at her. Sometimes the girl sounded so grown up, then ten minutes later, acted like such a child. "Peggy, did you ever wonder why Raymond Lister would tell you all this?"

"He said he didn't want me to feel uncomfortable around him. We stopped for chili dogs and lemonade. He likes the same stuff I do."

"What did he tell you about the rape?"

Peggy took a seat on the sofa and repeated what Ray had told her about the little whore he'd picked up, who, when they stopped for gas, claimed she'd been raped.

"And you believed him?"

"Why shouldn't I?"

"Gee, Peggy, I don't know. Maybe for the same reason I told you never to believe what boys told you in the back seat of their cars."

Her daughter sat up. "What reason would Ray have

to lie to me? And Vernon Pinckney? What's going on there? He never calls our house. You're not having an affair, are you?"

"Peggy! Why would you think such a thing?"

"I have to explain what I do with my life, why not you? You're the one wanting us to be friends."

"When was the last time I stuck my nose into your business?"

"You did it when I came in today."

"You got in the car with a perfect stranger. As your mother, or friend, I have every right to be concerned."

"He said he knew you."

"And you believed him?"

"Mother, are you telling me you don't know Ray?"

"Do you remember Ernie Kelly?"

Peggy glanced at the new coffee table. "Yes."

"I didn't know him either."

"Then what was he doing here?"

"Trying to make himself important. To me."

"But he hurt himself."

"I thought he was an obsessive fan, but he's sick. Ernie's in the hospital and getting the help he needs."

"Nobody's helping Ray."

Jean let out a long sigh. "This is why I really don't think you're old enough to get married."

"I waited until I was twenty-one, as you and Nana wished."

"It doesn't appear to be long enough. No wonder you make Mrs. Calhoun nervous."

"That woman is impossible."

"If I were Wesley's mother, I'd be advising him to call

the whole thing off."

"Mrs. Calhoun doesn't need any help . . . You'd really say that, if you were Wesley's mother?"

"Who'd want their son, and remember here, Wesley's an excellent catch—you've said so yourself—marrying a girl who'll jump into cars with strangers over the least little thing."

"It wasn't the least little thing! Wesley embarrassed me to death."

"Uh-huh." Jean stood up and headed for the kitchen, taking her drink with her. "How's that?"

Peggy followed. "I don't know if I'm hungry or not."

Jean picked up a pot holder, opened the oven, and pulled out a tray with aluminum foil covering it. "It's not for you."

"You're having someone over?" Peggy pulled her robe tight. She glanced at the door. "When?"

"I'm taking this down the hall to Avery."

"He's a carpenter. You can do better."

Jean put down the tray. "Like Wesley's mother is counseling her son right about now?"

Peggy turned her back on her. "Oh, Mother, I don't know how to talk to you anymore."

"Well, if I ever hear of you doing anything as foolish as you did this afternoon, we're going to have one of these heart-to-hearts again."

Peggy faced her. "Are you forbidding me to see Ray?"

Jean opened the refrigerator and took out some brown and serve rolls. "Until the transcript arrives. It'll be here tomorrow. Harry's sending it over."

"What transcript?"

"From Raymond Lister's trial."

"Mother, why are you doing this?"

"Because I don't want you to start out as I did."

"The way you did? What do you mean?"

"What I mean to say is . . . ." Jean looked around for a place to put down the rolls. She didn't seem to see the counter or stovetop.

"Are you ready to put those in the oven?"

Jean looked at the rolls, surprised to find them in her hands.

Peggy dug a tray out of one of the cabinets. "Mother, are you all right? You don't look good."

Jean stood, slightly hunched, arms slack at her side. Peggy put her arm around her and walked her into the living room. The two of them ended up on the sofa again, facing each other, holding hands.

"What's bothering you, Mother?"

Wiping tears away, Jean stared at the foggy glass overlooking the river. "It's not your fault. It's mine."

"I don't understand."

"Peggy, I need to tell you something. I have a confession to make and only my pride keeps me from telling you." She wiped more tears away, dabbing at them with a napkin brought along from the kitchen. "When I arrived on Nana's doorstep . . . ."

"Yes?" asked Peggy, holding her breath.

"Nana didn't believe I was married to your father until I showed her the marriage certificate. Only days later did I learn I was pregnant. Thank God I was pregnant with you."

"Nana didn't believe you and Daddy were married?"

"Why should she? Your father was ashamed to tell his mother that he had married a girl from the country. Then, later on, when I wanted to go to work, your grandmother said, 'Fox ladies don't work.' At least the ones in her house weren't going to. We had a terrible row. I lost that battle, but she did allow me to finish my schooling."

"Why are you telling me this?"

Jean squeezed her daughter's hands. "Don't you see? I wanted to control your life, as Nana tried to control mine. I flew into a rage because you got in the car with a perfect stranger. Something I couldn't control. Lister was the type of person I didn't want you to meet. Ever."

"I think you're paranoid. Next thing you'll say is Ray planned on catching Wesley and me . . . ."

Jean pulled her hands away. "Catch you and Wesley doing what? What were you doing up there—skinny-dipping?"

Her daughter flushed and looked at the floor.

"In the middle of the day! What were you thinking?"

She looked up. "Now you're sounding like my mother again. What's the problem? No one was there."

"Except Raymond Lister, a convicted rapist."

"I wish you wouldn't keep harping on that. You're beginning to sound like a broken record. Anyway, I did it on a dare from Wesley."

"Oh, yes, blame it on Wesley because you decided to participate. When did Lister show up?"

"He—he came by . . . . We, er—we couldn't get out of the water until Ray left."

"Wesley could've."

Peggy said nothing.

"But he didn't. And Lister looked like a real man to you, someone who would protect a silly little girl. Is that the attraction?"

"Really, there's no attraction, and I'm not a silly little girl."

"When Wesley comes over tonight, you should apologize."

"I don't need you telling me how to handle my love life."

"You're telling me not to see Avery McFarland."

"Now you're being hypocritical. You won't accept Ray, but you don't mind me marrying into one of the richest families in Columbia."

"I don't see anything hypocritical about marrying a snob, if you know what you're getting into."

Peggy sat up. "Are you calling Wesley a snob?"

"More than that. There's no hope for change. He'll contaminate whomever he marries."

"I can't believe you're saying these things. How come you never mentioned this before?"

"Because you never got into the car with a convicted rapist before."

"I don't understand. First, it's Raymond Lister, then, it's Wesley. Now it's Raymond Lister again."

"Peggy, it's a complicated world out there, and if you're lucky, you'll find someone, usually older, to help you sort things out. This is one of those times, and I'm telling you to stay away from Ray Lister."

"And don't marry Wesley Calhoun."

"Oh, yes, marry him. Just know what you're getting into."

"I—I don't understand . . . ."

"Dealing with Raymond Lister was dangerous. The transcript will confirm that. Skinny-dipping in Lake Murray could only turn out to be embarrassing, not at all like what Lister did. You're treating the two incidents as equals. Do you really think Wesley would ever force himself on you?"

Peggy glanced at the wrist where Wesley had grabbed her. To tell the truth, she wasn't sure. The red marks still showed. "I guess not."

Her mother took her daughter's hands. "Peggy, has Wesley ever forced himself on you?"

"No, but—"

"But what?"

"Wesley grabbed my wrist this afternoon and wouldn't let go."

"That's all? Really, I'm not talking about—when did he do this?"

"When I was trying to leave with Ray."

"I would've been disappointed in him if he hadn't. Do you honestly think Wesley would force himself on you?"

"No."

"Do you love him?"

"Yes."

"Then marry him." She pushed Peggy's hands away. "The hell with what anyone thinks. But remember, I don't plan to change for the Calhouns."

"You don't sound like you're sold on the marriage."

"Does Wesley love you?"

"Yes."

"Does he look at other women?"

"No." Peggy remembered how Wesley looked at her, how he liked putting his hands on her. "Never."

"Does Wesley drink? To excess?"

"I don't think Wesley likes to drink. It makes him sleepy."

"Does he do drugs?"

"Mother, why are you asking me these questions? You know very well Wesley doesn't do drugs."

"Young lady, does your fiancé do drugs?"

"No, but I don't see—"

"And where did he graduate in his law class?"

Now Peggy was no longer puzzled. "Top ten percent," she said proudly.

"And he took a job at what law firm?"

"The best in the city. You're right. I think I'll keep him."

"I would too. I had one, but he got away. And I wouldn't give a thought to what people think. Down deep inside, we all wish we had a Wesley Calhoun, in spite of their mothers." Jean got up and headed for the kitchen. "By the way, I'm expecting company tomorrow night. If I'm late, you'll be here, won't you? To get dinner started? I'll leave instructions."

"Yes." Peggy trailed her mother into the kitchen. "Who is it?"

"Dan Stafford."

"The policeman?"

Jean looked up from the oven and smiled. "Don't worry, dear. It's not what it appears."

❖   ❖   ❖

Harry Hartner's car picked up Melvin Ott at his home on the south side of Columbia. Ott lived in a duplex in an all-black neighborhood. Porch lights illuminated children playing in the dirt that made up their front yard. On the adjoining porch, a mother in a rocking chair nursed a baby. As Hartner's limo pulled up, the children stopped their playing and hurried over to the chicken wire fence to stare.

Ott must've been watching because as soon as the limo stopped, the elderly black man came out the door and hurried down the steps. Ott wore his usual brown suit with an orange shirt and tan tie. In his hand was a suitcase. At the gate he stopped, rubbed the children's heads, then continued out to the limo. Seeing his boss had a passenger with him, Ott took the jump seat, his back to the chauffeur. On top of the suitcase, he placed his brown fedora.

Hartner peered through the darkened window. "Why don't you move out of here? Lord knows you can afford to."

The black man glanced out the window as the limo moved down the street: cars up on blocks, no curbs or sidewalks to speak of, and boys loitering on every corner. There were few lights. The kids knocked them out for entertainment, and that told the city fathers it would be a waste of time to replace them.

"This here's my home. I grew up here. My grandchildren live here. Some next door."

"Well, I've often wondered why I don't have any trouble coming down here."

"Aw, Mister Harry, you always arrive in this big ole car so people naturally think you some kind of celebrity. Stay much longer and you'll get covered up with autograph seekers."

Which wasn't at all true but sounded good. The last time one of the locals had spray-painted his boss's car, Ott had searched out the teenager and whipped him with his belt—after taking away the boy's pistol and his knife. That caused several of the homeboys to come after Ott. Melvin killed one and wounded several others. Melvin Ott carried a snub-nosed .38 in the hollow of his back, a switchblade strapped to one of his knee-length socks, and an attitude far worse than these kids understood. Ott had lived here before the neighborhood had gone downhill.

After that, the gangs pretty much let Ott alone. There was one boy, however, sent south to get away from the problems of the inner city. That kid threatened one of Ott's grandchildren, and before the old man could find him, several of the locals brought the kid over, nose bloodied, clothes torn, to apologize. Ott told the kid to apologize to his grandchild. What he wanted was respect, and from Harry Hartner he got it.

His boss gestured at the passenger in the corner of the limo. "You know Dr. Fox, of course."

"Shore do. Nice to see you again. Hear your gal's getting married."

Jean smiled. "And I hope you'll come to the wedding."

"My Liza's looking forward to it. Got the invitation last week."

"Someone ought to enjoy it. It's driving me crazy."

Harry cleared his throat. "If we could get down to business . . . ."

"Why you picking me up, Mr. Harry? I coulda come down to the office. It's no trouble."

"Dr. Fox thought someone might be following her. She wants to hire you, for all the wrong reasons. Have you read the transcript?"

Ott glanced at the woman staring out the tinted window. "There were a few words I had to look up in the dictionary, but I finished it."

"Then you're on your way to Tampa. Rent a car and drive to Alamo. We want to know anything you can learn about this Raymond Lister."

"He the one causing Dr. Fox all this trouble?"

"I prefer to use the word 'client.'" Hartner glanced at the driver. The glass partition was up, and the driver was probably more concerned with getting out of this part of town than anything they had to say. "I think if our client has been this diligent in burying her past, it's our duty to respect her confidence."

Now both men tried not to look at the woman.

"So, I'm going to Tampa to find some way to bury Raymond Lister."

"A man who spends twenty years in prison may not have much of a past, but he will leave some kind of trail. Somewhere along that trail our client would like to think are the means to send Raymond Lister back to prison. Such as, where did Lister come by his operating capital? From Florida? And if so, doing what? Or is it generated here? We have no idea where Lister's staying, but wherever he is, it takes money to live. And if Mr. Lister has a job, we want to know about it. I'll take it from there."

"Dr. Fox, why don't you let me take care of him?"

Jean had been staring out the window. Now she turned to the elderly black man. "Because I'm a coward."

"Jean, I don't think you have to apologize—"

"Harry, please, I've seen you go downhill, not since the death of Elizabeth, like everyone thinks, but because you think Raymond Lister's going to do the same to me. I thought otherwise. I was wrong. But I don't want this done in Columbia. I'm not bringing my problems here."

"That's not cowardly, just plain common sense: to protect your family."

"He could've had money," Ott said. "I had some myself when I got out."

"Melvin, if you want to keep up this Uncle Tom image, you'd better have your broker stop calling the office. No—I'm not begrudging a man making money while he's in prison, but I am begrudging him the right to come into my town and upset one of my clients. Personally, I don't think Lister was smart enough to put away any money while in prison."

"Any way we do it, I can't see how word won't get around about Doctor—I mean, our client. All it takes is Lister opening his mouth."

"Not if what you come up with is so important that Lister will leave town and never return."

"There may not be anything."

"I'm willing to chance that," contributed Jean. "What I'm not willing to sanction is your killing him."

"And that, my dear, is your second mistake."

Jean gestured helplessly. "Harry wanted me to stop Lister before he left prison. He wanted me to fight the parole."

"She thought Lister might be rehabilitated."

"Well, he deserved the chance."

Hartner harrumphed. "And you've given him a chance, at you and Peggy. And Ruth."

Jean stared out the window as the limo passed an area lined with strip malls and mom-and-pop businesses. People hurried along, shoulders hunched over as if against the wind; a man tried to hitch a ride with somebody, anybody; and boys were popping hubcaps off cars, redistributing the wealth in this part of Columbia.

"I had to give Lister another chance. And to see if I could forgive him."

"And could you?"

"Your notes never gave me the opportunity."

"Just a gentle reminder of the realities of life. Mark my words, this game you want Melvin to run on Lister will fail, or worse, misfire."

"Well, I'm certainly not going to hire Melvin to kill him, then lean over the wedding cake and ask how the job went down."

"Lister's not the kind to understand anything but force. That's why I don't think you should go to the police. I don't think there's anything the police can do, and the story of what happened in Florida would still come out."

"Not if I take care of him first," said Ott. "And I don't

have to come to the wedding, if'n it'll upset you."

"And how would I face your widow?"

"Well, Dr. Fox," said Ott with a smile. "I wasn't planning on it coming out that way."

"But you can't be sure."

"There's no guarantee, but I'm the one to be worrying about that."

Jean leaned forward. "If the trappings of civilization have ensnared me, why can't I use those same webs to frustrate Lister and drive him off?"

Harry Hartner only shook his head.

Melvin turned to his boss. "I'll need some papers."

Hartner opened his briefcase and handed Ott a manila envelope. "I think you'll find everything in here."

Melvin leafed through the envelope, taking out sheets and stuffing them in his pockets.

"Melvin, you still carry that Gold Card?"

"Yes, suh, ah do."

"Put everything on it."

"I'm picking up the tab," Jean said firmly.

"That's not necessary, my dear."

"Save your money for Elizabeth's children."

"Dr. Fox, I can have some men watch Miss Peggy. Lister won't get no chance to hurt her. I can make those calls from the airport."

"Thank you, Melvin, but Peggy is liable to simply get in the car with him."

Both men stared at her.

"It's . . . it's some kind of father-image thing." Jean uttered a sick little laugh. "Raymond Lister comes to town and hits me where it hurts—with what Peggy wants or is searching for." She took the black man's hands. "Find something, Melvin. Do this, not for me, but so my daughter never has to learn about people such as Raymond Lister."

sixteen

eggy fumbled with the phone, knocking the instrument off the nightstand and to the floor. Without opening her eyes, she felt around for it. She could hear a woman's voice. When she opened her eyes, she saw the phone under the bed and sunlight coming through the shades. Her legs ached, as did her arms. Too much water-skiing. And sun.

Into the phone, she said, "What is it, Mother?"

"Peggy, this is Nana. What took you so long to answer?"

"I was asleep." Peggy looked at the digital readout across the room. "It's not even eight."

"It's time you were up if we're going to get anything done today."

Peggy swung her legs over the bed. Ugh! Her breasts were burned from yesterday's swim. Her butt, too, from the way it stung. "Er—what were you and I going to do?"

"Shop for bridesmaids' gifts, pick out the thank-you notes, and stop by the post office for more stamps."

"Did Mother put you up to this?"

"Put me up to what?"

"Calling to check on me."

"You told me you wanted to have all those things done before the wedding, my dear."

"I'll be right back."

Her grandmother was asking what she was talking about when the girl put down the phone.

Peggy went into the living room, pulled back the curtains, and looked over the river. Below her, traffic moved along the street, and on the river, several boats moved up or downstream. No one was in the living room or the kitchen, or the bathroom, or under her mother's bed. She checked the hall closets, then made sure the front door was locked. Peggy returned to the phone and reported what she'd found.

"Now, if you and Mother don't mind, I'm going back to sleep. I had a hard day yesterday."

"And let yourself be picked up by some stranger."

"Nana, you, too?"

"We have only your best interests at heart."

"I'm a grown woman. I can take care of myself."

"Not if you continue doing such foolishness."

When Melvin Ott arrived in Coventry he headed for the courthouse where Raymond Lister had been tried and sentenced. Ott wondered if he'd have to visit Raiford and hoped that wouldn't be necessary. He'd been in prisons before and they depressed him.

He parked in front of the courthouse and walked past the granite Confederate soldier, then up the stairs. An hour later he returned to his rental, stuffing an envelope into his pocket. The rental was being ticketed.

Melvin pulled out the envelope and showed the letter to the officer. The patrolman read it, tore up the ticket, and told Ott to have a nice day. Ott thanked the policeman, got in his car, and drove down the street to the law enforcement center.

"I'm Dr. Jean Fox and welcome to the real world. Ashley, our new engineer, told me I was wrong in my advice to Shirley Ann. Shirley Ann asked how much longer she should wait for her boyfriend to marry her. If you remember, Shirley Ann was twenty-four and her boyfriend, twenty-seven. Her boyfriend, who plays minor league baseball, said that as long as he's able to play ball, that's all he wants to concentrate on. I told her if she loved the young man and wanted to wait, have at it. It was her life. Ashley disagreed. Ashley, I have since learned, is an avid baseball fan, and she said any guy who hasn't made it out of the minors by age twenty-seven wasn't much of a prospect and to move on.

"Well, Shirley, there you have it from someone who knows baseball. Kyle, why didn't you know that? What? You are not a geek . . . . Oh, you take that as a compliment. Very well. Tom, welcome to the real world."

"Dr. Fox, my wife left me."

"Why is that?"

"She said she had to find herself."

"How old are you and your wife?"

"I'm thirty-four. She's thirty-two."

"How long have you been married?"

"Seven years."

"First marriage for both?"

"Yes."

"Any children?"

"A six-year-old girl."

"Tom, I doubt that your wife didn't know who she was—she just didn't like her job."

"She didn't have a job. She stayed at home with our little girl."

"That's the job I'm talking about. You're sure there's no other guy in the picture?"

"Not that I know of."

"Is it possible?"

"I don't think so. She's staying with her folks.'"

"Then it appears this problem has deeper roots. You've got a mother who doesn't want to raise her child and parents allowing her to get away with it. How often does she see the little girl?"

"Not much."

"Will she go for counseling?"

"We did a few times, but it didn't help."

"Why's that?"

"The shrink said my wife should be given the space to find herself."

"Tom, when you were a kid, did your mother warn

you about hanging out with the wrong crowd?"

"Yes, ma'am, she did."

"But you did, didn't you, hang out with the wrong crowd?"

"Sometimes . . . ."

"Tom, it's unfortunate that this has to impact your daughter's life, but I'm here to tell you that you've never stopped hanging out with the wrong crowd."

Peggy took her grandmother's arm as they walked into the center of the mall. From narrow, slanted windows in the roof, sunlight streamed down upon them.

"Now wasn't that nice," said Peggy.

The two women were on the ground floor, having left a restaurant offering cuisine from the Low Country of South Carolina. "A bit late for lunch, if you ask me."

"Sorry, Nana, but I need my sleep. I had a rough day yesterday."

"And we agreed not to talk about it. We can, however, talk about your mother. She's worried about you."

"And for the life of me, I can't understand why."

"Our meddling won't stop, child, even after you're married. Your mother and I will still be trying to raise you. Or are you too much in love with Wesley to notice us fighting over the details of the wedding?"

"I've noticed."

"Did you receive the transcript from Harry Hartner?"

"Yes. Nana, what's your interest in this?"

"The papers, what did they say?"

Peggy sighed. "I haven't read the whole thing, but I haven't found anything to contradict what Ray told me."

"Peggy, don't be a fool. Men are sent to prison because of what they've done, not on a lark. You would do well to have more empathy for the poor victim. If you can't empathize with her, I think your mother and I raised you rather badly."

"At the risk of being rude—"

"Then don't risk it. There'll be plenty of time, when you're my age, to shock people." Her grandmother started for the glass doors at the entrance of the mall.

Peggy followed her. "Ray might be telling the truth. Innocent people are put in prison every day. There weren't any witnesses, and the girl, whose name we'll never know because it's been deleted from the transcript, might've lied about the circumstances. If we could talk to her—"

Ruth stopped at the doors. "Peggy, it's that kind of talk that makes my hair stand on end."

"That I have an open mind—is that what frightens you? Mother encourages me to think for myself."

"There are some things you aren't supposed to have an open mind about, and what happened to that young woman in Florida is one of them."

"And I think you and mother are ganging up on me."

Peggy pulled back one of the heavy glass doors for a woman pushing a stroller. They smiled at the woman and her baby, then Ruth asked, "Did you ever consider that you might be wrong?"

"And did you and Mother ever think you might be wrong about Ray?"

"Peggy, what hold does this man have over you? What has he told you?"

"What did he tell me? He told me he was innocent."

"And that was enough to clear him, in your eyes."

"I'm giving him the benefit of the doubt."

"You're doing no such thing. You're using Raymond Lister to drive a wedge between you and your mother. Well, young lady, I have to tell you, you're no different from your mother when she moved out, citing her work for an excuse."

"And look what that got her."

"What will it get you, believing in Raymond Lister?"

"Ray isn't going to do anything to hurt me."

"He already has, child. He already has."

Raymond Lister was leaning against Arthur Propes' car when the older man came out of a house in a residential neighborhood. In the state capital, the escort services offered a good number of services for politicians and their hangers-on, here for midweek sessions, only leaving for the weekend to attend to business back home, and their wives.

Once an influential lobbyist respected around the capitol, Arthur Propes' fall had been quick. Lobbyists were supposed to give gifts, not take them, especially from sixteen-year-old girls. Talk started. The wrong kind of talk. If Propes could be this indiscreet—he was seen around town with the girl—how could you trust him on whatever issue he might be touting? More to the point, if someone's name became linked with Propes and his young bimbo . . . .

That wouldn't do, no, not at all, and slowly but surely, Propes had been dropped from the more important social events. At first the lobbyist didn't mind. He was comforted by his whore. When the girl left him for a Carolina football player, Arthur learned he was addicted to young flesh and he began using the very services he'd once supplied. The feeling of breaking them in was the best feeling of all. And his new friend helped him find girls just the right age.

"Have fun, Pops?" asked Lister.

"She was all right," said Propes, a pasty-complected man with thinning gray hair. "I like them with a little more spirit."

"Me, too. Maybe that's what we have in common."

That must be it, because Raymond Lister could come up with the most uncommon girls, and Arthur, well, he was too far gone to care. The rest of Propes' family was well aware of his addiction and sent a regular allowance, even going to the extreme of purchasing a condo in the state capital. The Propeses were scared to death the prodigal son would return home. Yes, everyone agreed, it was best for Arthur to stay in Columbia, and the family made sure he had the money to remain there.

Lister gestured at the house. "They love it when you take them."

Arthur nodded. All this talk was causing him to have another erection. Even at his age he could do it more than once, and it surprised these young girls what an old man could do. As his doctor had told him, his heart would give out well before his pecker.

"What's on your mind?" he asked, hoping Lister would go away so he could return to the whorehouse. Up and down the tree-lined street were few cars except those of the customers of this house.

"I have another girl for you, and you won't have to travel far from home. You wouldn't mind if she wasn't a teenager, would you?"

"They're not as playful. A little too serious for my taste."

"This one has plenty of spirit."

"Then I think I could fit her in." Arthur couldn't help but giggle at what he'd like to fit into some young girl. My God, if he didn't return to the whorehouse he'd have to go home and relieve himself, and he didn't mean take a pee.

"Let's go to your place."

"Er—Mr. Lister, really, I'm not into—"

"Oh, can it, Pops. That's where the girl is."

Propes waved at the young black man in the kiosk as he drove into the garage, but the young black man didn't seem to notice. After parking the car, Arthur got out, but Raymond Lister stayed behind.

"You aren't coming up?"

"Later. I've got to set up the girl for you."

Arthur gave his new friend a sly smile. "I under-stand. And I do wish you the best of luck."

Raymond didn't return the smile. After Propes left, Raymond got out of the car, carrying a cooler. Once he was in the elevator, he punched the button for the four-teenth floor, and while going up, he picked the lock housing the elevator's controls. In moments, he had the panel open and was checking the controls against a diagram in an oversized paperback manual.

When the bell rang signaling the top floor, Raymond shut down the elevator, and from the cooler took a small plastic box, about the size of a pack of cigarettes. He mounted the box inside the control panel and closed the circuits with bridge clips, then reached up and opened the overhead exit. After putting his billfold in a front pocket, he stuffed more items from the cooler in the rear pockets of his jeans.

He had to stand on the cooler to boost himself into the space between the sling which holds the elevator and the top of the cab. Then he climbed over the bar and took a seat above the sling, the elevator right be-low him. From the rear pocket of his jeans, Raymond took a remote control. He punched buttons and the elevator descended to the garage level as the counter-weight rose toward him.

When the elevator stopped at the garage level, Raymond looked around in the faint light of the shaft. There was the dust which had accumulated from con-struction, cables running upward, and the roller guides on each side of the shaft. He sat astride the bar, star-ing down into the darkness of the shaft.

"Well, sport, that was the easy part."

Raymond punched the remote, but nothing hap-pened. The elevator at the bottom of the shaft didn't move. He punched the button over and over again, but still the elevator didn't leave the garage level.

Raymond sighed. He pulled an antenna from his other back pocket, activated the relay attached to the antenna, and mounted the antenna and its relay on the beam he sat on. He tried the remote again. This time the elevator moved, and it was all Raymond could do not to flinch when the cab rose to stop just beneath his feet.

He affixed a relay antenna to the overhead shaft—he would place an antenna on every floor if he had to— then smiled. "Now we're going to have some fun."

Raymond lowered himself to the top of the elevator and back through the emergency exit, then dropped to the floor. He closed the overhead exit, brushed off his workman blues, washed his hands and face with a damp cloth, and hit the remote again. With a lurch, the elevator returned to the garage, where Raymond touched another button and the doors remained closed. He nodded to himself, then touched the button again and the elevator started back up.

During the return trip, Raymond wiped off the over-head exit and control panel and stuck the oversized paperback manual back inside the cooler. When the elevator opened on the top floor, he picked up the cooler and walked down the unfinished hallway to the rhythmic sound of hammering—the unit Avery McFarland had been assigned to next—then onto where the workmen were installing fixtures in the unfinished condos on this end of the building.

Raymond stood watching the work and eyeing some PVC pipe stacked near the open side of the floor facing the river. Plastic sheeting rustled in the breeze. Another storm was on its way, but Raymond had little interest in the weather. The weather would have no bearing on what he planned to do tonight.

When the black man was admitted to Johnny Mack's office, he was not offered a seat. The sheriff leaned back in his chair, stared at the black man, and worked a toothpick around his mouth. The deputy, who had ushered the black man in, stood by the door. People in the bullpen stared through the glass.

"Never met a colored private eye before."

Melvin Ott said nothing.

"What can I do for you, boy?"

"Need some information, Sheriff. I was hoping you might be able to help me out."

Johnny Mack glanced at his deputy and the deputy grinned back. "We don't care much for private detectives around these parts, white, black, or purple. This have something to do with a runaway gal or a messy divorce situation?"

"I brought a letter. You might want to read it."

"Why didn't you say so?" Mack sat up. "Working for some white man, are you?" He stuck out a hand, taking the letter. "Who is it? Somebody I know?"

Ott gave him the letter. "Yessuh, I do believe so."

Mack took the letter, leaned back in his chair, and started reading. Before he finished, he was sitting upright and motioning the deputy out of the room.

"And close the door."

Now people in the bullpen were really staring through the glass.

"Mr. Ott, you know I've got to check this out."

"Yessuh, I imagine you do. No offense taken."

"You know how it is. We get all kinds of weirdos in here. Now, if you'll have a seat I'll be right back." Coming around his desk, the sheriff asked, "Like some coffee?"

"Yes, suh, I'd like that very much, if you don't mind showing me where the machine is."

Mack slapped Ott on the back. "Machine hell! This job's tough enough without having a decent coffee maker on the staff." He led the black man into the bullpen where a woman was typing a duty roster. "Evelyn, you take care of Mr. Ott here. He needs some coffee and maybe a roll or two. You like coffee rolls, Mr. Ott? Evelyn makes the best. Anything you want, just ask Evelyn. And I'll be right back after verifying this with the judge."

seventeen

At Gladys Dockery's, two kids played under the wrought-iron stairway, swinging on a stick tied at the end of a rope. When Johnny Mack rounded the corner, he spoke to the children, who stopped their swinging and stared at the sheriff and the man who accompanied him.

Johnny Mack and Melvin Ott climbed the switchback stairs and the sheriff knocked on the door next to the fan blowing air through the upstairs apartment. Gladys Dockery appeared at the screen, wiping her hands on her apron. She pushed back the door. From beyond the kitchen came the sounds of a game show and a man competing with the contestants.

"Now wait a minute! Wait a minute! I know the answer!" screamed Lamar from the bedroom.

Gladys smiled at Johnny Mack but was puzzled at the appearance of the elderly black man. Melvin Ott stood behind the sheriff, remembering what Mack had told him about how life had been tough on Gladys Dockery. Her father had been crushed to death just before the sawmill had closed, then her mother had turned to whoring when her only son had been sent off to prison. To top it off, Gladys' husband had been in a wheelchair for the last, oh, ten years or so. No wonder the woman had prematurely grayed.

The Fox girl was Raymond Lister's daughter!

The thought struck Ott like a thunderbolt, and he had to grip the railing to keep from toppling over the side. My, oh my, but the skeletons white folks kept in their closets. Back when he'd first gone to work for Harry Hartner, his brother had found a job for him at one of the textile mills. Ott turned down that job and took a lot of grief from his wife. Now, his brother was unemployed, his job having gone overseas, but Melvin was still snooping around in white folks' business.

"This here's a private investigator, Gladys, from up Carolina way."

The woman gripped her apron. "Raymond—he's not in any trouble, is he?"

"No, ma'am, he's not." Ott moved from behind the sheriff. He held his hat in his hands. "Now why would you ask that?"

Gladys glanced from one man to the other, finally coming to rest on Ott again. "Sometimes Ray's temper gets the best of him. Johnny Mack can tell you. He and Ray went to school together."

"You knew your brother was in South Carolina?"

Gladys shook her head.

"Ma'am, I do credit work for people, background

checks when people apply for a job, and while I'm not at liberty to tell who's doing the inquiring, I would like to ask you a few questions about your brother."

She looked at Johnny Mack.

"I can vouch for him. Judge Clements sent him over."

"Judge Clements? He's the one sent Ray to prison."

"Mr. Ott knows all about that."

"That why you're here? To ask about that case? Ray's done his time."

"No, ma'am. I'd like to ask who your brother hung out with after being released from prison."

"What's that got to do with Ray getting a job in South Carolina?"

Ott said nothing, only stared at the woman.

Gladys looked at Johnny Mack, and finding no help there, said, "Ray wasn't here long enough to hang out with anybody."

"Maybe someone your brother ran into? An old friend?"

"He might've seen someone, but if he did, he didn't tell me."

"Did your brother have a job waiting in South Carolina, is that why he moved there?"

Gladys looked at the sheriff. "I don't like these questions, Johnny. Is Ray in some kind of trouble?"

"That's what we're trying to keep from happening. The judge wants to see Ray go straight. Me, too."

"Well, you know how he is—when Ray sets his mind to something."

"To what, Mrs. Dockery?" asked Ott.

"A job . . . ." Gladys glanced at her feet. "A girl, anything." Suddenly her back straightened. "If Ray had put his mind to it, there's nothing he couldn't've done. My brother could've been a success at anything if that woman hadn't ruined his life."

"Yes, ma'am. Did your brother know someone in South Carolina? Friends? Relatives?"

"We don't know nobody up there. Maybe it was somebody he met in prison."

"Did he mention any names?"

The gray-headed woman shook her head.

"Does your brother have a car?"

"An old Ford. He took it with him. It didn't run so well. Ray had to get it fixed at Worm's. He might've talked to those fellows while he was working on his car. Heard it took a week to get the new top in."

Mack and Ott had stopped by Worm's Garage. The woman's brother had repaired his car there, and Lister also had the money for the parts. Cash.

"Ma'am, where would your brother have gotten the money to fix his car?"

Gladys glanced at the sheriff. "I had some money. It was money Ray left behind. I held it for him."

"May I ask how much money that was?"

"Close to five thousand dollars," said Gladys.

The sheriff's mouth fell open. "Five thousand dollars—is that what you're saying?"

"Ray left some things behind. I sold them for cash and held the money for him."

"You held the money at home—not in a bank?"

The woman nodded.

"Gladys, that's just plain nuts, keeping that kind of

money around the house."

The woman set her jaw. "Raymond made me promise the money would be here when he got out and it was. I had it in a shoe box." She glanced toward the bedroom and the sounds of the man competing with the contestants on the game show. "Lamar didn't know nothing about it."

"Gladys, somebody could've knocked you over the head for that money, might've even hurt the kids."

"Well, they didn't." The woman gestured at the laundry hanging between porch and tree, the fan blowing air through the apartment, and the rusty barrel where trash could be burned. "Why would anybody think I had any money in here?"

"You don't have any more around, do you?"

"Fat chance. I've got four mouths to feed, and now, no car."

Ott asked, "So when you gave him the money and car, your brother left?"

"Yes."

"And he didn't tell you where he was going?"

"No."

"And he didn't hang out with any of his old friends while he was in town, besides the mechanics at Worm's?"

Gladys appeared to be making up her mind about something. "I don't want this to get back to Ray's parole officer, but I heard he and Calvin Burdett had drinks at Kirby's."

Ott had visited Lister's parole officer and he and the sheriff had been told that Lister had made each of his assigned visits and turned in the names of places where he had looked for a job. The pickings, however, were fairly slim in Alamo.

Ott now turned to the sheriff. "Where can I find this Burdett fellow?"

"Burdett's dead. Tell you about it in the car."

Ott nodded. "Did your brother meet any women while in town?"

Gladys glanced at her feet. "Ray wasn't here long enough to meet any women."

"No one from the past?"

"All those women would be married now, raising their families, some on their second marriages. Now if you don't mind, I'd like to get back to supper. It's been nice talking to you." To the sheriff, she said, "Come by anytime, Johnny. And don't worry, I ain't keeping any money around the house. I'm hoping Ray'll send us some, though." She closed the screened door and walked through the kitchen and into the room where her husband lay in the bed.

"Wait a minute! Wait a minute! I know the answer! Just give me a second! I know that answer!"

The children on the swing watched the two men come downstairs and disappear around the building. When the kids followed them around the corner, they saw both men climb into a patrol car.

Once behind the wheel, Johnny Mack said, "Burdett was killed northwest of Miami. A drug deal gone sour."

"You think Lister was involved?"

"Out of my jurisdiction. Besides, I've lost one friend. I don't want to lose another." He brought down his hands, slapping the steering wheel. "Goddamn Yan-kees!" He saw Ott's look. "Ever since the glass factory closed down, this whole town's gone to hell, the people, too."

"And ex-cons, whichever way they turn, don't get a fair shake."

"Spoken like someone who's been there."

"Served seven years for armed robbery."

"Then how'd you come by that license? They don't give private eye licenses to ex-cons."

Ott grinned. "I guess you figured it out, Sheriff. I have friends in high places."

"I sure have, Mr. Ott, I sure have. Now, before you upset anybody else, what else can I do for you so I can send you on your way?"

"I'd like to meet any women Lister hung out with while in town. There has to be somebody for a man just out of prison." Ott smiled. "I know there was for me."

Mack shook his head. "I don't know . . . a black man going around talking to a bunch of white women. You are going to keep me busy." His face lit up. "No, you're not. There was a woman—the night Cal was killed. This woman was seen with both Burdett and Lister at Kirby's Bar and Grill. I asked around when I got inquiries from Miami."

"Who was she, Sheriff?"

"Girl by the name of Donna Diaz. A spic."

Without any hint of a smile, Ott asked, "Now you wouldn't have any trouble with me talking with a spic, would you, Sheriff?"

Jean pulled into the condo's garage and parked. She snubbed out her cigarette—the tenth of the day—and glanced in the rearview mirror. Seeing no one, she strapped her purse across her chest, stepped out of the car, locking the doors behind her, and hurried over to the elevator. It was a standing joke around the station that the weirdos came out of the woodwork near a full moon. There had been plenty of those calls today.

The elevator came down and stopped, but the doors failed to open. She thumped the button again. What was going on? Glancing behind her, she saw Arthur Propes in his car. Propes wasn't moving, he was just sitting there. Had the old guy finally suffered a heart attack? Drinking, staying out late, trying to make it with younger women—it would come as no surprise. Jean took a couple of steps toward the car before realizing the person in the car wasn't Arthur Propes but Raymond Lister!

Frantically, Jean looked around. The doors of the elevator were still closed and Raymond Lister sat in a car less than ten feet away. The stairwell was behind Lister's car, and the security guard sat in the kiosk reading a magazine. Jean ran for her car, fumbling with the remote, finally unlocked the door, and once inside, slammed the door and hit the button, thumping down all four locks. She was dialing 911 when Lister got out of the car, walked over, and tapped on her window. Once he had her attention, he backed away and stood there, hands out, away from his body.

Jean glanced at the kiosk. The guard was just sitting there, letting Lister run amuck—in her building. Was this the security she paid good money for? Jean looked at Lister. He was standing there, like he wanted to talk.

The voice on the phone asked, "Can I help you?" When Jean didn't answer, the voice asked, "Is anyone there?"

Lister walked to the elevator and punched the button. The damned doors opened. For him, the damned doors *would* open.

"Is this some little kid?" asked the 911 operator. "If so, you've got to tell me what's going on at your house. Is there a problem with your mommy or daddy?"

Lister was back at Propes' car now, one space away, leaning against it, arms folded across his chest. Jean glanced around. The guard was reading his magazine, Lister was less than ten feet away, and she was hiding inside her damn car. She was either going to cower in here or have it out with Raymond Lister.

She turned off the phone and tried to lower the window before remembering she'd need the key. After the key was in the ignition and the window halfway down, she asked, "What are you doing here, Lister?"

"What are you afraid of, Murphy?"

Jean scanned the garage and the few cars that were parked there. She lowered her voice. "If you don't remember, you assaulted me. Answer the question: What are you doing here? You don't belong here." Jean stopped, remembering what happened last time she'd told someone they didn't belong here: Ernie Kelly.

"You can't tell me what to do. I'm not in prison any more."

"That's where you're headed, if you don't get out of here. This is private property. You'd better leave before I call the cops." She picked up the phone again.

Lister came off the car. "You won't call the cops and I'll tell you why. You don't want people to know how you screwed up my life."

"I screwed up *your* life?"

"And I'm not leaving until I receive an apology."

"Then I apologize. Now get the hell out of here and don't come back."

"A public apology. Everybody has to know. Peggy, your mother-in-law, the people at work. Everybody." He grinned. "All your listeners."

Jean shook her head. "No, no, I won't do that."

"Yes, you will or I won't leave town."

She put down the phone. "Lister, I can't. I have a new life, a position with my company, a daughter about to get married."

"I had a job, a girlfriend who married another man. I had my whole life ahead of me and you ruined it."

Jean felt close to tears. Head bowed, she said, "Don't do this to me, Raymond. I said I was sorry. Now go away and leave me alone. Leave my family alone."

"After you apologize for what you did."

Her head snapped up. "What I did? You're the one who raped *me*."

"If that's true, why did you just apologize?"

"Raymond, listen to me. I can't give you what you want. It would kill Peggy."

"Twenty years in prison about killed me."

"Please . . ." Jean was crying, tears running down her cheeks. "Please don't do this to me."

"You did it yourself. When my attorney asked if you'd enjoyed having sex with me, you lied. You lied on the witness stand."

"But I didn't like it. No woman likes being raped."

"You're still lying! And I'm going to stay here until you tell Peggy what you did to me."

"I didn't do anything. You did it to yourself."

"That's not what happened and you know it!" He stepped toward her.

Jean let go of the half-lowered window and jerked back. Lister had stopped. He was taking deep breaths. His hands clenched, again and again.

"What happened was . . . ." He cleared his throat and that seemed to bring his hands under control. "What happened was you wanted to get laid, and when it didn't turn out the way you wanted, you hollered rape. Your problem was you'd never had a real man before."

"Do you seriously believe that?"

"Of course."

"You believe all I needed was a good . . . screwing?"

"Every woman does. You got yours, then whined about how it was done. Date rape, marital rape, you bitches are all the same: shaking your asses at us, then, when you get what you want, whining about how it was done. You'll never keep a man that way, not a real one."

And at that very moment, Jean realized Raymond

Lister would never leave her or her family in peace. Melvin Ott had been right. It would come down to murder. That would be the only way to rid herself of this man. But Ott was out of town—where she'd sent him!

You dummy! Can't you do anything right?

No, no! Melvin's been on the case less than twenty-four hours. He needs more time. She had to stall, had to make time for Melvin to work his magic. That policeman, Dan Stafford—he was coming over for dinner. This was no time to panic.

Jean took a breath and let it out. "I wondered who was filling Peggy's head with all that garbage."

"Our daughter."

"*My* daughter, never your daughter."

"Really, Murphy, if I can't have her, why would you think I'm going to let you have her?" Lister turned on his heel and started across the garage.

Jean jerked back and jabbed at the button to raise the window. But Lister was heading toward the kiosk. Why?

If I can't have her, why would I let you have her!

Peggy! That had to be it. What had the bastard done this time?

Jean leaped from the car and ran to the elevator and slapped the button. The doors opened and Jean stepped inside and hit the button for the eleventh floor.

The doors would not close. Whatever she did, whatever button she punched, the doors simply would not close. Jean stepped out of the elevator and hit the outside button. Across the garage, Lister leaned against the kiosk, talking to the guard.

Where did they find these people?

The elevator doors closed behind her.

Jean whirled around. But the elevator was gone, heading upstairs. She only took a moment to curse, then she was running for the stairs, pulling open the heavy door, throwing it back, and starting upstairs.

Several minutes later, gasping for breath, Jean arrived on the eleventh floor. She leaned into the railing, catching her breath and listening to the sound of her footsteps dying away on the stairwell below her.

Eleven damn floors! Several times she'd thought she'd pass out. Once she'd even seen black spots as she'd fought her way upstairs.

Jean pushed off the railing, then stumbled over to the door and grabbed the metal handle. She pulled back, shoved the door out of her way, and fumbled her way into the hall. As she hurried past the elevator, its open doors mocked her. At her condominium, she fumbled for her keys, then realized her keys were in her car downstairs. Jean hammered on the door and called Peggy's name. Abruptly, the door opened and she fell into the arms of her daughter.

"Peggy, thank God! Lock the door!"

Her daughter wore a robe and her hair was in a towel. "Mother! Are you all right?"

"Yes, yes." Jean pulled herself away, trying to catch her breath. "Just lock . . . the door."

"Mother, what's wrong?"

"Er—I took the stairs."

"But why?"

"The elevator didn't work."

"The elevator . . . didn't work?"

Jean couldn't talk. Not only was she out of breath, but her legs felt weak. Her daughter helped her into the living room and over to the sofa. Damn that Raymond Lister!

"Mother, you're too old to be taking the stairs. I don't care how much you work out."

"How was I . . . to get up here? The elevator didn't work."

"You might've used the stairs to the street level, then taken the elevator from the lobby. Wesley and I have done that when the elevator's busy."

Of course! Why hadn't she remembered the elevator in the lobby? Because the only one she'd ever used was the one from the garage. Another round to Raymond Lister.

"Have them send up my keys right away."

"Your keys?"

"They're in the car. See if Avery will do it."

Peggy stared at her for a moment, then went over to the phone and called the carpenter on his cell phone. When she returned, she said, "He said he'd go down right away. Mother, if you're so security conscious, why in the world would you leave your keys in your car?"

Jean had no answer for that. "Did you . . . did you buy the groceries I need for dinner?"

"Yes, but I don't think you're up to having guests tonight."

When her mother struggled to sit up, Peggy pushed her back down. "You stay right there, and if you want

me to stay home tonight—I had a talk with Nana today. She thinks you and I need to straighten out a few things."

❖   ❖   ❖

Ott climbed the stairs of the run-down building. Trash accumulated in the halls, paper peeled from the walls, and junkies shot up under the stairs. Melvin also heard racial slurs hurled in his direction. Evidently, the building was not meant for niggers. He kicked a syringe out of his way, then an empty wine bottle. So be it.

A door stood open on the right, and Ott knocked on it. He pulled out his pistol, then took off his fedora and hid the .38 behind the hat. From the apartment came the sounds of Oprah. Uh-huh. Seemed like some colored folks were allowed in this place after all.

A middle-aged white man dragged himself out of a worn recliner and trudged over to the door; hair in his eyes, two days' beard, maybe three. He didn't turn off the TV. Oprah was interviewing women who would do anything not to have sex with their husband.

"Yeah?" asked the white man. "What you want?"

"Looking for Donna Diaz. They said you'd know her room."

The middle-aged guy looked Ott over. "Who's looking for her?"

Melvin smiled. "Perhaps someone with the same interest as you have in Miss Diaz."

"Well, you'd better get your ass out of here. Ain't no niggers allowed in this building."

"Donna Diaz ain't no nigger." Melvin smiled again. "Matter of fact, neither am I."

The man stepped into the hallway and Melvin backed away. The white man's belly hung over his jeans. From the look of it, the guy had been working on that belly a good number of years.

"Oh, you one of them smart-ass niggers."

Melvin produced the gun from behind his hat. "Wrong again, sir."

The man gaped at the gun. He even stepped back.

"Now what room did you say Ms. Diaz was in?"

The man pointed down the hall. "Three fifty-three, and she's an ugly-looking bitch if there ever was one."

A nasty scar marched across one cheek of Diaz's face. It couldn't be over a couple of weeks old and wasn't healing properly. The woman definitely needed medical attention. Diaz hung her head as Melvin entered the apartment. He looked around. Nothing but a mattress on the floor and a crate used for a table. Melvin tried to place the crate's smell. Cantaloupes? Bananas?

The woman wore a dirt-smeared blouse and a pair of slacks with a tear down one leg. Ott put a hand under the woman's chin, raising her head. She pulled away. It was an ugly tear, which, from the look of the other cheek, had once been a lovely match.

Diaz reminded Melvin of a girl he'd met while serving with the Marines and kicking some serious ass in Santo Domingo. That woman had tried to talk Melvin into bringing her back to the States. He explained that there was only one thing worse than being a black man in America and that was being married to one.

He reached for the woman again. "I want to see it."

Diaz sneered. "Oh, one of them kinky guys, are you?"

Melvin took the chin and held it where he could examine it. Not enough light, so he walked Diaz over to the window.

The woman pulled away. "This ain't part of the deal." She smiled wolfishly. "You have to pay extra to see the scar."

"That why you think I'm here?"

"They said I'd get down to niggers sooner or later. Old niggers, too, it seems. Well, here I am. Are you ready?" Diaz laughed as she unfastened her slacks. "You might be the beginning of a big night for me. Bring any rubbers? I'm clean out."

"You don't have to do this, girl."

"Why?" Diaz pulled down her slacks where they caught on her hips, exposing a dingy pair of panties. "You gonna give me something for nothing?"

"Come into the light. I want to see that scar."

"You can see plenty from where you're standing."

"Come here!"

Diaz broke down and started sobbing but still didn't move. "Why you doing this to me? If you wanna fuck, get on with it. Then get out!"

"Girl, I don't want you."

Diaz wiped the tears away. "The scar's too much, is it?"

Melvin's answer was to open his arms, and suddenly Diaz was there, letting him wrap his arms around her. It was similar to the night when his daughter had told them she was pregnant and with no husband in sight. His daughter spent a good bit of time in his arms that night, while her mother wore out the rug, pacing back and forth, raving and ranting.

"Why're you here, old man?"

"For Raymond Lister."

Diaz pushed him away. She wiped her face, then blew her nose on a soiled piece of tissue. "Raymond sent you?"

"I don't think Raymond Lister cares one way or the other about you."

"Then where's the asshole? I'd like to know."

"Why's that?"

"I'd like to kill the bastard!"

Melvin smiled. "Killing him would be easy. How would you like to go one better?"

eighteen

*P*eggy looked through the peephole in the front door. See, Mother, I can be as security conscious as you think you are. On the other side of the door stood the detective, and you would've thought he might've dressed up, coming over for dinner. True, he wore a suit, but the gray suit looked like the one he'd put on this morning, and his hair was a mess. Her mother could do better. And what had her mother meant when she'd said, "Don't worry, Peggy. It isn't what it looks like"?

What else could it be? Her mother was taking up with a policeman; before that, a carpenter. Was she going through some kind of a midlife crisis? If so, what a time to be leaving home. Before opening the door, Peggy told herself, smile, baby, smile. No matter what you're thinking, no matter how you feel, you need the practice for when you're Mrs. Wesley Calhoun.

"Lieutenant Stafford, please come in."

"Miss Fox." The policeman produced a bottle from behind his back. "For dinner." He handed over the wine. "Will you be joining us? Though I'm not sure what the younger generation drinks these days."

"Probably the same as the older generation, just too much of it." She gestured toward the living room. "Please have a seat. Mother will be out in a moment."

"'Dan,' please."

"If so, then I must be 'Peggy.'"

The policeman didn't go into the living room but followed her into the kitchen. He sniffed, then glanced at the stove. "Ah, green olive steak. Smells good, but I think your sides are burning."

Peggy clunked down the wine bottle and snatched a pot off the stove. When she lifted the lid, she found the broccoli stuck to the bottom, and the vegetable didn't slide around when she tilted the pot from side to side.

"Oh, no! I didn't put in enough water! Why does she ask me to help? She knows I'm helpless in the kitchen."

Stafford took the pot and shook it. The broccoli slid across the bottom. "Nope. Just in time." He held the pot under the spigot and turned on the water. "Don't worry. Nobody'll notice. In the South, you have to cook the fool out of vegetables or people don't think they're done." He slid the pot back on the stove and turned down the heat. "You just had the burner up too high."

"I think you've done this before."

Stafford opened the oven and looked inside. "Unfortunately, I know what good food tastes like, so I have to cook for myself to have something edible to eat. Ah, yes, green olive steak. One of my favorites. Someone must've told your mother."

From the kitchen door, Jean said, "No, but if I'd known you could cook, I would've invited myself over to your place."

Peggy whirled around. "Mother!"

Jean wore a green embroidered crinkle dress, tan sandals, and silver earrings. She inclined her head toward Peggy. "Such a sense of propriety, and this from a girl who went skinny-dipping yesterday."

Peggy flushed and fled the room.

Stafford watched her go. "You certainly know how to clear a room, Dr. Fox."

"'Jean,' please. May I offer you a drink?"

"Anything with bourbon in it, and while you're building it, I'll finish up in here." He found an oversized plastic spoon and used it to dip the sauce on the meat. By the time Jean returned, Stafford was running a cloth around the sink. He stopped to take a sip. "Perfect. And I might hire you to tend bar."

Jean took in the spotless sink and counter area. "And I might have to marry you. Every working woman deserves a wife." She put down her drink, opened one of the drawers, and gathered up some silverware. "Take off your jacket and make yourself comfortable."

Stafford reached for the silverware. "Why don't you finish in here while I set the table."

"Ah, a sensitive male," she said, turning loose the silverware. "I'll be putty in your hands."

"More likely, I sensed the way to your heart was through your head, not your stomach."

"Then have your way with me, sir. Just be here afterwards to clean up." She opened a cabinet. "Tea?"

He gestured at the bottle on the counter. "That's mine. It'll go with green olive steak."

Jean checked the bottle. "Perfect. The table mats are in the hutch. What were you telling Peggy about cooking?" she asked through the serving window.

"When I was a kid, an old black man dragged me off the street and put me to work in his restaurant, washing dishes. Later on, I became a cook. I was practically raised in that restaurant."

"By this old black man."

"Well," said Stafford, finishing the silverware placement on the table, "when Moses pulled me off the street I was running with a gang, leather jacket and all. He saved me from that, though he'll say all he was looking for was a dishwasher."

Jean put cut glass salt and pepper shakers on the serving window, then a couple of wine glasses. "Why'd you stay with him? A life of crime must've looked more exciting—to a kid."

Stafford set out the shakers and glasses. "I was planning on going back to breaking and entering after the heat was off. By then, too many of my friends had been picked up and sent off to prison."

"So you're a thief who became a cop."

"Moses gave me a place to sleep, plenty to eat, and only made me go to church once a month."

"Only once?"

"He said the rest was up to me."

"Did you go more often or should I ask?"

"Made all kinds of excuses not to go that once. Moses

said it was a condition of employment. So there I was, the only white face in the whole choir." He returned to the kitchen. "But I sure did learn to sing."

"While this was going on, where were your parents?"

"My father disappeared. You know the story, went out for a pack of cigarettes and never came back. Mother waitressed, trying to put food and liquor on the table. Sometimes we had to go without, and you can guess which one we went without. When she remarried, there was no place for me. The food in that restaurant was damned good. Probably why I stayed. Moses never stopped me from going back for seconds."

She was staring at him. "Dan, why are you telling me all this?"

"I thought you asked."

"No. It was more than that. It was like you were answering an ad for a job. For a cook."

"Nope. I had other work in mind."

They were staring at each other when the doorbell rang. Jean broke off their stare to answer the door, but only after straightening the thick, brown paper protecting the hallway's carpet and glancing through the peephole. It was Wesley Calhoun.

"Come in, Wesley," she said, opening the door.

The young man wore a blue knit shirt, white pants, and loafers without socks. His dark hair was neatly combed and appeared to be slightly wet.

Jean headed for the bedrooms. "I'll tell Peggy you're here. This is Lieutenant Stafford of the Columbia Police Department."

Stafford extended his hand. "Nice to meet you." They

shook hands. "Drink?" asked the detective, walking into the living room.

"I don't think so. I'm driving."

"Good thinking."

Jean came out of the bedroom and found Stafford had moved her drink to the coffee table, the one re-placed by Columbiana Towers. She still wasn't satis-fied with how it fit in with the rest of the furniture, but it would have to do. She took a seat alongside Stafford.

"Did Wesley tell you what he and Peggy were doing yesterday at Lake Murray?"

"No, he didn't."

"Well, Wesley, will you tell him or shall I?"

The young man flushed. "We were skinny-dipping, though I don't think there's any law against it."

"Indecent exposure."

"You're not going to—"

"You said you didn't think there was a law. There is." Stafford grinned. "But I wasn't there. I don't know if you two looked indecent or not."

Jean slapped his arm. "Dan! That's my daughter you're talking about."

"And about to become someone's wife. Congratula-tions on your impending marriage, Wesley."

"Thank you, sir."

"'Dan,' please." Then to Jean, "I'm not here in my official capacity, am I?"

"That's up to you."

Peggy came out of her room. She wore a pure white sleeveless blouse and charcoal slacks, and carried a black purse. A platinum necklace hung around her sunburned neck and it matched large earrings and a tiny wrist.

"Boy, am I glad to see you," said her fiancé.

"Why?" She looked at those on the sofa. "Mother, have you been giving Wesley the third degree?"

"No. I let Dan do that."

"That is absolutely horrid of you. And your guest. Wesley, let's leave before I make a scene." She headed for the door.

Stafford watched Peggy go. "Nice to meet you, Wesley, and good luck."

"Nice . . . nice to meet you."

"Wesley," called Peggy from the door, "are you coming or not?"

"Yes, dear." Her fiancé trotted off after her.

Stafford smiled as the door closed behind the young people. "I don't think you have anything to worry about. Peggy's whipping him into shape nicely." He stood up. "I'll check on dinner."

Jean got to her feet and followed him into the kitchen. "When you told me about your past, did you think I might have a past as interesting as yours, one I'd like to share with you?"

From the oven, Stafford looked up. "Well, do you?"

"Just who are you, Mister?"

The deputy stood in the crossroads where the shoot-out had occurred between Raymond Lister and the drug dealers. Melvin Ott was the only other person there, and with the aid of a rather strong flashlight, the black man was examining the former service station.

"I asked you a question, Mister."

Ott wandered over to where the deputy stood beside a patrol car parked next to Ott's rental. The deputy wore a tan uniform and matching Stetson. Ott was still in his sport coat, tie, and fedora.

"I was going off my shift," said the white man. "Me and the missus were going bowling. Then the boss calls and tells me to meet you out here and fill you in."

"Sorry to ruin your evening, but I'm looking for whoever survived the shoot-out that took place here a few weeks ago."

"Well, if that's all you want, I can tell you only one got away and he drove away."

"Was he wounded?"

"Not that we could tell."

"Which way did he go?"

The deputy pointed in the direction of the rammer, the guy driving the Chevy, had pulled out of the bean field. "That-a-way."

Ott glanced down the road, then back at the deputy. "And he was the only one to get away?"

The deputy hitched up his Sam Browne belt. "That's right, the only one."

"Is that all you can tell me?"

"This guy you were asking about, Calvin Burdett, was found face down about where I'm standing."

"I'm not interested in Burdett. My only interest is in the ones that got away. The ones you didn't put in your report."

The deputy's hands came off his belt. He spread his feet. "Mister, are you calling me a liar?"

"I'm just trying to understand something—something that won't go any further than this field."

The white man looked over the rows and rows of beans. "I guess my wife will have to forget about bowling tonight."

Ott said nothing.

"Well, to tell you the truth, the boss told me to make sure you got enough information so you wouldn't come back."

Ott merely stood there, waiting for the deputy to continue.

"We wrapped up this one nice and tidy and the county came out of it with over six hundred thousand dollars. There may have been more—sure there was, but scavengers got it. You know how long it would take to wrap this up if we did it by the book?"

"What do you figure happened?"

"You sure this won't go any further?"

"Deputy, all I'm doing is trying to trace a man who I think was here that night. More than that, I'd rather not say, only because it might change what you're about to tell me."

The deputy kicked a rock. It went sailing out of the crossroads. "There was a beige Cadillac over there, and beyond it, in the corner of the field, another car, probably the rammer. The one that got away. Here"—the deputy pointed at his feet—"was the second Cadillac, a real dressy thing."

"Pimpmobile?"

"Right. Owned by a black guy out of Miami by the name of Cricket Kerns. Little guy who talked with a squeaky voice. Had two bodyguards. One was killed outright. Cricket went over the hood—you could see from the streak of blood—and fell off about here. But that wasn't where we found him."

"And where was that?"

The lawman pointed at the narrow porch of the old service station. "In there."

Ott studied the porch as the deputy pointed at the ground about twenty feet away. "Now this Burdett fellow—he was found about there. Shot from behind. Actually under the arm. Probably by the guy in the rammer."

"Did Burdett kill anyone?"

The deputy shook his head. "Carried a nine millimeter, but it hadn't been fired. Found on the ground near the body."

"Let's see if I've got this straight: Burdett was shot in the back by the man who got away, but the man I'm looking for—"

"Killed Cricket Kerns and one of his bodyguards. With a shotgun. But made it look like Kerns done it."

"So there are two missing people?"

The deputy pointed at the service station. "Yes, sir, that would be right. One hid behind that brick pillar and used a shotgun to carve up the pimpmobile. The other bodyguard, man by the name of Freddie Noyles, must've been behind it. Noyles got away, with his bag."

"How do you know?"

"'Cause there were suitcases in the car for the dead

men. They were leaving the country." The deputy gestured at the field behind him. "One of their bags was found over there. The scavengers missed that one."

"Then it wasn't a drug deal gone sour."

"No, but that's the way the sheriff said to close it. Didn't matter to me none. Sons of bitches come in here, messing around in our county. They oughta stay in Miami and shoot it out there." The deputy spit on the ground. "Word on the street is, Freddie Noyles—that's the one got away—is down in the Caymans, trying to free up some of Cricket's money. He won't be able to do it. You've got to have the right codes. I doubt Noyles has them."

"How do you know this?"

"We ran everybody through the NCIC and asked around in Miami. You know, just to cover our ass. These days Feds pop up everywhere, and I still ain't sure you ain't one of them. What we found was the mob was leaning on Cricket pretty hard. Cricket planned to get out but didn't make it. Pedro Gomez, the rammer— he's down in Brazil, but Freddie Noyles, he's got to try to pry that money out of the Caymans." The deputy eyed the black man who was taking in the scene, trying to see in his mind's eye what had happened that night. "That help?"

"Yes, sir, and I think you'll still have time to join your wife for bowling."

"Hell, Mister, I don't want to go bowling. That Betsy McGowen talks a blue streak. I was hoping you might need a little more help, government agent or not."

"Well, if you could come up with some pictures of

this Noyles fellow, that would help."

"Going down to the Caymans, are you?"

"I was thinking that might be the next stop."

"Shit," said the deputy, "Freddie Noyles must be some special kind of nigger—sorry, didn't mean that the way it came out—and you must be—"

"Some special kind of nigger," said Melvin Ott with a slight smile.

They were washing dishes together: Stafford running them under the spigot and using a brush on the stubborn spots, Jean stacking them in the dishwasher.

"Did you really tell your listeners it was a waste of money to have a computer in the house?

"I did."

"Hard to believe in this day and age."

"Music and drama classes have been cut back or eliminated to make way for computer labs." She took another plate. "Besides, all children do is play games and chat with their friends. Is it really necessary to encourage a child to become more of a couch potato?"

"There must be something you can use a computer for."

"Word processing, like on a typewriter."

He chuckled. "You really are a hard case, but my partner's wife swears by you."

"Oh, Detective Greene—who was here the night—"

"Ernie Kelly almost died." Returning to his dishes, Stafford said, "I heard you paid for Kelly's surgery."

She shrugged. "I asked my attorney if we could give Ernie some help."

"You have many people who stalk you?"

"Well, I am a rather large fish in a small pond."

"Why don't you take your show to Atlanta?"

Jean looked up from sorting silverware in the dishwasher. "It's been suggested, but I'd have to move away from Peggy and Wesley. And Ruth."

"You could always sell your show to some syndicate and demand better protection, as part of your compensation package." He handed her the ceramic dish the green olive steak had been cooked in.

"Perhaps."

"I heard that bit you did on Princess Di."

Jean almost dropped the ceramic dish. That was the day she'd left the station and rushed over to Ruth's. Her Princess Di comments had been on the tape Kyle had put on. It was one of his favorites because it generated so much mail.

". . . . saying she wasn't much of a mother."

Jean settled the dish into the rack. "A single mother's job is to raise her children, not improve her love life."

"I noticed you never remarried."

"I put my time where my mouth is."

"But I would think that a child needs two parents."

"I hear that all the time—from people trying to justify all their romances."

"But many divorced people, and their children, go on to make blended families."

"Those are not the ones who call my show."

They continued washing the dishes in silence, stacking and racking them. Once finished, Stafford asked, "Why did you invite me over tonight?"

"I was trying to make up for all the times you asked me out and I couldn't go."

"I don't believe that any more than I believe what you told me the last time I was here."

"Dan, there's no reason to be rude."

"Police business is rude and intrusive by its nature."

"So you've decided you're here officially?"

"Actually, I thought there was something you wanted to tell me."

"Sorry to disappoint you." Jean wiped her hands on a cloth. "But I've put the Ernie Kelly incident behind me. Perhaps you should leave and we'll charge it off to experience."

"What experience," he asked, taking the cloth from her, "how to lie your way out of attempted murder?"

"Attempted murder? You think I tried to kill Kelly?"

"No. Avery McFarland did. You're an accessory."

"Dan, what is your hang-up with this? Why would I want to kill Ernie Kelly?"

"I didn't say it was intentional."

"Then what are you saying?"

"That Kelly pressed his attentions on you. McFarland interceded on your behalf. It makes you an accessory for not coming forward—because excessive force was used." Dan gestured at the door of the kitchen. "Perhaps you have McFarland's cell number, you know, because there's only you and your family on this floor. Perhaps Columbiana Towers Corporation gave McFarland's number to you—because my partner learned that Jamie

Stubbs knew of the restraining order."

"I didn't have his number that night, but I have it now."

"And why is that?"

"Because my daughter . . . ." Jean stopped. Didn't want to go there.

"Well?"

"Dan, I wouldn't be surprised if Peggy was the one who instigated the skinny-dipping at Lake Murray. Her grandmother and I can't wait for her to be married. We want her to settle down, and we can't believe that Wesley Calhoun is that interested in someone so flighty."

Stafford considered this. "Okay. Then, would you care to explain why a pair of your pantyhose was found in a dumpster behind this building?"

Jean had to stop and think. "There is a central collection system for our trash, but I don't see what that has to do—"

"These hose were found in the building contractors' dumpster—one Avery McFarland would have had access to. Now if Kelly attacked you, as I think he did, and McFarland intervened, I see nothing in that but self-defense, but when your pantyhose ends up in the wrong place, it makes me want to ask questions, about all that blood on the glass wall in the next room. Avery McFarland is a brawler, and he has a particularly nasty reputation."

"So he told me. He also said you'd persecute him until you pinned something on him. I guess he was right."

"So the question becomes: why weren't the pantyhose

in your trash? Because John Greene or myself might have found them, torn and stained, and asked more questions?"

"How do you know they were mine?"

"I ran a test."

"I don't think you have that right."

"I can do anything I want—if I'm not found out and it's not used in court."

She turned away. "And I think it's time you left."

He followed her out of the kitchen. "Why? Because I've come too close to the mark?"

"I'll get your coat."

"I can get it myself."

He followed her to his jacket, which lay across the back of the sofa: Jean coming from around the front, Stafford approaching from behind. Both reached his coat at the same time, both picked up the coat at the same time, and each looked at the other.

"Evidently you can't wait to get rid of me and I can't wait to leave."

Jean let go of the jacket. "I'd say that about covers it. I'll show you to the door."

"I know the way."

She followed him down the hallway, both of them tromping across the thick, brown paper. "Thanks for bringing the wine."

He turned around. "And thanks for dinner."

"You cooked it as much as I did."

Stafford stared at her for a long moment, then his arms were around her, pulling her into him, his lips on hers. Jean fought to get free. He was trying to force himself on her . . . .

Stafford turned loose. "Sorry, but I wasn't going to leave without finding out what that was like."

Jean backed away, wiping her mouth and reaching for the phone. To call the police. But Stafford was the police. She was supposed to be safe with him.

He was staring at her. "Jean, are you all right?"

"I just didn't expect it. We were having this argument, then suddenly you were kissing me." Jean shrugged, trying to buy time, trying to understand her feelings toward this man. Maybe she shouldn't sort things out, just go with the flow. That would be a change. "How was it for you?" *Now where had that come from?*

"How was it . . . " Stafford smiled. "It was nice."

"I wish . . . I wish I could say the same, but you were in such a hurry."

It took only a second, then Stafford's coat was on the floor, his lips on hers, and this time they didn't stop until needing to come up for air. At the last moment, his tongue flickered inside her mouth, sending a tingle throughout her body, all the way to her toes. Maybe they even curled. Jean didn't know. She was having a hard time remaining on her feet. What was happening here?

He said, "That was much better."

Jean kept a hand on him, keeping Stafford close but feeling the wall between them, a wall of her own making. The same kind of wall between her and her daughter. Lister hadn't had to tell Peggy a damn thing. She couldn't have a relationship with Dan, or any other man, or her daughter, unless she told the truth. But not just yet. Not just now. She was enjoying the moment. So this was what it was like to go with the flow.

She said, "It's much better done together."

"That's not all I'd like to do," said Stafford with a grin.

Jean glanced at the floor. "No, no. I'm not ready for that." I'll never be ready for that.

"Sorry. Caught up in the moment."

She nodded quickly. But it was all right. This was how it was when two people were attracted to each other . . . felt safe in each other's arms. There was banter, a kind of playfulness between them, like in the kitchen. Even during supper. Anticipating things to come. It would even be all right if they—

"Jean, do you need to sit down? You don't look so good. I have to tell you that I'm not used to my kisses having that kind of effect on women."

"I guess I thought you were rushing things."

"I don't get much time off, and well, I was attracted to you the first time we met."

"Even when suspecting me of something I didn't do?"

"But you did."

"Then how do we work this out?"

"By your telling me the truth."

"Dan, I have told you the truth."

Stafford retrieved his coat from the paper covering the carpet and opened the door. "Good night, Jean. I won't forget the kisses, but I also won't forget the lies."

Lister waited for Stafford to leave the Columbiana before he took the elevator to the top floor. On the way up, Raymond didn't allow the elevator to stop, and, as he rose in the shaft, he donned a pair of latex gloves like those used by policemen to investigate crime scenes. In one pocket was the remote control. In another, tools for picking locks, and it took all the way to the fourteenth floor for Raymond to calm down.

Having a damn cop over for dinner! How fucking obvious! Didn't she think he knew what she was up to?

He'd been in the kiosk when the cop had rolled into the garage and flashed his badge. Raymond thought he was a goner, and the guard part of the setup. But the guard had simply said, "Yes, Lieutenant Stafford, Mrs. Fox is expecting you." The fucking cop had stared at Raymond, as if taking a mental snapshot for the next time they met.

The next time! Damn woman! Screwing with him. He'd show her and he'd show her tonight!

When the elevator stopped, Raymond found himself slamming his fists against the wall. He glanced around, temporarily disoriented. Sweat ran down his face. His shirt was soaked. He had to get hold of himself or he was going to screw up everything but The Woman's life. He used the remote to open the elevator doors, took a breath, and let it out. Everything was all right, everything was going according to plan. He could hear Fox's guardian angel, that fucking carpenter, hammering away. Well, sport, your late night hours are all behind you.

Raymond slipped down the hall, leaving the elevator doors open, and he didn't enter McFarland's unit until hearing the tapping of the hammer begin again.

McFarland looked up from his position on the floor. "What the hell you doing here?"

Raymond made his eyes wild. It wasn't difficult. They were still wild from the ride up, and on his way down the hall, he had pulled out his shirttail and mussed up his hair. "It's that Fox girl. Not the mother but the daughter. There's been an accident. The phone's out. Fox said you had a cell up here."

McFarland stood up, reaching for the phone. It was then he noticed the gloves on Raymond's hands. His hand came away from the phone. "I don't believe—"

Raymond met him before the carpenter could set himself, slamming a fist into McFarland's face.

Take that!

The blow dazed McFarland. He fell back and his head bounced off the counter. When his head came back up, Raymond crossed with a left, dropping the carpenter to the floor.

And that, you fucking woman!

A blow across the back of the head and McFarland went down for good.

Fucking woman! Fucking . . . woman.

Raymond stood there, listening to his breathing and for sounds from the hall, then bent down and wrapped a bandanna around McFarland's face, soaking up the blood dribbling from the man's mouth. He hoisted the wiry man over his shoulder and carried him to the door.

The hallway was empty. The Smiths, who paid the full price to live up this high, were in Europe. Raymond carried his burden past their condo, then the elevator, and down to the fourteenth floor's plywood door, where he picked the lock with McFarland lying across his shoulder. Once the padlock popped open, Raymond knocked the lock to the floor, pushed the door out of the way, and carried McFarland across the unfinished floor to the stack of pipe he'd noticed earlier in the day.

Plastic sheeting rattled in the night, and from the street came the sound of traffic as Raymond dumped McFarland on the stack of white pipe. He ripped the sheeting with a lock pick, then stood there, lighting a cigarette as a light rain blew through the hole in the plastic sheeting. The carpenter moaned, moved around, and started sliding down the stack of pipe.

Raymond stuck a foot out, stopping him. "Uh-huh. Not yet, sport."

While Raymond held McFarland in place, he got the cigarette going, and after a couple of drags, tossed it to the concrete floor. Only then did he pull his foot away.

McFarland started down the pipe, and when he didn't slid off by his own inertia, Raymond gave the unconscious man a little shove. McFarland was followed over the side of the building by several pieces of pipe kicked off behind him.

In Propes' condo, Raymond wove his way through the darkness and over to the bar. He flipped on a tiny light and poured himself a drink.

Arthur Propes appeared at the bedroom door in a

robe. "Did you bring her?"

Raymond whirled around, almost knocking over his glass, his mind not on any girl. "She—she was with her boyfriend."

"Boy—boyfriend?"

"Don't worry. I'll have her here in the morning."

Propes nodded and shuffled back into the bedroom.

Raymond returned to his drink. It seemed like the world had gone to hell since he'd been away. Every perversion was tolerated, but it had been his ticket into the Columbiana. Just watch for the old, rich guys who lived alone. None of them could live *that* alone.

Raymond wondered if he'd have to do something about Propes. Probably, but not at the expense of enjoying the moment. Raymond took his drink to a chair overlooking the river and waited for the sirens to begin.

nineteen

"Where are you, Melvin?"

Harry Hartner was breakfasting on the terrace with his wife—grapefruit and bran flakes because of a doctor who wouldn't allow him to enjoy life. It's not the cholesterol that gets you, but the heartache, as any fool should be able to see. But his wife was with him, making sure he stuck to his diet.

So nice, out here on the terrace, until the sun climbed into the sky and the humidity blew in from the ocean. In August, he'd take the family down to Pawleys Island: three grandchildren and no mother. No father either, but that SOB would never see the beach again. He had made damn sure of that. Harry sighed. All in all, the beach would never be the same.

Ott's voice came over the line, bouncing off a satellite and sounding like that was just what it was doing. "I'm in the Caymans, Mr. Harry."

Hartner dropped his spoon, spattering grapefruit

juice across his chest. "You're where?"

His wife looked up from the morning paper.

"The Caymans, and don't worry about those commercials, Mister Harry, they take the American Express card down here. I'll be all right."

"Yes. I'm sure you will."

Hartner wiped grapefruit juice off his glasses. Good thing he stuck a linen napkin in his collar whenever eating, despite how dowdy it made him look. They got over three dollars to launder a shirt these days. Highway robbery.

"Melvin, would you be so kind as to explain why you're in the Caymans?"

His wife glanced at him again, then went back to her paper. On the phone, Melvin told his employer what he had learned in the bean fields northwest of Miami.

"And you think this will help our client?"

"I don't know, but it can't hurt."

"Well, stay in touch. There have been other developments that might require your expertise. That carpenter, Avery McFarland, fell to his death from the top floor of the Columbiana last night."

Silence on the other end of the line, then, "First, Ernie Kelly, now this carpenter. The police shore gonna take an interest in our client now."

Sitting on the chaise lounge, Peggy saw her mother stir in the bed. Peggy pushed a blanket off and went over to take a seat on the edge of the bed.

Her mother turned over and looked up, then around the room. "How did I get here? I don't remember . . . ."

"I had Lieutenant Stafford bring you in here."

"You had . . . Dan bring me in here?"

"Dr. Knight gave you a sedative and I told Stafford he could come back in the morning. He's out there now, waiting to give you the third degree."

Jean tried to sit up. Peggy pushed her back down. "Don't rush this. You've had quite a shock. I know how much you thought of Mr. McFarland."

"Avery . . . ."

Tears came to Jean's eyes. Avery was dead because of her. Who'd be next? Ruth? Wesley? Certainly not Peggy. Peggy was useful to Lister because she gave him power over a mother who feared what people would think if she revealed her past.

"The way Stafford talks, it's like he thinks you had something to do with Mr. McFarland's death."

Jean sat up, pushing her daughter away. "I believe I did and I want to see him."

"Mother, what in the world are you talking about?"

"Later, Peg. Tell Dan to give me a few minutes."

Peggy was staring at her as she went out the door.

Jean put her feet over the side of the bed and stood, using her hands to steady herself. Dr. Knight shouldn't've given her that pill. She needed to think, which wasn't easy. Still, Lister's challenge rang out loud and clear as she stumbled over to the dressing table.

"If I can't have her, why would I let you have her? If I can't have her, why would I let you have her? If I can't have her . . ."

steve brown

Well, dammit, he couldn't! Avery wouldn't want her to cut and run. Avery would want her to stand and fight, to defend her turf. Problem was, Lister was letting her know how far he was willing to go if she didn't say she'd lied on the witness stand, that she'd enjoyed her "good screwing."

Inviting Dan Stafford over for dinner to fire a shot across Lister's bow. It sounded so clever. So smart. Lister hadn't gotten the message. Maybe never would. What could she do? Maybe nothing.

The face in the mirror knew the score. Just past forty, and for the first time, feeling it. Crow's feet around the eyes, the gaunt look that comes from too much exercise and dieting, lines of age beginning to crease her cheeks. And the gray was there. Face facts, woman, this is beyond your capacity, and the face in the mirror is telling you that. Jean stumbled back to the bed.

The portable on the dresser rang. Without thinking, she picked it up. "Yes?" It was Harry Hartner talking about Avery's death.

"Terrible business. You think Lister . . . . This is not a secure way to talk. Perhaps you could drop by the office this afternoon."

"Have you come up with anything?"

"Someone else brutalized by Raymond Lister."

Jean laughed. "I know someone who was brutalized by Lister, but she doesn't have the nerve to come forward. No, Harry, it's time I go to the police."

"Jean, I don't think—"

"I have to find a way to live with myself. Going to the police might be a start."

"But the police—isn't that a bit extreme? Melvin's still on the job."

"No. I'm finishing Raymond Lister and finishing him now."

"I can't say I agree with your decision, but call me if you need anything."

"I'll do that."

Jean put down the phone. She was staring at it when Peggy burst into the room, slamming the door behind her.

"Mother, I want to talk to you!"

"I take it you were listening in on the extension."

"You're trying to pin this on Ray, aren't you?"

"I don't think I have to pin anything on anyone. The record speaks for itself. Raymond Lister raped . . . raped . . . ." Jean found, not only could she not tell her daughter who Raymond Lister had raped, she couldn't even draw a breath. Jean gripped the edge of the nightstand and finally got out, "He's a rapist . . . and went to prison for it."

Finally, she could breathe. Jean turned loose the nightstand and straightened up on the side of the bed. Uh-huh. You thought you could lock away the rape in some small compartment of your mind, but Lister had broken in. Again.

Peggy was saying, ". . . half a mind to move in with Nana until the wedding's over. I can't take much more of this bickering."

"Peggy, you talk as if Raymond Lister's a member of this family."

"Well, he is, isn't he?"

Jean's hand came up to her mouth. "My God, what do you mean?"

"You know exactly what I mean. All I'm waiting for is for you to say it."

"Say what?"

"No, Mother, I won't do your dirty work for you." And Peggy left, slamming the door behind her.

Jean sat there, listening to her daughter storm out of the house. My God, what had the girl meant? She didn't suspect . . . ?

Jean got up and went to the door. Stafford was on his feet, looking at the door Peggy had disappeared through. "You okay?"

"Just a mother-daughter spat. Peggy doesn't want me to go in to work." What was wrong with her? Hadn't she decided to tell the truth, even before Harry Hartner called. But while fighting with Peggy, the words wouldn't come.

"I don't want you to go into the office either," Stafford said. "Besides, we need to talk."

"Put on some coffee, would you?" As she closed the door, Jean wondered, with Avery dead, what exactly would they talk about? It couldn't be that Stafford actually cared for her? What man could care about such damaged goods?

Peggy met Raymond Lister going down in the elevator. She looked at him. "What are you doing here?"

"I have a friend who lives here." He smiled. "Matter of fact, I have two friends."

"That's nice." Now Peggy realized where she had seen

that smile before. In the mirror. "I don't suppose you're speaking of my mother?"

"I doubt she'll ever be my friend."

The bell signaled their arrival at the garage.

"Because the two of you are too stubborn to work things out." Leaving her father behind, she walked briskly over to where her car was parked.

Raymond was thrown off stride. Work things out? Work what out? With who? The Woman? What was the girl talking about? But she was getting away.

Raymond hurried after her. "Like to get another chili dog and lemonade?"

Peggy used a remote to unlock the door of her sports car. "Why couldn't you just come out and tell me? Why all these games?"

"I—I don't know what you're talking about."

She sighed as she opened the door. "No, Ray, I don't want a chili dog and lemonade. I need time to think."

Raymond's mind raced, trying to figure how to handle this. Damn! He'd thought he could talk this girl into anything. "I have a friend who wants to meet you. I told him I'd bring you upstairs."

His daughter slid behind the wheel. "Who?"

"Arthur Propes."

"Ugh!" said Peggy, making a face. "I don't know if you know it, but Propes is a real sicko. My mother told me all about him."

Raymond put both hands on the window sill and leaned down. "Your mother has a lot to say about people. I'd hate to hear what she has to say about me."

"You're right about that."

"Well, if there's anything I can do, let me know."

"I don't think that's what either of you want. I think you only want to manipulate me."

The Paradise Casino was alive with activity, though it was early morning. The founders of the Cayman Islands' banking system understood the psychology of people receiving ill-gotten gains. Those people weren't content to sock money away for the future. They had to let go, to burst out—in song, in gambling, in drink, in getting laid. Simply put, they wanted to celebrate victory over the schmucks who rose early, went off to work, and brought home barely enough to make ends meet. But that wouldn't happen in the Caymans, so a regular shuttle service was set up between their pristine islands and the wicked Bahamas.

Freddie Noyles had taken that shuttle the night before and was busy spending his retirement income, but what the hell, once things cooled off in Miami, he'd be back in the action. Everybody needed a bodyguard and he was one of the best. Even Cricket said so. The problem was Cricket Kerns was dead, and without the numbers in Kerns' head, Freddie wasn't going to get any money out of these damn banks, which was where the banks made their squeeze. More than one depositor had failed to return to cash in his chips, having cashed them in otherwise.

Freddie was considering his predicament while sitting at the roulette wheel. Maybe that's why his luck was so bad. Another guy stood on the other side of the table, but the son of a bitch was winning, and the hell of it was, the old guy paid for his chips with an American Express card. Freddie had never seen an American Express card used to cover bets. Maybe that was the guy's luck. Or the brown fedora on the railing next to him.

Freddie turned away in disgust. Nothing to cash in made it easy. He took a seat at the bar and ordered a drink. A few minutes later, the old man joined him.

"Buy you a drink?" he asked, placing his fedora on the bar.

"On what? Your fucking Gold Card?"

"The card belongs to my employer." Fedora grinned. "But the winnings are all mine."

Freddie downed the rest of his drink. "I like your style, old man." He motioned for the bartender. "Hit us again"—Freddie snatched the card out of Fedora's hand—"and put it on this." The bartender mixed their drinks. "You were hot in there, why'd you quit?"

"I always quit while I'm ahead. It wouldn't take more than a couple of turns of the wheel and I'd be up shit creek. And out of a job."

Freddie laughed. This guy was all right.

The bartender served their drinks and moved a discreet distance away.

After a sip of his drink, Fedora asked, "How much did you leave behind in that bean field north of Miami?"

Freddie about fell off his stool. "Just who the hell are you, man?"

"Your newest friend."

"The hell you say." Freddie slid off the stool and backed away.

"Cool it, Freddie. You can't be extradited. Matter of fact, no one's even looking for you."

"Then what's your game?"

"Sit down—if you want the money you left behind in that bean field."

"I don't think I'll be doing that."

"Oh, you prefer to try to get Kerns' money out of his bank instead of the trunk of his car?"

"Sounds good to me." Freddie started for the door, giving the old guy a wide berth.

"I'm not going to track you down twice. You'll never see that money again. Almost a half million dollars, and I know who has it."

"Then go get it yourself, man."

Fedora laughed. "Do I look like someone who can take a half million dollars away from some cracker with a shotgun?"

When Freddie reached the entrance of the bar, he glanced back. The old guy was just sitting there, sipping his drink. He made absolutely no move to follow him. Hell, he wasn't even looking at him.

Freddie scanned the casino. The other guy would be white, that's the way they'd work it. Send the black guy in to . . . what? Freddie knew he couldn't be extradited or he wouldn't be here trying to pry Cricket's money out of that damn bank. He was having little luck prying anything out of anyone. The whole fucking island had an attitude—when you came on intense, they looked at you like, what you doing, man? Aren't you rich like everybody else? If he could get his hands on Cricket's money, he'd be set for life. But he couldn't, and it looked like he never would.

The old guy was still sitting there. Ordering another drink. Probably on his employer's credit card. Who was this nigger anyway? No Fed would use an American Express. They'd impress you by flashing the green. Just one of the boys, they'd say. Look at all this bread we're knocking down. Want a cut of the action? This is what you've got to do.

And the old guy was really old. He shouldn't be going up against any cracker with a shotgun. When Freddie returned to the bar, he asked, "Just tell me one thing, man, that American Express card you used, you said it belonged to your employer. Who you work for? The Feds? Dade County Metro?"

Melvin Ott looked at him. "Why, Freddie, I work for you."

Jean took a cup of coffee from Stafford after sitting on the sofa. He had stood when she returned to the room. There was no embrace. Stafford's eyes were bleary, his clothes rumpled. He needed a shave.

"Where's your partner?" In the forty-five minutes Jean had taken to dress in hopes that Stafford would leave, she had put on makeup and changed for work. She sipped from her cup.

"John's probably in bed by now." Stafford rubbed his eyes as he sat down. An empty coffee cup sat on the table in front of him. "Like I should be."

"Why aren't you? I'm not sure if you're here in your official capacity or not."

"I'm not and you have to believe that."

Jean put down her cup. "What do you want, Dan?"

"First, how do you feel?"

"A little groggy, that's all. I shouldn't've taken that sedative. It's going to make for a very long day."

Stafford looked out the window and across the river. "My partner's not here because he doesn't think you had anything to do with McFarland's death."

"Good, but are you going to tell me why Greene doesn't think I was involved in Avery's death?"

He looked at her. "You knew McFarland well enough to be on a first-name basis?"

"Is that an official question?"

"No. It's something I want to know."

"I never knew Avery until the night Ernie Kelly fell across the table and almost killed himself. Before that, we were nothing more than nodding acquaintances in the hall. Later, we had a drink in the unit where he was installing cabinets. Avery showed me why I should buy cabinets from him. Now I won't be able . . . ."

Stafford reached for her.

"No, no," Jean said, backing away. "I'm okay. You brought your partner along to check me out? You didn't trust your own judgment? I guess that's flattering in its own way. What possible interest would the police have in what happened the night Kelly was injured?"

"The department doesn't. I want to know."

"Why should you care?"

"Because I care about you."

"How could you? I'm a suspect. Or was."

Stafford didn't have an answer for that.

"Why don't we take a few days to sort things out?" Stafford got to his feet. "To see if I'll forgive and forget."

The doorbell rang.

"I'll get that for you."

"I'm well enough to answer the door." Another lie, thought Jean, as she hoisted herself off the sofa and stumbled across the room. She needed to talk with Peggy, but wasn't that just another way of stalling? What did it matter who she told first? Dan, Peggy— Ruth already knew and she'd weathered that little storm.

Little storm, my ass! The looks people gave you, the shift in chemistry, the balance of power. Twenty years ago her life had been ripped apart. She was the one who had put it back together.

Jean glanced through the peephole. A Chicana stood on the other side, looking in the direction of the elevator. Jean opened the door. "What can I do for you?"

As the woman faced her, Jean saw the scar: a long gash across the fleshy part of the cheek. The dark-skinned woman wore a white blouse, no jewelry, and a navy blue skirt. On her feet, a pair of sturdy work shoes. In her hand, an umbrella.

"Dr. Fox?"

"Yes?"

The woman glanced at Dan behind Jean. "Name's Donna Diaz. Melvin Ott told me you might be looking for a maid."

twenty

Raymond Lister's plan had worked so well that he failed to consider something might go wrong. True, occasionally something didn't fall into place as he expected, like Peggy's catching a ride from Lake Murray with him or the fact that Fox had a radio show, but given enough time to consider these factors, he was able to work them to his advantage.

On the plus side, there had been Arthur Propes, whose condo and car he was using. Using right now, he might add. Scrunched down in the front seat, Raymond watched Dan Stafford leave but not Jean Fox; so he was quite confident going upstairs, right to her door.

The door opened, but it wasn't The Woman who met him. It was Donna Diaz. "Hi, ya Raymond. How you doing?"

Raymond's mouth fell open. Forgotten was the clever line designed to rattle The Woman and force her to admit she had wronged him twenty years ago.

"Hey, Ray, aren't you going to say hello? Or are you just going to stand there with your mouth hanging open."

"Where's . . . Fox?"

"Gone to work. Did you forget this place has a front door?"

"What the hell are you doing here?"

"Got a job working for Dr. Fox. Can you believe that? I listen to her every day."

"A job? Doing what?"

"Cleaning house."

Before he knew what he was doing, Raymond had the woman by the arm. "They already have a maid. What are you really doing here?"

"Let go the arm! You want me to call the cops?"

"I'll wring your fucking neck."

"And I'll have Dr. Fox's attorney on your ass. That's who found me and sent me here."

Lister's hand dropped off Diaz. Maybe he should shut up and listen. Like he learned to do in the slammer.

Diaz pointed at her scar. "You don't leave me alone, I'll send you back to prison for sure."

"If you were going to do that, you would've done it in Florida."

"Raymond, you are so screwed up you wouldn't recognize the truth if it bit you on the ass." A sad look crossed her face. "You know, I really had a thing for you, until you did this to me. At first I thought it was me, then I realized you're screwed up when it comes to women. Dr. Fox explained. You can't connect without beating hell out of them. To you, that's courting. But I'm not here to straighten out your ass. Her lawyer's got papers ready for you to sign." Diaz smiled. "You and I are going to settle out of court."

"Settle what . . . out of court?"

Diaz pointed at the scar. "This, asshole."

"Fuck you, too."

"Raymond, let me clue you in. Not only are you going to fix my face, you're going to apologize for what you done to me. You fucking ruined my life. I couldn't get a job after you did this. Nobody wanted anything to do with me."

"I don't either."

"I'm having surgery next week and you're to come up with a thousand bucks."

"I'll pay nothing."

"Oh, you'll pay."

"I don't have any money."

Diaz leaned against the door jamb. "Johnny Mack said you had five grand your sister squirreled away for you."

Raymond stared at this woman. How did these people know everything? "I—I spent it."

"Then you'd better work two jobs cause you're gonna need the money."

"I ain't gonna work two jobs for any woman. And I ain't gonna pay for no surgery. I have no idea how you got that scar."

"That detective friend of Dr. Fox has got affidavits from the people at Kirby's Bar and Grill. Get it through your head, Raymond, you've met your match. Not in me, but in Dr. Fox."

Raymond's breath came fast and furious; hands clenching and re-clenching at his sides. "If you take . . . if you take me back there . . . I've got all kinds of friends there, too."

Diaz rolled off the jamb. "You ain't got friends like Jean Fox, respectable folks who can have you locked up before you can say 'Johnny Mack,' and you know whose side the sheriff's gonna come down on, not some ex-con's. He'll be listening to Judge Clements about how you violated your parole."

"What if I just up and disappeared? Left town?"

Diaz smiled broadly. "Now you're getting the picture, Raymond. Now you're getting the picture." And Diaz slammed the door in his face.

Raymond stood in the unfinished hallway, hands clenching at his sides, breath coming in short gasps, and as he did, Arthur Propes stepped off the elevator and walked toward him. When Lister hadn't returned, Arthur had decided to go looking for him, and Arthur thought he had a good idea where he would find his new friend.

"That the girl?"

Raymond let out a breath. "What? Oh, no. That's the maid. She's not here, but she'll be back."

Propes backed away. "Sorry, but I don't want anything to do with the Fox girl."

Lister followed Propes to the elevator, thinking, trying to figure this out. There could be only one reason why Propes wouldn't want to get it on with Peggy Fox. "You've made a play for her before, haven't you? When she was younger?"

Propes said nothing, only punched the button for his floor.

"And she turned you down, maybe even told her mother." Raymond slapped Propes on the back, almost knocking him over. "You dumb shit, don't you know you'll always need a pimp to get laid?"

Propes punched the button as Raymond turned his thoughts back to his current predicament. So Fox thought she had him, did she? Well, there was always Plan B.

The doors opened, and as they stepped on the elevator, Propes bit his lip. "I think it's best we don't see each other again, Mr. Lister."

"Okay, Pops, but you'll never find another pimp like me." He put his arm around the older man. "Mind if I get my gear out of your place before I go?"

It was raining when Peggy returned to the garage. She parked alongside Propes' car—where she saw her father sitting, car pointing outwards, as if ready to leave. Storm clouds were brewing. Her father looked like he might go off half-cocked and really get into trouble.

Peggy got out of the car and walked over. "What's wrong, Ray?"

"Nothing!" It was almost a shout, and Ray did not turn his head nor did he look at her.

With anyone else, Peggy would've left well enough alone and gone upstairs. She wouldn't even be talking to someone like Raymond Lister. But Raymond Lister was her father, and while driving around Peggy had sorted things out. Her mother was going to have to

admit Ray was her father, and her parents had to learn
to live with each other. After all, they were her parents,
no matter the circumstances of the conception.

"Tell me what's wrong. Maybe I can help."

Lister faced her, and as he did, clenched the steering wheel. To Peggy, it looked like the wheel might snap
in two at any moment.

"Are you all right?"

"No, dammit!" He took his hands off the wheel and
held them in his lap. But they wouldn't stop moving.
Over and over again, they clenched and clenched and
clenched. "Your mother . . . ."

"What did she do this time?"

"I try and try. I really do, but I don't think it's going
to work out. Your mother doesn't want it to."

Peggy put a hand on her father's shoulder. "What
did she say?"

"It's not what she said. It's what she did. She hired
that goddamn spic!"

"Who?"

"Your new housekeeper."

"Ray, you have to understand that Mother's a real
fanatic about cleanliness. Whoever the new maid is,
she won't last long." Peggy ran a hand up and down
her father's arm, trying to calm him. In his lap his
hands continued to work, clenching again and again.
"Everyone should be given a second chance. That in-
cludes our new housekeeper. Now, tell me, what did
this woman do?"

"You wouldn't understand."

"I'll speak to her. Mother doesn't have to know. We

can work things out."

Lister whirled around and Peggy stepped back. If looks could kill . . . .

"She came on to me!" shouted her father.

"The new maid?"

"I know what you're thinking: once a rapist, always a rapist. You're like everyone else." Raymond faced the steering wheel and this time Peggy let him go.

Someone in the family had to be the peacemaker. Usually it was Nana, settling arguments between her and her mother. Now, it appeared, she was the only grown-up in the family. "Stay right there, Ray. I'll be right back."

Peggy took the elevator to the eleventh floor, introduced herself to the new housekeeper—who had a horribly scarred face—and confronted the woman with her father's accusations. To her surprise, the maid only put down her dusting cloth and stepped over to the phone in the kitchen, where she hit the speed-dial.

"What are you doing?"

The woman waved her off, then, into the phone said, "Dr. Fox, please. Donna Diaz calling."

Peggy tried to take the phone away. "You don't have to call my mother. We can work this out."

Diaz dodged away, taking the phone with her. "I'm to report any contact you have with Raymond Lister. Yes, Dr. Fox, Peggy has come home. The problem is: Lister told Peggy *I* came onto *him.*"

Pause.

"I don't think I'm in any danger, but I'll leave by the

lobby." She handed the phone to Peggy. "She wants to talk with you."

Peggy was staring at the maid as the woman picked up an umbrella from the hallway floor. Into the phone she said, "Mother, what's going on?"

As Peggy listened, Diaz watched the girl's face fall. When Peggy hung up, Diaz asked, "What did your mother say?"

"She said if I didn't like the way she was handling my father, perhaps it would be best if I moved in with my grandmother until the wedding was over."

"All in all, a very smart thing to do. That man will poison your mind."

"What's going on here, Ms. Diaz?"

"Your mother's teaching you how to handle a bully, and if you're smart, you'll watch and see how it's done."

After Peggy disappeared upstairs, Raymond sat in Propes' car and smiled. He was totally relaxed, hands at his sides. He could handle his daughter. He could still handle any woman. If it'd been a son he would've seen through his old man's bullshit, but Peggy was just another woman. With his daughter under control, Raymond sat back and assessed his position, which was Plan B.

The Woman had money, especially through her mother-in-law, and the old lady knew about him. He could see it in her eyes the day he'd asked for any odd jobs that needed doing around the old lady's house. That was when Plan B had been born, and it felt good to have a fallback position.

Shit, but the money he'd be rolling in, and anytime he wanted it, as much as he wanted. Leave town, start a new life, and always have a place to come back for a new stake. How many times would Fox wish she was dead? More than once a day—for the rest of her life.

A delivery truck pulled into the garage and parked in front of his car. A nimble black man hopped down from the truck with a package under his arm and hurried over to the elevator.

Raymond leaned out the window. "Hey, you're blocking my car."

The black man stopped, peered at Raymond, and then came over to the car and flipped over the box. It had no bottom; there was only a pistol in the black man's hand. The gun was thrust into Raymond's face.

"Good to see you again, motherfucker. Put your hands on the steering wheel where I can see them."

A chill ran through Raymond as he did what he was told. Where did he know this guy from? He wasn't from the joint, or was he? All niggers looked the same to him.

"Who the hell are you?"

"Remember my voice? I remember yours." The black man laughed. "Best of all, I remember your shotgun. You still got that shotgun? Can it be traced back to what happened in the bean field?"

The nigger on the other side of the Cadillac! He should've waxed his ass while he'd had the chance.

"What you want?"

"Money. I want all that money you took from the drug deal."

"I didn't take it, you dumb fuck. I left it for the cops to find."

Freddie jammed the pistol in Raymond's face and Raymond jerked back. "Hey, motherfucker, don't play games with me. Nobody walks away from that kind of money. And look where you're living, the car you're driving."

"I take that money and it would've queered the deal I'm working on."

"What deal?"

"None of your business."

Freddie glanced at the cars in the garage of the Columbiana. "You thinking of robbing these rich white folks? You running some kind of scam? Man, how'd you even get in here?"

Raymond said nothing.

"Uh-huh. Well, let me tell you how I see it. You took that cash and hid it with the shotgun. Now you're waiting for things to blow over. But I figure the money's around here somewhere, and the shotgun that killed my friends."

"I don't have the money, nigger."

"What else would you be doing here? No man's crazy enough to walk away from that kind of money. You've gone to ground, motherfucker, and I'm going to hang around until you surface. With the money." Freddie backed away, keeping the pistol trained on Raymond as he climbed back into the truck and drove off.

Raymond took his hands off the steering wheel. Damn! When things went wrong, they really got fucked. And there was no Plan C.

Out of the corner of his eye, Raymond saw Peggy exit the elevator. His daughter threw a suitcase and overnight bag in her sports car, then got in. Raymond climbed out of his car and walked over.

"Where you headed?"

His daughter cranked her engine and shifted into gear. "I'm staying at Nana's until the wedding. I think you and my mother deserve each other."

twenty-one

That night when Jean returned to the Columbiana, a thunderstorm greeted her. There was also no guard in the kiosk, the gate was up, and Propes' car was parked over the line again. She'd have to speak to him about that. And the guard in the kiosk, why did she even try?

Jean snubbed out her cigarette and got out of her car after looking around, then punched the button for the elevator. The floor indicator said the elevator was at the garage level, but no matter how many times Jean punched the button, the doors wouldn't open. She'd have to speak to someone about that, too.

Just as she was about to take Peggy's advice about the stairwell to the elevator in the lobby, the doors opened. Jean glanced at them, then at the heavy metal door leading to the stairwell. Outside, lightning crackled and rain poured. The sooner she was upstairs, shoes kicked off, and a nice, strong drink in her hand, the better. She stepped inside the elevator and punched the button for the eleventh floor.

The doors didn't close, but as she was about to step off and use the stairs, the doors closed in her face. Jean waited, but the elevator didn't move. Why hadn't she taken the damn stairs? She slammed her hand on every button, including "Door Open."

Nothing.

Then the elevator began to rise.

Whew! She didn't want to think about being trapped in an elevator overnight. But when the eleventh floor passed, fear gripped her again.

Remember, you punched every button.

So why hadn't the elevator stopped at any of the other floors?

The elevator finally stopped at the fourteenth floor, but the doors didn't open. Jean punched eleven again and nothing happened. Then the doors opened and Raymond Lister stood there.

From his office, Dan Stafford dialed Jean's number. After getting her answering machine, he hung up and called the radio station. He was soon connected with the station manager. Stafford recognized the voice as belonging to the slick-looking guy who was in Jean's office the night her car had been trashed.

"Dr. Fox left a half hour ago," said Tony Nipper. "You can probably reach her at home."

"I tried there."

"Well, she and Mr. Pinckney may have gone out to dinner. They did have something to celebrate."

"What was that?"

"Dr. Fox is up for Talk Show Host of the Year."

At the mention of Pinckney's name, Stafford felt a twinge of jealousy. But how could you be jealous over a woman who'd run him off earlier in the day? Still, he was worried about her. And nobody had to know. He was a policeman calling on official business.

"Does Dr. Fox have a cell phone?"

"Only in her car." A small chuckle. "If you listened to her show you'd know that cell phones are no-nos. Life is too stressful to add cell phones to the mix."

"But for emergencies?"

Another chuckle from Nipper. "I can see you don't know Dr. Fox very well. There are no emergencies allowed in Jean Fox's life."

Stafford hung up and dialed the car phone. No answer. Stafford tried her condo again. Still no answer. Only a machine. He slammed down the phone.

It rang instantly and he snatched it up. "Stafford here."

"Can you and John catch a call at the Coliseum? With this rain, we're stacked up with fender benders."

"What's coming down?"

"Some kids breaking in, another of those black gangs."

"In this weather?"

"In this weather."

"Bad guys don't like bad weather."

"Just check it out, would you? I don't think the campus police would call us for nothing."

"You've got it."

Stafford hung up as his partner strolled into the room. John Greene tossed his beret into the air, then caught it on his finger as it came down. The black man slung the beret around and around, making the hat circle his finger.

"Business or pleasure?" he asked.

"Near the Coliseum."

"In this weather?" The beret slipped off Greene's finger and soared across the room, landing on another detective's desk. "What are they doing—fighting over a place in line?"

Stafford stood up. "They want someone who can talk to those black gangs. That's what happens when you're lucky enough to be paired with a black man."

"I don't know how to talk to those people," said Greene, fetching his hat. "I was raised in the suburbs. Being black is my burden."

Stafford dialed Jean's number again. No answer. Then the car phone again. No answer there either.

"Who you calling?" asked Greene.

"The captain. I want to know if it's too late to change partners."

Greene snorted, slapped the beret on his bald head, and left the room. Stafford had it bad for this radio chick, and John hoped they didn't get jammed up anytime soon. You didn't want to go through any door with a distracted partner.

Jean cowered in the corner of the elevator. "What are you doing here, Lister?"

"It's time you and I talked, Murphy." There was a wildness in Lister's eyes. His hands clenched as he blocked the entrance of the elevator.

"Anything you want to say, you can say through my attorney."

"Through your attorney." Lister blinked. "We're not married. It never went that far." He stepped inside the elevator. "You really think you can get rid of a man like me. I'm not Ernie Kelly."

Jean was taken aback. All those years in prison must've scrambled his brain. "It's kidnapping if you don't let me off this elevator."

"Oh, you're getting off." Lister grabbed her by the arm. "This is your stop. Your very last stop."

The call came over the radio. Greene was riding shotgun so he took it. "Car 54, where are we?"

Stafford glanced at his partner, then shook his head and watched the road through wipers having a hard time keeping up with the downpour. Bad guys breaking into places in this weather. Well, it would be a new MO.

The voice on the radio said there was a call for Dan Stafford. Would he like to take it over the air?

Stafford frowned. Whoever was listening could hear everything. If a snitch was calling, he was blown. "Okay. Put it on."

It was Johnny Nipper from the radio station. "Lieutenant Stafford, Dr. Fox's daughter just called. She can't locate her mother and is going over to the Columbiana to check on her. I told her you might swing by and see if her car's there."

"What about Vernon Pinckney?"

"He's already home. I just spoke to him."

"Columbiana's on our way. Tell Miss Fox to stay put."

As he hung up, Greene said, "The Columbiana isn't on anyone's way to the Coliseum."

But Stafford was making a U-turn in the middle of the street, spraying water and fishtailing in the rain. Once the sedan was headed in the opposite direction, he floorboarded the accelerator. Around them, horns blared, cars skidded. Greene flipped on the blue light, and Stafford slowed at the next intersection, then the next, running one light after another.

"You know," said his partner, buckling up, "you're handling personal business during office hours. And interrupting another call."

"I'm checking out a complaint called in by a concerned citizen. He thinks there's something funny going on, and so do I."

"That's for the uniforms. We have a call to answer at the Coliseum."

Stafford made another turn, then glanced at his partner. "You want out?"

"Of course not. Bad guys would have to be crazy to be out in this stuff, and crazy I don't need."

Jean tried to shake off Lister, but his hand clamped down hard, shooting pain all the way up into her shoulder. Jean thought she would faint. Her legs weakened. The hallway swam. It wasn't only the pain, it was the whole scene . . . when she was nineteen.

As they headed for the plywood door, Jean fought with Lister, trying to free herself. It was no use. Lister's huge hand was like a vise on her wrist. She screamed for help, but no one answered.

"No one's up here. That's why I chose the top floor."

Jean glanced behind her. None of the doors in the unfinished hallway had opened. But the elevator doors were still open. How did he do that?

"Raymond, let me go! No one has to know about this. Not the police, not even Peggy."

He leered over his shoulder. "You see, you really did like it . . . the first time."

"Raymond, you've got to believe me. I didn't want to be raped."

Jean remembered the recorder in her purse. The purse was strapped across her chest, as she always wore it to prevent it being snatched. As she was being pulled through the plywood door, her free hand found the recorder in the side of the purse, ready to be pulled out for dictation, mike set at maximum. She had to say something . . . before the fact. But who should she address this to? Dan or Peggy?

Still being pulled across the unfinished units, Jean said, as loud as she could, "If you think raping me's going to make me submit, it won't. I'll report you to the police again. Peggy will know you for what you are."

He ignored her.

"Did you hear me, Raymond? I said there will be consequences if you rape me again."

Lister only continued to pull her across the cluttered open space.

"You'll be returned to prison. You'll never see Peggy again."

Still nothing from Lister.

She saw a stack of sheetrock ahead. It appeared to be their destination. At the sight of the flat, level surface, Jean's knees buckled. She stumbled but wasn't allowed to fall. Lister was strong enough to hold her up with one hand and pull her along. Now the tears started.

"Raymond, please don't do this. That . . . that policeman who came over for dinner last night. I think he's interested in me. Please don't mess me up again."

Lister pulled her past the sheetrock, but Jean couldn't see this because of the tears. "I have money! I'm about to sign a new contract and move to Atlanta! How much do you want?"

"Shut up. It's gone too far for money."

Jean brushed the tears away and scanned the open space with its plastic sheeting rippling in the wind. West Columbia was a blur across the river. Construction gear and supplies were scattered around the open space, but they were all dry. Funny what the mind focuses on in times of danger. She noticed Lister had not stopped to lay her out on the sheetrock but was dragging her toward the edge of the building.

He was dragging her to the place where Avery

McFarland had fallen to his death! Lister had no intention of raping her! He planned to kill her!

There was the stack of white pipe that the police said Avery had sat on before going over the side. The pipes were repacked and stacked well away from the edge. But the way Lister was dragging her, he wouldn't take the time to make this look like any accident. He would simply fling her off the side of the building.

"Oh, my God, Raymond. Don't do this!" Jean grabbed one of the support beams as they passed by, and just as quickly, her hand was pulled off as Lister made his way across the cluttered floor.

Lightning cracked and Lister had to raise his voice to say, "You've given me no choice, no way out."

"I have money!"

Lister snorted. "You have more tricks up your sleeve. This has to be finished and now." He threw out a hand. "Just look at this weather. It'll be hours before they find you."

Forgotten was the recorder whirling away in her purse. All Jean could think was how much she'd underestimated Lister. She'd wanted to get him out of her life; now she was about to be removed from his! Permanently. She should've been thinking about leaving some sort of message that would convict Raymond Lister of her murder, but all that would be heard later on the tape would be Jean begging for mercy—and Raymond Lister's wild laughter.

twenty-two

Freddie Noyles got out of his car, pulled his nylon jacket up over his head, and hurried across the street to the parking garage. Lister had disappeared inside just before some woman in a white BMW had driven in. Did the two of them have something going? Was this more leverage he could use against this honky? Freddie shook off the rain, dropped his jacket back on his shoulders, and ran a hand across his hair. As he stood by the kiosk, the phone rang.

Freddie looked around. No one home, and wherever the guard was, he sure as hell wasn't going to hear that phone in all this rain. There was nothing in the garage but expensive cars. Where the hell was the guard?

Drops of blood dripped across the floor. More blood led to either the elevator or the stairwell door. Freddie couldn't tell which, and after a few hesitant steps in that direction, he damned well wasn't going to find out.

Time to shag ass. He pulled up his jacket and started out of the garage but was stopped by a light coming down the street. A flashing blue light coming right toward him!

Cops!

It was all Freddie could do not to run. Cops who saw a brother running out of a place like this; they'd shoot first, ask questions later. But who said they were coming here? Who was to say he wasn't the guard on duty?

Freddie stepped inside the kiosk, shook down his jacket, and faced the street, putting his hands on the control panel. He tried to ignore the phone. In a few seconds the cops would be gone and he'd be long gone. Lister had been a hard case back in the bean field and hadn't changed worth a damn. Killing the guard, then . . . then what? None of this made sense.

Oh, shit! The police were pulling in here! Why not? There was a dead man around here . . . somewhere.

The car stopped in front of the gate. Its windshield wipers threw water left and right and the blue light on the dash flashed. Freddie's legs trembled. He just might pee on himself. The driver stuck his head out the window; some brown-haired white dude.

"Raise the gate, okay?"

Freddie scanned the controls. The ringing phone, the panel with all its buttons, and the flashing blue light. Freddie hit a button and the gate rose on his right.

"Wrong gate, buddy," said the policeman.

The cop in the passenger seat leaned down so he could get a look at Freddie through the windshield. He was a black guy wearing a purple beret. At least it looked purple in the blue light.

"Sorry." Freddie hit the other button. "First night on the job."

The cop nodded and drove his car through the gate and over to the elevator, dripping water as it went, and washing away the bloodstains, Freddie hoped. He glanced at his own car across the street. He had to get out of here! He didn't give a damn where Lister was—that asshole!

The phone finally stopped ringing. Yeah. That's all he needed was one of those cops to come over and ask why he didn't answer the damn phone. One of them was out of the car now, but the one wearing the beret stayed inside while the first cop punched the button for the elevator after checking out a white BMW. The car belonging to Lister's woman.

Now the other cop was out of the car. The cops talked among themselves, then the one in the beret started Freddie's way, walking quickly. The other cop disappeared inside the stairwell, and Freddie heard his feet slamming into the metal as he made his way up the stairs. The heavy door closed and the cop wearing the beret was in his face, asking a question.

"Er—what'd you say?"

"I said, do you have the number of the elevator people? We think someone might be stuck in the elevator on the fourteenth floor."

Freddie's crotch warmed over and piss started down his legs. Maybe nobody would notice in all this rain. But something they would notice was the blood. Freddie covered the drops of blood with his feet as he faced the control panel. There was a drawer on either side. Freddie opened the drawer as the cop stepped into the kiosk and opened the other drawer.

The black cop said, "If this is your first night on the job, maybe it's best I give you a hand. We don't know how long the woman's been up there."

Damn! thought Freddie as he fumbled through the drawer. He'd never get out of here. EMS would be on their way, then the fire department, more cops, TV crews. Shit. Lister was probably screwing her right now—in the fucking elevator. Why did things like this always happen to him?

What was it he was looking for? Oh, yeah, a phone number for the elevator people.

Peggy hung up the phone at her grandmother's. "I'm going home, Nana."

"In this weather? Why, child?"

"Because mother's not at the station or the condo or answering her car phone, and that was the booth in the parking garage I just called. There was no answer."

Ruth left the chair she was sitting in. "I'll change and go with you."

"No. I almost didn't hear her, but Mother was reaching out to me today and I don't want to miss the connection."

"You can't get away with this!" screamed Jean as Lister dragged her toward the open space.

A new sheet of plastic had been nailed over the opening where Avery McFarland had gone over the side. Lightning ripped a hole in the night. Through the sheeting the lights of West Columbia across the river were a blur.

"Didn't I get away with offing your buddy, that guy who thought he was so fucking tough?"

Jean looked at the sheeting Lister was pawing at. Lister had killed Avery McFarland and now he would kill her, then hang around and court her daughter, maybe even seduce her into going away with him and being the father Peggy never knew!

She would not let that happen! And from her rape training Jean remembered to twist her hand around, snapping her hand against where Lister's finger and thumb came together—and run for the door.

Stafford took the stairs two at a time before he realized there was something under them. He went back to the turn and saw a pair of feet sticking out below him. Stafford vaulted over the railing and landed on the floor, going to his knees . . . and finding . . . Jamie Stubbs back from suspension and with his head bashed in. Dead, but the body still warm.

Stafford was on the third floor before he realized buildings this size had more than one elevator. He left the stairs and ran to the bank of elevators. One indicator said its elevator was on the fourteenth floor, the other on the seventh.

Stafford slammed his hand against both buttons and cursed loudly until the elevator arrived. When it did, he leaped inside and hit the button for the eleventh floor. The doors took forever closing. He had to go to the eleventh floor and make sure Jean was all right. Telling John that there was someone trapped in the elevator on the fourteenth floor was only good—

The fourteenth floor!

The floor where Avery McFarland had fallen to his death. And there was a body under the stairs, and the other elevator was hung up on the fourteenth floor.

Stafford hit the button for the fourteenth floor. If Jean was home, she was on the eleventh, safe and sound, but if she was on the fourteenth floor . . . .

But why would she be up there?

Lister came after her, and though Jean had slipped out of her heels, he caught her at the plywood door.

"Come back here, bitch! I don't have all night."

Jean fell back into Lister and her purse slid off. Out fell the tape recorder. It skidded across the concrete. Lister saw it and had an idea. He picked up the machine and held it to Jean's face.

"Speak into it!" he ordered.

"What! What?"

"Tell Peggy you lied. How do you turn this . . ." He

saw the recorder was already on and threw the machine across the open space where it hit a beam and fell to the floor. That was quickly followed by her purse. "You'll try anything, won't you?"

Now she was in his face. Leaning into him, Jean shouted, "That sounds more like you! What do you really want, Raymond? Or are you just plain nuts!"

Lister raised his hand and Jean flinched. When she looked again, he was flexing that hand.

"You don't think . . . I know what I'm doing. You don't think I'm . . . in control here? You don't think I can't make it . . . outside. I know what's . . . important. Peggy won't have to worry about Propes. He'll never bother her again. My sister was wrong. I do know how to take care of my family." Dragging Jean behind him, Lister started for the side of the building again.

Head spinning, Jean had to follow. "You don't have to do this. Everything's all right. You and I can be with Peggy."

"*No!* You'll always be there, hassling me. You've always been there, fucking with me. You'd do it again."

"I won't! Just let me go!"

He turned on her, stopping a few feet short of the plastic wall. "The recorder—I saw it. You were going to put me on the radio. Don't tell me you . . . weren't."

It was then that Jean realized she'd been beaten. Whipped. After all her hard work, all that she'd done to keep a sense of self after being raped, her mother-in-law's constant meddling, the additional responsibilities she'd taken on—now her life came down to this: a few more steps, then oblivion.

Her plan to drive Lister away—instead of driving him away, she'd driven him insane. She'd been clever, oh, so very clever, but now all she was left with were the lights across the river blurred by the rain, the plastic billowing in the night, and Raymond Lister clawing at the plastic with his free hand—which he found impossible to do with a woman hanging all over him.

Because Jean wasn't trying to get away any longer. She was clinging to him, mouth at his ear. "I'm taking you with me, you bastard!"

A streak of lightning ripped open the night, illuminating a woman hunched over a man teetering at the edge of the open space near a support beam. Jean was determined this man wouldn't live in the same world as her daughter. If it was the last thing she did, she'd protect her baby from this monster.

They stumbled back from the edge. "Let go of me, bitch!"

"No!" Jean felt her jacket part in the back, so tightly had she wrapped herself around this man. "Neither of us will have her! We'll go over the side together! Ending this like it should've been done twenty years ago."

Pulling her off with those huge bear-like paws of his, Lister walked them back over to the edge. "Damn woman. What did you think . . . you could do?"

When he brought Jean toward him to toss her away, she slashed him across the face with her nails. "Try explaining that to the cops, asshole."

Lister jerked away, stepping parallel to the plastic wall. "You goddamn bitch!"

He brought his hand back, then remembered what

he was there for. Raymond swung the woman around and threw her against the plastic wall, and hopefully out of his life.

Jean hit the plastic at the time a gust of wind slammed into it. She was thrown into Lister, knocking him back and landing at his feet. While she was shaking her head to clear it, Lister reached down and grabbed her by the front of her jacket. Lifting her up again, he went to work on the plastic with the other hand. But a woman who hadn't allowed a man to touch her in the last twenty years—had grabbed him by the crotch and was hanging on tight.

Lister screamed and backed away but couldn't get away from her. When he brought up a hand to hammer her off, the motion threw him off balance and he fell back. He landed against the plastic wall, one hand holding onto the front of Jean's jacket, the other flailing out behind him.

Rain pelted the plastic, and Jean felt herself being pulled over the side as the sheeting gave way. One of the support beams was nearby. If she could just reach that beam . . . .

She got a hand on the beam, but Lister's weight dragged her fingers across the surface, snapping off one nail, then another. Slowly but surely, the plastic parted behind Lister and Jean felt her jacket separate.

At the plywood door, Dan Stafford stood, heart in his throat. This was why they warned you never to become involved a case. Involvement could immobilize you, like the scene at the edge of the building. Should he shout? Would that save them or put them over the side? It really didn't matter. He could see he was going to be too late.

Lister's size was too much for the plastic and Jean's jacket. The plastic separated behind him, as did the jacket across Jean's back. Rain whipped through the opening, hitting Lister in the back of the head, Jean in the face.

"Help me, Murphy!" he shouted. "Help me!"

Jean's fingers scraped across the beam. "I wish I could, Raymond. I really wish I could." Her last finger caught on a rivet, her remaining nail snapped off, and she began to follow Raymond Lister over the side.

But Dan Stafford was there, snatching her around the waist, his other arm grabbing the support beam. So Jean hung there, fourteen floors above the ground, watching Raymond Lister pinwheel around and fall to his death.

Then she was in Dan's arms, being held, but most important, being walked away from that awful edge, walked away from that screaming, gyrating figure falling to the street below. Jean never heard Lister finish his fall. She was sobbing into Dan's chest.

He looked over her shoulder at the ripped and torn plastic. The wind, now having a toehold, lashed at the material, ripping it apart. "What was that all about?"

Jean leaned into his chest, catching her breath, her heart racing; her mind, too. She didn't want to lose this man. "Ernie Kelly sent him . . . to harass me. It got out of hand."

Stafford hugged her tight. "Good. For a moment I thought Raymond Lister might've found you."

Jean pushed him back where she could see him. "You know about him?"

Stafford nodded.

"And still want me?"

Stafford ran a hand across her cheek, damp from her tears, damp from the rain. He kissed her gently. "Of course, but why didn't you ask for my help?"

"I'm—I'm used to taking care of my own problems."

Stafford pulled her into him. "Not any more you aren't."

Jean hugged him, a sense of relief washing through her. "Good, because I've got a lot to tell you."

about the author

Before he began his writing career, Steve Brown was a program director at a radio station. He lives with his family in Greenville, South Carolina. Brown is also the author of *Black Fire*, featuring a modern-day Scarlett and Rhett, *Of Love and War*, a love story set against the backdrop of the Japanese attack on Pearl Harbor, and the Myrtle Beach Mysteries. You can contact Steve through www.chicksprings.com.